"Stay."

He sounded rusty, as if he didn't know how to ask for what he wanted. He tried again. "Talk to me. Tell me about..." What? Her life? What she expected the "right" man to be like? "A movie. I haven't been to one in a long time. What's the last one you went to?"

Fiona relaxed, as he'd hoped she would. While he measured sugar, she told him about a thriller with a huge budget, big stars and an unlikely plot.

They hadn't even been there twenty-four hours.

How, in such a short time, had he gotten to the point where he had a thought like *I need her?* He hadn't kissed her, hadn't touched her beyond a hand on the shoulder, didn't know that she felt anything at all for him.

He didn't *need* her. That had been a ridiculous thought. But he wouldn't mind if snow kept falling for another day or two.

Dear Reader,

I confess to thinking it's great fun to tweak classic romance plots–you know, secret baby, marriage of convenience, snowbound hero and heroine.... And I admit to having a special fondness for the snowbound plotline. There are so few ways, in the modern world, we can isolate two people, trapping them together for days and days as the sexual tension rises to an unbearable level....

But let's face it, the odds aren't great, are they? Every time I read one of those books, I'd think about how, with my luck, I'd be more likely to end up snowbound with a sexy guy and his wife and kids. Since I write (and love) romance, that's not a workable scenario. So what can I throw into the stew to give it an unexpected taste? Not a baby–newborn babies are a common element in the classic take. They nap so conveniently, you know. I didn't want convenient for this book, I wanted *inconvenient.* No, what if our heroine were to have a teenager with her? Ooh, better yet: what about *eight* teenagers?

Yes, the plucky heroine is chaperoning a high school trip when in the midst of a blizzard she finds herself snowbound at a Cascade Mountain lodge with eight feuding, funny, sometimes depressed teenagers for whom she's responsible–and their reluctant host is a brooding man hiding out from the world after returning from being wounded in Iraq. Now, there's a mix!

I hope you have as much fun reading *Snowbound* as I did writing it.

Best,

Janice Kay Johnson

Snowbound

Janice Kay Johnson

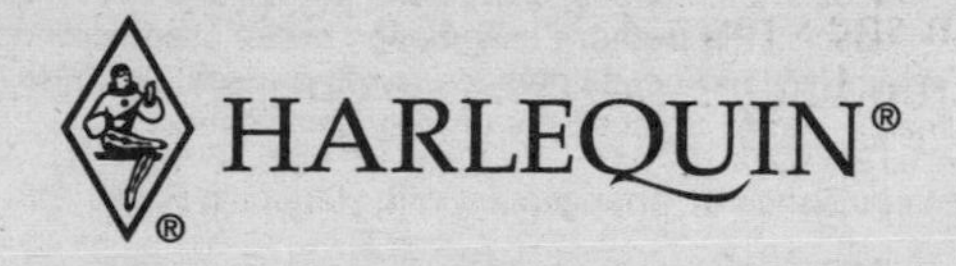

TORONTO • NEW YORK • LONDON
AMSTERDAM • PARIS • SYDNEY • HAMBURG
STOCKHOLM • ATHENS • TOKYO • MILAN • MADRID
PRAGUE • WARSAW • BUDAPEST • AUCKLAND

ISBN-13: 978-0-373-71454-4
ISBN-10: 0-373-71454-8

SNOWBOUND

This edition published by arrangement with Harlequin Books S.A.

www.eHarlequin.com

Printed in U.S.A.

ABOUT THE AUTHOR

Janice Kay Johnson is the author of nearly sixty books for adults and children. She has been a finalist for the Romance Writers of America RITA® Award for four of her Harlequin Superromance novels. A former librarian, she lives north of Seattle, Washington, and is an active volunteer at and board member of Purrfect Pals, a no-kill cat shelter. When not fostering kittens or writing, she gardens, quilts, reads and e-mails her two daughters, who are both in Southern California.

In December 2007 *Christmas Presents and Past*, Janice's first book for the Harlequin Everlasting Love line, will be published.

Books by Janice Kay Johnson

HARLEQUIN SUPERROMANCE

998–HIS PARTNER'S WIFE†
1009–THE WORD OF A CHILD†
1040–MATERNAL INSTINCT†
1092–THE GIFT OF CHRISTMAS (anthology with Margot Early & Jan Freed)
1140–TAKING A CHANCE††
1153–THE PERFECT MOM††
1166–THE NEW MAN††
1197–MOMMY SAID GOODBYE
1228–REVELATIONS
1273–WITH CHILD
1332–OPEN SECRET**
1351–LOST CAUSE**
1383–KIDS BY CHRISTMAS
1405–FIRST COMES BABY

HARLEQUIN SINGLE TITLE

WRONG TURN
"Missing Molly"

SIGNATURE SELECT SAGA

DEAD WRONG

†Three Good Cops
††Under One Roof
**Lost...But Not Forgotten

CHAPTER ONE

FIONA MACPHERSON was starting to get scared.

The rhythmic *thwap, thwap, thwap* of the tire chains helped her shut out the chatter of the eight teenagers behind her. With the snow falling so hard, she felt as if she and the kids were in a bubble, darkness all around, the headlights only reaching a few feet ahead. Snow rushed at the windshield, a white, ever-moving veil.

She shouldn't have taken this route—a thin line on the map that promised to cut north of the projected path of the storm.

"This way's good," Dieter Schoenecker had said, when she told her vanload of students what she intended to do. "We cross-country ski at a place up near High Rock Springs."

Hadn't she been a high school teacher long enough to know better than to take a sixteen-year-old's word for anything?

Not fair. *She* was responsible, not Dieter, and she had had some doubts about whether the line on the map was too skinny. But it *was* a highway, it headed westbound, and they should have been able to make it across the Cascade Mountains before the blizzard arrived.

Only, they hadn't. They'd left Redmond, out in the high desert country of eastern Oregon, hours ago, right after the Knowledge Champs competition had ended. They should have been close to home in Hawes Ferry south of Portland by now, or at least descending into the far tamer country in western Oregon. Instead they were in the thick of the storm. Fiona was struggling to maintain twenty miles an hour. It had been at least two hours since she'd seen another vehicle.

We should have turned back when we stopped to put on chains, she thought. And when they realized they no longer had cell phone reception.

The voices behind her had died out, Fiona realized.

"You okay, Ms. Mac?" one of the boys asked.

Despite the fact that her neck and shoulders ached and her eyes watered from the strain, she called back, "Yep. You hanging in there?"

Nobody had time to answer. A jolt shuddered through the van as it hit something and came to a stop, throwing Fiona against her seat belt.

"What happened?" Amy cried.

"We probably went off the road," Dieter said.

Fiona made everyone but Dieter stay in the van. She and he put on parkas and got out. With the engine turned off, it was utterly silent outside, the headlights catching the ghostly, slow fall of the snow and the white world they found themselves in. Tree boughs were cloaked with white, as were rocks and shrubs and ground.

"Awesome," he said.

She opened her mouth to snap at him, then stopped

herself. He was young. She should be grateful he didn't realize how frightening their situation was.

With the single beam of light from the flashlight that had been in the glove compartment, they could see that the van's right front wheel rested against a mound. Turning, she cast the thin beam in a semicircle and realized that the road—or what must surely be road—curved. She'd gone straight.

"Try reversing," Dieter suggested. "A couple of us can push, too."

Moments later, they were on the road again. Fiona waited until the boys clambered back in, bringing a burst of cold with them and shaking off snow. This time, Dieter got in the front seat.

"You know the rules," she began.

"Yeah, but maybe I can help you see."

After a moment, she nodded, then with a hand that had a fine tremor put the van in gear and started forward.

Where were the snowplows? she wondered in frustration, but knew—they would be working on the more traveled highways.

I've endangered these children's lives with my bad decision. She felt as if ice were running though her veins.

"What if we get stuck?" Amy asked, in a high, frightened voice.

"We've done fine so far."

"But..."

Dieter said, "They don't close passes without sending, like, a state patrolman over it to be sure no one is stranded."

Fiona was momentarily reassured until she thought about how many roads there would be to patrol. And, because this snowfall was so heavy, anyone coming behind them might find the highway totally impassable.

Out of the van back there, she'd realized how bitterly cold it was tonight. If they got stuck, she could run the engine and the heater off and on, but none of them were dressed for more than a dash from the parking lot into a building. She, Dieter and Hopper were the only ones with real winter parkas.

"Tell me if you see any sign of habitation," she said softly to Dieter.

Leaning forward, staring at the same white kaleidoscope she was, he nodded.

Fiona blinked hard to ease the strain on her eyes.

Stay on the road, keep going and sooner or later they'd break free of the storm.

It was the staying on the road part that was the real challenge.

JOHN FALLON hadn't intended this trip to be a race against the storm. Once he heard the weather reports, he'd decided to move up the shopping expedition to town he had planned for next week. But the storm wasn't supposed to hit until the middle of the night or the following morning.

He was coming out of the country store with his arms full of groceries when he saw white flakes swirling from the sky. Given that he had an hour's drive deeper into the mountains and the blizzard, the sight wasn't welcome.

Nodding at townsfolk when he had to, he took the time to pick up his mail, go to the tiny liquor store and then to top his Toyota 4Runner's tanks at the Chevron station before setting out for the lodge. With the snow coming down harder, he skipped his usual stop at the library to pick out new books and check his e-mail.

Within half an hour, he was cursing under his breath. The snow was falling heavily—more like a midwinter storm than a pre-Thanksgiving one. Good thing he'd stocked up. If it kept on like this, the plows might take a week to get to his place. The Thunder Mountain Lodge, of which he was now proprietor, was the last dwelling on the west side of the mountains. Just past the lodge, the highway closed for the winter unless the snowfall was light.

If this storm was any indication, snowfall was going to break records this season.

He wouldn't mind. When he bought the lodge in December last year, John had intended to keep it operating, but he hadn't done much advertising and he found himself looking forward to midweeks when he had the place to himself.

Families were the most annoying. Cross-country skiers, snowshoers, hikers; they were okay. They tended to be out all day and come back tired. They'd eat quickly and gratefully, maybe sit in front of the blaze in the huge, river-rock fireplace that was the lodge's heart, then disappear into their rooms. But families… They were another story. The mothers always wanted to talk and the kids yelled and ran around and knocked things over. Families wanted suggestions for activities, baby bottles heated at odd hours, snacks for the kids after the kitchen was closed.

He'd had a particularly hellish group in August. Ironically a church group. Teenagers. They'd taken over the lodge as well as all five of his cabins strung along the river. They sang songs, they built bonfires, they flirted and wrestled and ate like there was no tomorrow. They *swarmed.*

John just wanted to be alone. Didn't seem like too much to ask, did it? He'd bought the damn place because it was about as isolated as you could get without roaming with Kodiaks in Alaska. Paying guests would give him enough income to get by, he'd figured. He would cook, serve, clean. Give him something to do. Otherwise, he'd keep to himself.

He just hadn't realized how busy Thunder Mountain Lodge was. One person after another told him, "We love the lodge. We come every year. It has to be one of the most beautiful places on earth." He also heard how refreshed they were after their stay.

They should have been here at the same time as the church group.

He had closed up the cabins for the winter, on the advice of the old curmudgeon he'd bought the lodge from, turning off the water and wrapping pipes. He'd done that just a few weeks ago. The lodge itself had six guest rooms along with his quarters in the back, plenty for the backcountry skiers and snowshoers who came in the winter. He had a couple scheduled to arrive tomorrow. Something told him they wouldn't be coming.

Wouldn't break his heart.

But he did wish he'd gotten down to town and back a few hours earlier.

The last half hour was a bitch, with the snow piling up at record speed and visibility close to zero. His mind kept flashing back to the sandstorms in Iraq, as blinding and bewildering.

Damn it, don't do this. Focus.

He knew every turn, every landmark. Even so, with the advent of darkness, he almost missed his turn. The massive, wood-burned sign that read Thunder Mountain Lodge carried a swag of snow and was already buried up to the bottom of the letters.

The lodge was half a mile farther, down a winding driveway that dropped toward the river. This privately owned land was heavily forested, the old growth here one of the attractions.

John had left the shed doors open and now drove right in. He was going to have to get out the shovel if he wanted to close them.

Unload first.

Making several trips, he carried the groceries and booze into the big, empty kitchen. Mail he left on the farmhouse table that sat in the middle. Once he'd put away the perishables in the restaurant-quality refrigerator, John put his parka and gloves back on and went out to shovel enough to close the shed doors. Having already worked up a sweat, he cleared a path to the front steps and the steps themselves, too, even though he'd likely have to redo them come morning if he needed to go out.

Then he stood for a minute in the dark, only the porch light and dim glow coming from the windows, and listened to the eerie hush snow brought when it wrapped the world in white batting.

For that brief moment, his soul felt at peace.

IN BACK, at least two of the girls were crying, one quietly, one not so quietly. Fiona simply didn't have the energy to try to reassure them. In fact, she'd have liked to cry herself.

They'd gone off the road twice more. With all three boys pushing, each time they'd made it back onto pavement. This last time, the snow had been knee deep. That meant the undercarriage was pushing through snow. Clammy with panic, Fiona started forward again. Now even the sound of the chains was muffled. Thank God, the highway didn't seem to run next to a river or creek. If they slid down an incline…

Don't think about it.

For the thousandth time, she told herself, *if we keep going, we'll eventually come out of the mountains.* Studying the map all those hours ago, she'd noticed a couple of little towns dotting the line of the highway once it crossed the pass and descended toward the Willamette Valley and Portland. There would be lights. Heat. Food and safety. Although it had been scarcely noticeable at the time, they must have gone over the pass an hour or more ago, because the road was definitely descending now, although not steeply.

But it seemed, if anything, that the snow was falling harder. Or perhaps her eyes were just so tired, she was less capable of seeing through that driving veil of white. Her neck and shoulders and arms were rigid. Somebody would probably have to pry her fingers from the steering wheel.

Her *frozen* fingers, she thought morbidly. After the van disappeared into a snowbank and its tracks filled in. Or perhaps her fingers wouldn't be frozen anymore, if nobody found the missing teacher and her pupils until spring.

"Wait a minute!" Dieter jerked. "Did you see that?"

She braked. "What?"

"I think…wait. Let me get out." He reached back for his parka, grabbed the flashlight from the glove compartment and sprang out, disappearing immediately in the dark.

Fiona just sat, too exhausted to move. Too exhausted to worry, even when he didn't come back for several minutes.

"Where'd he go?"

"Why are we stopped?"

One of the girls, voice high and rising, "Are we stuck?"

Fiona was too exhausted to answer, as well.

The passenger door opened again, and Dieter said exultantly, "There's tire tracks. And a turn here. I think there's a sign. I bet it's Thunder Mountain Lodge. Remember how I told you my family comes up here?"

Tire tracks.

"What if whoever made the tracks came *out?*" Kelli asked. "And they're, like, gone, and even if we find the lodge it's cold and dark?"

A lodge. Fiona's mind moved sluggishly over the idea. "We could build a fire," she said.

Voice pitched so only Fiona would hear him, Dieter said, "If this is Thunder Mountain, the next town is something like another hour. And that's when the road's plowed. I don't remember much in between."

The others were offering opinions, but she ignored them.

"Okay," she said. "I'm going to back up. Can you guide me?"

He left the passenger door open and talked her through backing up ten yards or so. Then he shone the flashlight on the tracks in the snow. Now Fiona could see them, too. A vehicle had come from the other direction and turned into an opening between trees.

Please God, she thought, *let the driver have known where he was going. Don't let me follow someone else as desperate as we are.*

"See?" Dieter turned the beam on a dark bulk to the right as she turned into the road or driveway or whatever it was. "Let me go look."

She watched as he plowed his way through and took a swipe at whatever it was with his bare hand. Clumps of snow cascaded down, exposing writing that the dim beam picked out.

He yelled, "It is Thunder Mountain Lodge. Cool!"

When he got back in, Fiona asked, "Please tell me it's not another five miles."

He laughed exultantly. "Nope. It's like…I don't know, a quarter of a mile. Half a mile?"

"Okay," she said. "Here goes."

Whatever vehicle had gone before her had obviously passed by a while back; it was a miracle that Dieter had spotted the tracks, vanishing fast under fresh snowfall. She kept losing sight of them in the white blur.

The kids in back were talking excitedly now that salvation was at hand. Dieter started telling them about this great old lodge, the ancient trees and the river just below.

"There's this *huge* fireplace," he was saying, when the van lurched and the front end seemed to drop.

One of the girls screamed. Fiona braked, out of instinct—they had already come to a dead stop. Dieter jumped out again, coming back to shake his head.

"I don't know if we can get it out."

"Can you still see the tire tracks?"

He looked. "Yeah."

"It can't be that far. We'll walk." She turned. "Everyone, bring your stuff, especially if you have any food left over from lunch or dinner." They had stopped at a hamburger joint on the way out of Redmond. "Put on all the clothes you brought."

She took her purse, but left the tote that held only the schedule for the day, competition rules and her notes on questions she would drill students on in the expectation they'd be asked the same ones again someday. Once everybody was out, she made them line up single file behind Dieter, bringing up the end herself. Then, feeling silly, she locked the van.

"Lead on," she called.

Her face felt the cold first, then her feet. Was this the right decision? she worried, as they stumbled through the dark and falling snow led by—God help them—a sixteen-year-old boy's memory of a winter vacation.

Well, she had no choice—not after she'd gotten the van stuck. Within minutes, she was almost too cold to care.

"I see lights!" Dieter exclaimed.

Fiona blinked away the flakes clinging to her lashes and peered numbly ahead. Was that a dim glow, or a mirage?

"Keep going," she ordered, her face feeling stiff.

Gradually she saw them: golden squares of windows. Not brightly lit, but as if there might be lights on deeper inside the lodge. Or maybe firelight was providing the illumination.

They were staggering, a ragged line of kids and Fiona, when they reached porch steps. Freshly shoveled, she saw in amazement, as if someone had been expecting them.

On the porch that seemed to run the width of the rustic lodge, her students clustered, waiting for her.

The door was massive, the knocker a cast-iron bear. She lifted it and let it fall. Once. Twice. Then again.

She was about to reach for the handle to find out if the door was locked when the porch light came on, all but blinding her, and the door swung open.

Framed in the opening was a man with a scarred face who said, "What in hell?"

Fiona's knees weakened and she grabbed for the door frame. "Can we please come in?"

WATCHING THEM file past him, not just a couple of stranded travelers but a whole damn *crowd* of them, John felt a wave of incredulity. What kind of idiots had been taking the pass in this blizzard? How in God's name had they found the lodge?

And how long was he going to be stuck with them?

They all went straight to the fireplace and huddled in front of the fire with their hands out toward it as if asking for a blessing. None made any move to shed jackets, and he realized studying their backs that most of them weren't dressed for the weather at all. Athletic shoes and jeans were soaked to their knees and probably frozen, too.

Was he going to have to deal with frostbite?

"How far did you walk?"

One guy turned his head. "Just, I don't know, halfway from the turn?"

The voice gave him away. He was a kid. John looked down the line. They were all kids!

"Isn't there an adult with you?"

"Me." The woman who'd been the first to come in turned to face him, pushing back the hood on her parka. Dark, curly hair framed a face on which he could read exhaustion. Her eyes, though, were the pale, clear grey of the river water cutting between snowbanks. She was young, not much older than her charges, her body as slight as those of the teenage girls. "My name is Fiona MacPherson. Thank you for taking us in."

"What were you doing out on the road?"

She explained. They'd competed in a high school Knowledge Champs tournament in Redmond, and were returning home over the mountains.

"We came over this morning on Highway 22," she explained, sounding meek. "But the weather reports said a storm was coming from the south, so I thought I'd take a more northerly route back."

"This highway closes in the winter. You're probably the last ones over it."

"I didn't know that."

And parents trusted her to be in charge? He shook his head.

"You're damn lucky to have made it." John waved off whatever she was going to say. "You all need to get out of your wet clothes. I don't suppose you have anything to change into?"

Eight—no, nine—heads shook in unison.

"Get your shoes and socks off. I'll see what I can find."

He started with the lost and found. Seemed like every week somebody left something. Sunglasses, single gloves, bras hanging on the towel rack in the shared bathroom, long underwear left carelessly on the bed, you name it, he'd found it. If one of the girls wanted birth control pills, he could offer her a month's supply. Bottles containing half a dozen other prescription drugs. Pillows, watches, but mostly clothes.

John dragged the boxes out and distributed socks, one pair of men's slippers, sweatpants, a pair of flannel pajama bottoms and miscellaneous other garments. Then, irritated at the necessity, he raided his own drawers and closet for jeans, socks and sweaters.

Without arguing, they sat down on chairs and the floor as close to the fire as they could get and changed, nobody worrying about modesty. Not even the teacher, who wore bikini underwear and had spectacular legs that she quickly shivvied into a pair of those skintight, stretchy pants cross-country skiers wore these days. They looked fine on her, he saw, while trying not to notice.

"We were so lucky to find you," she told him, apparently unaware that he'd noticed her changing. "I couldn't see anything. But Dieter—" she gestured toward one of the boys "—saw tire tracks. I don't know how. Then he spotted your sign. He and his family have stayed here before."

"You're not the old guy who was here then," the kid said.

"I bought the lodge last year."

"It's a cool place! My family and me, we've come a couple times. Once in the summer, when we stayed in one of the cabins. Last time we skied."

"It's not skiing when you have to plod instead of riding up the hill," one of the girls sniffed. Literally—her nose was bright red and dripping.

"Sure it is," the first boy argued. He was at that ungainly stage when his hands and feet were out-sized and the rest of him skinny. Crooked features added up to a puppy-dog friendly face. "You don't think when they invented skiing they had quad chairlifts, do you?"

"My great-great-whatever came west in a covered wagon, too," she retorted, with another sniff. "I'd rather fly United, thanks."

The rest chimed in with opinions; John didn't listen. He looked at the teacher. "Anyone going to miss you?"

"Oh Lord! Yes! We were having trouble with cell phone coverage." She gave him a hopeful look. "Do you have a land line?"

"Out here? No. And cell phone coverage is lousy for miles around even when the weather's good. Unfortunately, my shortwave radio had an accident and I haven't got it fixed." If what his idiot guest had done to it with spilled coffee could be called an accident. And he should have taken the damn thing to town to be worked on, but hadn't felt any urgency. Stupid, when a guest could have an emergency at any time.

"Well, we'll try again anyway. Kids, anyone who brought a phone. If you reach someone, tell them to start a phone tree."

Six out of the eight kids pulled tiny flip phones out of a pocket or bag. John suddenly felt old. When he was sixteen, nobody'd had a phone. Or wanted one.

The teacher was the only one who got lucky, although he gathered the reception wasn't good. The kids all put theirs away, shaking their heads.

She kept raising her voice. "Yes, Thunder Mountain. You'll call the parents?" Pause. "It's snowing there, too?"

That caused a stir.

"Wow."

"Cool."

"We don't get snow that much. I wish I was home."

"We have more here."

"Snowball fight!" another boy said. This one's face caused a shift in John's chest. He looked too much like the teenage boys hanging around on dusty streets in Baghdad. He might be Hawaiian or Polynesian. Something just a little exotic, skin brown and eyes dark and tilted.

"Yeah!" The third boy, short and stocky with spiky blond hair. Sweatpants from the lost and found bagged on him. "I will so take you down."

Girls giggled. Like a litter of puppies driven by instincts they didn't understand, the boys began shoving and wrestling.

Dark heads, laughter. A group of boys much like this, clowning around. A mud-brick wall. Rusty dust puffing under their feet, a couple of dirty soccer balls lying forgotten.

With a physical wrench, John pulled himself from the past. He tolerated guests at the lodge. Teenage boys, he avoided. Their very presence brought back things he couldn't let himself remember. How was he going to endure this group?

The teacher—Fiona?—evidently sensed his longing. After telling the kids that the principal would call all their parents, she said to John, "I hope you won't be stuck with us for long. Um… Do you have any idea when this storm is supposed to end?"

"A couple of days, at least. And I'm at the bottom of the highway department's list for plowing. Could be a week before they get here."

The longest week of his life.

Just like that, he was propelled into another flashback.

He was driving a truck, the sun scorching through the window and sweat dripping from his helmet, dust from the convoy ahead turning his and everyone else's face to gray masks their mamas wouldn't have recognized. Women walking along the side of the road in dark robes—how in hell did they stand the heat inside them? Kids giving the convoy wary, sidelong looks. Men staring with flat hostility. M-16 in his lap, John scanned the people, the side of the road, the rooftops of the sand-colored mud buildings for anything that looked wrong.

As quickly, the vivid memory faded and he was

back in the lodge, only the teacher looking at him a little strangely.

Not the longest week of his life, he apologized silently, if anyone was listening. He'd lived a year of longer ones. Survived them.

If living half in the past, hiding out in the present, could be called survival.

CHAPTER TWO

"A WEEK!" the teacher exclaimed, and John had the sense she was repeating herself.

Yeah, he'd definitely tuned out.

"But…if the highway department knows we're stranded here, surely they'll plow this far sooner than that. You can't possibly have enough food to keep us that long."

"This is a lodge. I take in paying guests. Since I just stocked up, we won't starve."

"Oh." She nibbled on a delectable bottom lip, full enough to make his groin tighten.

Damn. Why her? The subject of women wasn't something he'd wasted any time thinking about since he got out of the VA hospital.

"Do you have any guests right now?" she asked.

John shook his head. "Expected a couple today. Don't suppose they'll make it."

"So you have enough beds?"

This was a woman who knew how to stick to the essentials.

"We'll have to make some up."

"We can do it. I don't want to put you out any more than we have to."

You want to share mine?

Right. That was happening.

Nice, he thought somewhat grimly, to know that his libido *had* survived.

"I'll show you where the bedding is."

She ordered them all to come. "You can make up your own beds."

"We get our own?" a blond pixie asked.

"Two to a bed," Fiona MacPherson decreed. "We'll stick to our buddy system."

Made it harder for a boy to sneak into a girl's room, John diagnosed with wry amusement. Chaperoning this bunch for a week would be a chore. The school ought to give her a nice fat bonus once she returned the kids to their parents' custody. Unless, of course, she was in hot water for setting out in the first place on the foolhardy venture to cross the pass.

They trooped upstairs. He showed them the shared bathrooms, each boasting a deep, claw-foot tub, double sinks, piles of towels and open shelving for the guests' toiletries.

"Oh, eew," one of the girls exclaimed. "We don't have toothbrushes or anything!"

He almost kept his mouth shut. Bad breath might make the chaperoning easier. But that was just plain mean. He might be a recluse, but he was also an innkeeper.

"I keep extras for guests who forget them. Remind me and I'll go get some."

"Bless you," the teacher murmured, apparently not having considered the benefits of halitosis.

He handed out flannel sheets and duvet covers, they

picked partners and rooms. Fortunately two of the rooms each had a pair of queen beds, so the three boys went in one of those and three of the girls in the other. Another pair of girls shared a room and Fiona claimed the first room at the head of the stairs.

John went in with her to help her make up the bed. Setting the armful of linens on a chair, she looked around with approval.

"Dieter told me the lodge was really nice. This is lovely."

He'd bought the place as-is, but it was in good shape. Her room was typical: polished plank floors with a rag rug to add warmth, a bed built of peeled Ponderosa pine and covered with a puffy duvet, antique pine dresser with a mirror that showed a wavery reflection. The artwork varied from room to room, giving each character. She was in the one he privately thought of as the Rose Room, with cottage-style paintings in which roses smothered fences and arbors and tangled in old-fashioned hedgerows. He tended to put women in here.

With quick, efficient movements, he and Fiona made up her bed with snow-white sheets and duvet cover. When they'd finished, she looked at him over the bed.

"I don't think you told me your name."

"Fallon. John Fallon."

Her smile was a thing of beauty, somehow merry and so warm he had the sudden illusion of not needing the fire downstairs. "It's nice to meet you, John Fallon. You're a kind man to try to hide how much you wish we hadn't shown up on your front porch."

He thought of himself as a decent man. Decent enough to do the right thing when he had to.

"I usually have guests. You're not putting me out." What was a little white lie?

"We're just surprise guests."

And nonpaying ones, he presumed.

Again, she seemed to read his mind.

"I'll make sure you're reimbursed, at least for the food. I teach at a private school." She nodded toward the voices drifting from the other bedrooms. "Most of their parents are pretty well-to-do."

He only nodded. "That would be appreciated."

Again her teeth closed briefly on her lower lip. "I hate to ask, but… We ate at four o'clock. I suspect the boys especially are starved."

John had once been skinny like the one kid. He seemed to remember eating from morning to night and never feeling full.

"Sandwiches?"

"Sandwiches would be great." She treated him to another smile, this time relieved.

They met at the foot of the bed and had one of those awkward moments where they both hesitated, started forward, shuffled, until he finally waved toward the door. "After you."

It seemed to him that her cheeks were a little bit pink. Did she feel some of the pull that had him half-aroused and uncomfortable?

He couldn't imagine. With his scarred face and obvious limp, he was more likely to be an object of pity than lust. His throat momentarily tightened. Had that moment been so clumsy because she'd been trying to defer to him since he was disabled?

"I'll get started on food," he said shortly, and left her to the kids.

Like a bunch of locusts, they showed up in the kitchen all too quickly and began filling plates. A couple of the smaller girls barely nibbled—one was Asian, a tiny thing with glossy black hair down to her hips, the other thin and plain with braces that pushed her lips out. Those two, he remembered, had taken the room with one bed, and now were quieter than the others.

Two girls were arguing loudly about some math question, while another flirted with the stocky boy who seemed more interested in piling food on his plate. The teacher looked dead on her feet.

She swayed, and John stepped forward, but she rallied and said, "Wow! This is great. Thank you."

They took seats around the long, farmhouse table that occupied the middle of the enormous kitchen, John at her right side.

"Everyone, our host is John Fallon." She reeled off their names, most of which he'd likely need to hear again.

The tall, skinny boy who'd stayed here before was Dieter Schoenecker, the stocky one had the unlikely name of Hopper Daniels, and the third boy was Troy Thorsen. Nordic last name, which didn't explain his racial heritage.

The girls were a blur. Kelli—with an i, she made sure to tell him, last name he didn't catch, Amy Brooks, who seemed given to posing and flipping her hair,

Tabitha, Erin and…that left someone out, but he couldn't remember who. Probably the plain, quiet one.

Watching the speed with which the food disappeared, John took mental stock of his larder. They'd be okay for a week, he figured; he kept an emergency supply of canned goods he could dip into if need be.

Fiona took half a sandwich and ate it slowly, as if she had to remind herself to take a bite and swallow. Clearly they'd driven across the mountains that morning, and had probably made an early start to have had time for any kind of competition during the day. Driving for hours through the blizzard had to have wrung her out.

"Why don't you hit the sack?" he said quietly. "They're still wound up. I can sort them out later."

"I'm responsible…"

"You look ready to collapse."

Dieter Schoenecker, who sat on her other side, heard. "Ms. Mac was Superwoman today."

She managed a grin and pretended to flex a bicep. "That's me. Speaking of which—" she pitched her voice a little louder "—have I mentioned that I have X-ray vision? I see through walls."

"Ahh! Ms. Mac doesn't trust us." The Hopper kid clasped his hand to his chest and fell back in his chair.

She just smiled. "Bathroom on the right side upstairs is for girls, left side for boys."

"Toothbrushes." John pushed back his chair and stood. His bad leg chose to cave, and he had to brace his hand on the back of the chair until the spasm let up. Without looking to see if anyone had noticed, he left the kitchen.

He grabbed a basket and piled it with toothbrushes,

toothpaste in sample tubes, dental floss, the small bottles of shampoo and hand lotion he put out when readying a bathroom for guests, and a couple of packages of feminine products. It might embarrass the girls, but if they were here for very many days, odds were a couple of them would need something.

Fiona stood when he came back. "I'll take that up." She looked into the basket. "Oh, thank goodness. I didn't even think of that as a problem. I'll distribute all this." She raised her voice. "I'm going to bed, kids. Help Mr. Fallon clean up, then I expect you to get ready for bed, too. It's been a long day."

"Do we have to turn the lights out?" Amy looked genuinely horrified.

"No. You can read, talk, listen to music, whatever. Just keep it down, and be considerate of each other."

"If you need anything during the night—" John pointed to a door at the back of the kitchen "—that's where I'll be."

Nods all around.

He walked the teacher to the foot of the stairs.

Standing one step up, she was at eye level with him. "Did I tell you when I called that our principal said they had four inches and snow still piling up even in Portland? It's amazing that you have electricity."

"We operate on a generator. There aren't any power lines out here."

"Oh. That makes sense." She gave a small shiver. "I can't believe how lucky we were. I didn't want the kids to know, but...I was so scared."

Feeling cruel, he said, "You should have been. Without winter gear..."

Her chin came up. “This blizzard wasn’t predicted so soon. And none of the meteorologists expected it to be so major. It’s only November!”

“You ever noticed how ski areas open Thanksgiving weekend? Means they’ve been getting snow for weeks.”

“That’s true, but we’re not at that kind of elevation here…” She trailed off, then sighed. “You’re right. We should have never set off without being prepared. I knew we had chains, and I’ve driven in snow, so I got complacent. But my dad kept down sleeping bags in the trunk whenever we traveled during the winter.”

“Smart man.”

“You saved our lives.”

“No. It sounds like Dieter did.”

Her face softened. “He did. He’s an amazing boy. Really brilliant. I mean, they’re all smart, but not like him. And he’s so…together. Mature and, I don’t know, comfortable with himself. Which, let me tell you, is rare in sixteen-year-olds.”

The boys he’d known in Iraq were younger in years, if older in experience. Living in a war zone did that to kids.

He jerked his head toward the kitchen. “They all that age?”

“Willow is fifteen. She’s our only sophomore. And Troy and Erin are seniors, so they’re seventeen. The rest are juniors.”

John nodded.

“It’s nice of you to take charge. I really am tired.”

“Go. They’ll be fine.”

“I know. You’re right.”

Still she didn’t move, and he thought how easy it

would be to step forward, wrap a hand around the back of her head and kiss her.

Something on his face may have given away the tenor of his thoughts, because her color rose and she groped backward with one foot for the next step.

"I don't know what I'm just standing here for. Tiredness, I guess. Um, good night."

He dipped his head. "Good night."

John stayed at the foot of the stairs watching until she disappeared above with the basket of toiletries. He should have offered her a nightgown; he had a few of those in the lost and found, too. All were sturdy flannel. He didn't know if any newlyweds had ever honeymooned at Thunder Mountain Lodge, but if so the brides had remembered to take home their lacy negligees.

John frowned, trying to remember whether the kids had called her Miss. Or was it Ms.? Young as she looked, she could be married. No, he decided; if she was, she would have called her husband tonight, not the principal. And she'd asked him to phone parents. She hadn't said anything about him calling a husband.

Heading back to the kitchen, he was irritated to realize that he felt relieved.

FIONA HAD NEVER been more grateful to be able to brush her teeth. As she did so, she thought about their host. He'd been remarkably kind so far, but he'd looked so grim all the while!

She wondered what had happened to give him the limp and the scar that ran from his jaw down his neck and beneath the collar of his shirt. It looked…not brand-new, but not as if he'd lived with it for years, either. Several times she'd seen a spasm of pain on his face, too, so the injury to his leg obviously still troubled him.

Well, she could hardly ask, and hoped the kids would be tactful enough not to. Or, more realistically, she should hope that they were too self-centered to care about John Fallon's history.

Fiona brushed her hair with her own brush from her purse, then gazed at herself in the mirror. What had he seen when he looked at her? A couple of times she'd imagined… But that was silly. He probably thought she was an idiot who hadn't showed any more sense than the teenagers would have.

She sighed. Sad as it was to admit, he was right. It terrified her still to think what might have happened if Dieter hadn't spotted those tire tracks. The fact that they were safe and warm tonight was a miracle.

In the bedroom, she hesitated over what to wear—or *not* wear, finally leaving on the pants he'd lent her and her turtleneck. Just in case she had to get up for some reason during the night.

The bed felt wonderful, the fluffy duvet heavenly atop her. Tension drained out of her, and Fiona closed her eyes.

The moment she did, white swirled beneath her lids, as if the sight had been imprinted on them. She squeezed her eyes tighter shut and fought to picture something or someone else.

What she came up with was John Fallon's face as they'd stood at the foot of the stairs. Lean, tanned, with strong cheekbones, dark bristles on jaw and cheeks, a fan of lines beside watchful brown eyes, and a mouth he kept compressed. The scar, puckered and angry. Maybe, she thought, his mouth was tight against pain and not from impatience or irritation.

But there had been that moment when she'd have sworn his gaze had lowered briefly to her mouth. The muscles in his jaw had knotted, and something had flickered in his eyes.

Had he kissed a woman since he'd been hurt?

How silly. He probably had a girlfriend, or even a wife who happened to be away right now. She doubted he had looked at her with desire—even momentarily.

He was being as polite as he was able, and she would have to do her very best to be sure they weren't any more trouble than they had to be. It was absurd for her to wish that the unsmiling lodgekeeper would look at her with just a little more warmth.

Still, she held on to the image of his face until exhaustion overcame her.

FIONA AWAKENED to the sound of a squeal, then hushed giggles. Huh? She opened her eyes and stared at a strange, pitched ceiling. For a moment she felt completely blank. Then it came back to her.

Snowstorm, hellish drive, the lurch as the van dropped off the road, the tramp through knee-deep snow in the dark.

She had slept… She turned her head and found an old-fashioned clock on the nightstand. Twelve hours? Was it possible?

Galvanized, she jackknifed to a sitting position. Her

students! And here she'd gone to sleep vowing to keep them out of their host's hair.

No slippers, but she'd left her borrowed wool socks on. Fiona paused to peer in the mirror and shuddered. She'd scare the kids.

No choice. She needed the bathroom, and *now.*

Raucous laughter came from one of the girls' rooms followed by someone shushing.

"Hey," she said, flapping a hand as she went by.

"The bathtub is so-o amazing," Tabitha called after her. "Mr. Fallon said it was okay to use as much hot water as we wanted."

The idea of sinking into a deep tub of hot water was irresistible. On the other hand, putting on dirty clothes when she got out was less appealing.

Water splashed the floor in the bathroom and toothbrushes, hairbrushes and makeup were scattered over the counter. Dirty clothes were heaped in a corner. Sitting on the toilet, Fiona gazed at the pile wide-eyed. Had John Fallon come up with *more* clothes…?

Then she spotted the neat pile of folded laundry on the slatted shelving unit beside the towels. As if in a dream, she investigated. There were her jeans and yesterday's socks, neatly rolled. He'd washed and dried their clothes last night.

"I'm going to marry him," she said out loud.

If he had a clean shirt she could borrow, she could leave off her panties and handwash them. She could have that bath.

Realizing she hadn't looked outside yet, she went to the window. Beyond the eaves, snow still fell and the world beyond was completely white. What if they had slid into a ditch last night, instead of making it safely here?

She shivered and turned quickly back to the bathroom.

Fiona brushed her tangled hair and went out, stopping once again in the door to the girls' bedroom. This time she saw that Hopper sat on the floor with his legs outstretched and Amy, Tabitha and Kelli lounged on the beds.

"Where's everyone else?"

Kelli shrugged. "Still asleep, I guess."

"I see it's still snowing."

"It's really pretty outside."

"Have you had breakfast?"

"Uh-huh. There's a toaster, and this really great bread, and muffins, and when he saw we were up, Mr. Fallon scrambled some eggs. And then he gave us the laundry."

"I couldn't believe it when I saw he'd washed our clothes. It's like..."

"The shoemaker and the elves." Tabitha nodded. "The bread tasted like it was right out of the oven. Do you think he slept at all?"

"I don't know." Fiona scrutinized them. "He loaned you some more clothes."

"They are *so* too big." Amy gazed down at herself with comical dismay. Actually the flannel shirt she wore draped becomingly, giving her a waifish look but for the swell of breasts.

"I'm going to go borrow something, too," Fiona declared. "And then take a bath. Don't let Willow or Erin beat me to it if they appear."

"We won't."

She'd barely reached the first floor when John Fallon materialized in front of her.

"Oh! You scared me. I didn't see you."

"I was adding wood to the fire."

Their host was even better looking in the light of day. He'd shaved and wore a heavy, cream-colored, Irish knit sweater over jeans. His dark hair, brushed back from his face, was just long enough to curl over the collar of the sweater.

"Thank you for washing our clothes."

He nodded. "I set some more out in the kitchen, if you want to borrow something. Once everyone's up, I'll run another load."

"Are we leaving you anything to wear?"

"Enough."

Was he always so closemouthed, or was it just Fiona who brought it out in him? Weren't innkeepers supposed to brim with *bonhomie?*

"Um…I think I'll go pick something out." She started toward the kitchen.

He followed. "Breakfast?"

"I'm going to take a bath first, before the kids use up all the hot water."

"The lodge has several water heaters. It's not good for business to make guests take cold baths."

"No, I suppose not. I should warn you, though, that unless they're reined in, my group may challenge your capacity. Have you ever had a lodgeful of teenagers before?"

He seemed to shake himself. Or had he shuddered?

"Yes."

"They shower a lot. They're awfully conscious of how they look." And smell.

"I remember."

She sniffed. "Did you bake that bread fresh this morning?"

"Figured we'd need it."

"Did you ever go to bed?"

His big shoulders moved. "I get up early."

She opened her mouth.

"No more thanks." Was that a trace of humor in his eyes? Or was she imagining it?

Like the living area with its enormous, river-rock fireplace, the kitchen was vast, the cabinets rustic, the floor slate. There was plenty of room in the middle for a table that would seat at least twenty.

Almost at random, she chose a red plaid flannel shirt from the neat piles on the table. "If you'll excuse me…?"

He stepped aside.

Clutching the shirt, she hurried upstairs. Ugh. Nothing like letting a man you'd barely met see you first thing in the morning.

Willow had joined the others, and called after her, "I want a bath, too!"

"I had dibs on it."

She locked the door and started water cascading into the tub before she noticed a cut-glass bowl of bath beads on an antique wood commode situated perfectly to hold a glass of wine, say, or candles.

The tub was definitely big enough for two.

She dropped a white bead in, and soon the scent of gardenias filled the steamy air.

She ached as if she'd competed in a triathalon yesterday. Sinking into the hot water was heavenly. The foot of the tub was slanted, and she barely held her chin above water. She actually floated, and gave a moan of pleasure. Someday, she, too, would have a bathtub like this.

If the water hadn't cooled, she might never have been able to make herself get out. That, and the realization that her stomach was rumbling. She'd barely had a bite or two last night, and the hamburger she'd eaten at three-thirty or so yesterday afternoon seemed like an awfully long time ago.

Her bra would do for another day or two, but she added her panties to the pile in the corner and slipped on the jeans. She would offer to do the wash; somehow, the idea of the handsome, scarred stranger downstairs plucking her dirty panties from the pile and dropping them in the machine was too much for her.

The flannel shirt, well-worn, hung to midthigh and she had to roll the sleeves four or five times. Fiona dried and brushed her hair, leaving it loose around her face, then hung her towel on a rack and left the bathroom.

The sound of running water came from behind the closed door to the boy's bathroom. Someone else was up, then.

When Fiona stopped in the door to the girls' bedroom, Willow jumped up. "My turn."

Erin had appeared now as well, and she shrugged. "I have to go get something clean to put on first anyway."

As usual, she looked exquisite this morning, her black hair glossy in a plait, her skin smooth. Fiona had never seen her break out in acne, sweat or even frown. The only adopted child of a cardiac surgeon father and a mother who designed exquisite linens that sold at high-end department stores, Erin was invariably composed and quiet. She was a straight A student and the star of the Knowledge Champs and Hi-Q teams, but no more than a ripple on her brow would show when she made a mistake or was outmatched. Fiona often wondered if she was anywhere near as serene as she appeared, or whether she suffered from the pressure of having to live up to such high-achieving parents.

Fiona made a face. Big assumption on her part. Maybe Erin's parents were easygoing despite their career successes. Fiona had only met them once.

"Sleep well?" she asked, as they went downstairs.

Erin nodded. "Except Willow kept talking in her sleep."

"Could you understand what she was saying?"

"Once in a while. But it didn't really make sense. Like once she said, 'Why did you fall down?' And when I asked what she was talking about, she said, 'You fell over that blue thing.'"

Fiona laughed. "That sounds pretty normal. Dreams hardly ever make sense."

"I guess that's true." At the foot of the stairs, she looked shyly at Fiona. "Do you ever have ones where you can fly?"

"Not fly, but bounce. And stay up for a long time. Do you actually soar?"

"Uh-huh. Everything's tiny below."

Somehow that seemed rather aptly to symbolize Erin, who often kept herself apart from her peers. Fiona didn't remember, for example, ever seeing her with a boy.

"Does the dream worry you?" she asked carefully, as they entered the kitchen.

"No." Her voice was very soft. "Except I'm scared of heights. So it seems weird."

Yes. It did.

"You okay rooming with Willow?"

"Sure. Are these the clothes we can borrow?" Far and away the most petite of the girls, she lifted garments until she found a turtleneck that was clearly a woman's. More from the lost and found, Fiona surmised.

Unless it belonged to John Fallon's currently absent wife.

"Come and get some breakfast after you've had your bath."

Erin nodded and left Fiona alone in the kitchen. She sliced bread and popped two pieces in the toaster, then gazed at the small paned window beyond which she saw nothing but floating white flakes.

"Can I get you some eggs?"

Fiona jumped, turning. "You should clear your throat when you come into a room."

He lifted his brows. "Like a butler? Ahem, ma'am?"

She laughed at him. "Exactly."

"I feel like a butler some of the time. Invisible." He looked surprised at his own admission.

"You own the lodge," Fiona protested.

"But guests feel as if they're paying for me to wait on them. Which puts me in the servant class."

"Really? Do they talk as if you aren't there?"

"Not everyone. But some do."

She studied him. "You don't sound as if you're used to it. Which means you haven't been doing this long."

"I'm learning on the job." His expression, never forthcoming, closed completely. "Your toast has popped up. And you didn't tell me whether you want eggs."

"If you mean it, I'd love some. Scrambled," she added.

He nodded and got supplies from the enormous refrigerator while she buttered the slices of toast and slathered on jam that looked and—when she took a bite—tasted homemade.

In only moments, it seemed, John set the plate of eggs on the table in front of her.

"Will you sit down with me?" she asked. "I suppose you've long since eaten."

"I wouldn't mind a cup of coffee. You? I'm sorry, I should have asked sooner. I didn't know whether the kids should be drinking it, so I didn't offer any."

"I'd love some."

She began eating hungrily while he poured coffee and sat at one end of the long table with her, pushing a mug toward her. "I'm starved," she admitted, between bites.

"Stressful day yesterday."

"You can say that again."

"This Knowledge Champs. Did your students win?"

"We actually have two teams. The A team did pretty well. They won one round and tied another. The B team got creamed. Partly because Amy and Hopper were too busy flirting to pay attention."

"Ah." His mouth relaxed into something approaching a smile. “Amy being the one constantly fiddling with her hair.”

“I swear, I’m going to make her put it in a ponytail before the next competition.”

Fiona finished her toast and considered the muffins.

“Applesauce or blueberry.”

“You made them yourself?”

“Yes.”

How like him. A succinct answer, no desire to expand the way most people would, admitting that they’d always liked to cook or hadn’t liked to cook but found they were good at it, no, *The recipe is my mother’s.*

So, how to learn something about him? *Are you married?* seemed too bald.

“Do you have kids?” she asked.

“No.”

Argh.

“Me, either,” she said. “Someday.”

He nodded, although whether concurring or simply acknowledging what she’d said, Fiona couldn’t guess.

“Do you usually have guests year-round?”

“Generally just weekends in the winter.”

“Don’t you get lonely?”

Again she thought she saw amusement, as much in a momentary narrowing of his eyes as on his mouth. Did he know perfectly well what she was getting at?

“No.” After a moment, he added, “I prefer the solitude.”

Fiona hid her face behind the mug and took a sip of coffee. “Then I’m doubly sorry,” she said, setting it down, “that we’ve had to impose ourselves on you.” She tilted her head. “I hear some of the kids coming right now.”

He rose, lines appearing between his brows. "I shouldn't have said that."

She looked at him. "Is it the truth?"

Very stiffly, he said, "I served in Iraq. When I got back..."

Behind him, Dieter and Troy wrestled to determine who would get through the doorway first. "Food," Dieter moaned. "Let me at the food."

When she looked again at John Fallon, it was to see that he had once again wiped his face clean of expression. Whatever he'd been going to say—and, from what she'd read about the problems of returning veterans, she could guess—would remain unspoken unless she wrenched it out of him.

Darn it, did the boys *have* to show up, just when the conversation was getting interesting?

CHAPTER THREE

WILLOW AND ERIN came into the kitchen right behind the boys, Willow with wet hair slicked to her head. If Erin had bathed, she'd somehow kept hers dry.

John took orders for eggs and disappeared into the pantry.

"Can we go outside after breakfast?" Dieter asked.

"Have you looked out the window?"

"Yeah, it's still snowing. Major cool!"

"Do you know how easily you could get lost out there?"

"Come on," he coaxed. "We'd stay right by the lodge."

"Clothes are another problem. We can't keep asking Mr. Fallon to wash them so we can go out and play."

His face fell. "Oh. Wow. I wish I had my ski stuff."

Personally Fiona would settle for a couple of pairs of clean underwear.

"We'll see," she said. "I'm going to offer to do the laundry this morning. Maybe we could do a load of wet stuff later."

They cheered just as John return from the pantry with a big bowl.

"They want to go outside," she explained to him. "I'm concerned about our limited changes of clothes."

He thought he could come up with a few pairs of quilted pants and more parkas and gloves. "The lost and found is full of gloves. And hats."

No surprise; those were the small items easy to misplace. She could lose a glove at home or in her car.

When she was done eating, she insisted on carrying her own dirty dishes to the sink and then he showed her the laundry room. "I'll get a load running," she said with a nod. "And I'll organize the kids to wash dishes. You shouldn't have to wait on us."

He opened his mouth and closed it.

"What?"

He shook his head. "Just...you don't look like a schoolmarm. But you have it down pat."

"I've been teaching for five years now."

"You don't look old enough."

Two personal observations in a row. Were either compliments?

"I'm twenty-seven."

"So you started teaching right out of college."

Fiona nodded. "I've been working on my master's degree at Portland State for several years. Summer quarter and sometimes an evening class."

"Better salary?"

She sighed. "Of course. But also, I'm learning. I used to think I wouldn't be interested in administration, but maybe someday."

This was when the conversation was supposed to become reciprocal. *Yeah, I thought about minoring in education but...*

Even though he didn't say anything in response, he

didn't seem in any hurry to leave the small laundry room. In fact, she was suddenly aware of how close he was to her, and of how alone they were even though she could hear the kids' voices coming from the kitchen. Not that she wasn't aware of him every time she saw him, but now she found herself noticing the deep chocolate shade of his eyes, the fact that he'd apparently nicked himself shaving that morning—and how fresh and puckered that scar was.

When her gaze touched on the scar, something flared in his eyes and he took a step back.

Before he could speak, Fiona said hurriedly, "What about you? Before…Iraq. Were you career military?"

For a moment he didn't answer, and she thought he wouldn't. Then, with obvious reluctance, he said, "No. National Guard. Before, I was an engineer."

"Really?" Oh, no; had she sounded surprised? Please God he hadn't noticed. "What kind? Did you design bridges?"

"I was a mechanical engineer. Mainly robotics to increase workplace safety."

"From that to innkeeper." She'd meant the words to be light, but she could tell he didn't take them that way.

A muscle spasmed in his jaw. "That's right. Now, if you'll excuse me?"

"I'm sorry. I didn't mean…"

"Nothing to be sorry for." He walked away, his limp pronounced.

Why had her asking about his past distressed him? Had he had some kind of breakdown when he got back from Iraq? Like the Vietnam vets who'd gone to live in the woods? Was the only difference that he'd been able to afford to buy this place?

The kids were all in the kitchen, Willow as usual looking shy and apart from the group, Erin equally apart but serenely so. John was nowhere to be seen. Fiona carried a basket upstairs and collected dirty clothes.

Going back through the kitchen, she said, "Boys, you get KP duty this morning. When everyone's done eating, it's your job to wash the dishes."

Inevitably Hopper grumbled, "Why us?"

"Because we're all going to take turns." She surveyed the table. "Tabitha, Erin and I are going to make lunch. Willow, Kelli and Amy will do the lunch dishes. Dinner we'll discuss when it gets closer."

Smiling, she left them groaning and whining. Some of them had looked shocked enough, she had to wonder if they were required to do chores at home. That was the thing with a ritzy private school—the kids came from a whole different world than the one in which she'd grown up. They were more sophisticated in many ways than the teenagers with whom she'd gone to school. They compared Thai food at a restaurant to food they'd had in Thailand, snorkeling off Belize to experiences on the Barrier reef. They wore designer clothes, had every electronic gadget and drove BMWs the minute they turned sixteen.

But there were also huge gaps in their knowledge. They spoke of maids instead of having to carry out the garbage. She doubted most of them knew how to mop a kitchen floor or scrub a toilet. Maybe even how to wash dishes, although they were smart kids—they'd figure it out. They seemed not to have been expected to be responsible for much of anything. She had one student in her U.S. History class who'd wrecked two cars since March, and both times his parents had just bought him a new one.

Many of her students were great kids; some, like Erin, were clearly driven. But others were spoiled and simply marking time. She had two this year in Knowledge Champs that she suspected were merely padding their résumés for college: Amy and Troy. Amy was also one of the weakest participants. But Troy was different.

As a senior, he was on the A team. He was smart. But she'd also found him to be lazy. He often missed practice. His grades were top-notch, but when she looked at his file she saw that he had participated in very few extracurricular activities in his first three years of high school. That had changed this fall, when he joined Knowledge Champs and won a part in the fall musical.

Well, it wasn't her business, but it would be interesting to see how they responded to her expectations if they were stranded at Thunder Mountain Lodge for long.

And even more interesting, she decided, as she set the washing machine to a normal cycle and started picking out light-colored garments, to see whether John Fallon opened up to her—or started hiding out in his quarters.

Of course, she shouldn't care, considering she'd never see him again after the snowplows came through. What was it he'd said? *I prefer the solitude.* But then, with the way he looked at her sometimes, she wondered whether that was true.

Would he tell her how he'd been hurt if she asked? Or would he be offended by her nosiness?

She frowned and closed the lid on the washer. Probably the latter, and she wouldn't even blame him.

But she couldn't stop thinking about him. He was an enigma: an intelligent, well-educated man who'd presumably had a high-paying job and yet was now cooking and cleaning up after strangers at this remote lodge, glad when he had his midweek solitude. A man who hid his pain, who had been dismayed by the sight of the woman and kids on his doorstep but had been kind in large and small ways since then. He was a man who looked as if he badly wanted to kiss her, and yet he seemed to have forgotten how to flirt.

More assumptions on her part, Fiona thought with a sigh as she headed back to the kitchen to see how the kids were doing with cleanup. She was tantalized by him, so, ergo, he must be attracted to her.

Because she was so irresistible, of course.

Another sigh. She was pretty on a good day, which this was not. True beauty, she'd never achieve.

Face it: she was unlikely to have a shot at learning what had wounded John Fallon psychologically as well as physically. And, honestly, even if the attraction was reciprocal, where would they go with it, living several hours apart as they did?

Stick to fixing the kids' problems.

"Watch it!" she heard one of the boys say, followed by the crash of a dish shattering on the slate floor.

Fiona winced and hoped the man she'd been obsessing about was out of earshot. Clearly she would have to supervise the kitchen crews.

It might have been far more interesting to have been stranded here *without* eight teenagers.

GETTING THE KIDS out the door was a chore, even after John went to the effort to round up a fair selection of parkas, gloves, hats and several pairs of boots. One girl—Amy—didn't want to go. John was sympathetic until she started to whine.

"It's cold."

"Come on, you gotta be on my team," Hopper coaxed.

"I don't like getting cold."

"But you ski!" one of the other girls said in apparent surprise.

Her lower lip was getting pouty. "Not when it's snowing like this."

Troy Thorsen grabbed a hat and put it on her, pulling it down over her ears even as she shook her head madly, fighting him. "You have to come out, or we won't have even sides."

She yanked it off and threw it at him, her eyes flashing. "I don't *have* to do anything."

Their teacher intervened. "No, you don't. Amy, if you'd rather stay inside, that's fine. Mr. Fallon has a good library. You can pick out a book and read in front of the fire with me."

"But, Ms. Mac!" the skinny kid protested. "Aren't you coming out?"

"Are you kidding? Not a chance."

"Bummer," somebody muttered.

Kelli sniffed and pointedly turned her back on Amy. "Let's just go out. It doesn't matter if sides aren't even."

"Yeah," a couple of them agreed. All began zipping parkas and donning hats.

Amy smiled at Hopper, the boy she'd been hanging on. "You could keep me company. We could play a game. Or, like, explore the lodge." *Be alone,* her tone promised.

Yanking on gloves, he missed the full wattage of her smile and possibly her implicit promise. "Nah, it's going to be cool out there. I'll see you later, okay?"

Standing to one side, John saw anger flare on her face.

Then, "Oh, fine!" she snapped. "I'll come already." She appropriated a parka the girl in braces had been reaching for, picked out a faux-fur headband that left her hair to ripple down her back and chose gloves.

"Cool!" Hopper declared, as oblivious to the cold-shoulder she gave him now as he'd been to her earlier, flirtation.

Coatless—she'd loaned hers to one of the girls—Fiona followed them out onto the porch. "Remember, you'll stay right in front. I want to be able to see all of you whenever I glance out."

"Yes, Ms. Mac," they all said dutifully, meanwhile rolling their eyes.

Shaking her head, she came back inside and shut the heavy front door. "Want to bet on how long they last out there?"

"I'm going to say ten minutes for the one who didn't want to go."

She laughed. "Hopper may live to regret not falling in line."

"Or be very, very grateful he ticked her off early on."

This smile was wry. "Amy is a bit of a handful. She's an only child, which doesn't always mean spoiled…"

"But in Amy's case does," he said bluntly.

"I shouldn't have said that." She seemed perturbed at the idea of criticizing one of her charges. "I'm an only child myself."

Interesting. He wouldn't have guessed. Nodding in acknowledgment, he changed the subject, "If you'll excuse me, I have work to do."

"Can I help?"

He shouldn't succumb to temptation. Spending time alone with her wasn't smart. But she was not only the first woman to interest him since he'd landed stateside, she was also the first person of either gender he'd had any inclination to talk to.

So he said, "If you want to clean bathrooms."

He was ashamed of himself for sounding ungracious. She'd been more than generous in getting the whole group to help out. Once upon a time, he'd known how to make pleasant conversation. Not so long ago. Before…

John willed his mind to go blank.

Fiona helped hold him in the here and now. "Our bathrooms?" She sounded horrified. "We can clean them ourselves."

"We'll just do a quick swipe. Before your charges come in and need hot baths again."

"Oh, dear. They will, won't they?" She nodded.

"Fine. But they won't have made their beds, either, and we're not doing that for them."

She sounded so fierce, a trace of amusement stirred in him. He hardly recognized it. He'd lost his sense of humor along with so much else in Iraq.

Climbing the stairs, he asked, "Are you going to be in trouble over this?"

"With the school, you mean?"

He nodded.

"I don't know. I hope not. I did call my principal before we left Redmond, and he agreed that it made sense to take the alternate route. And it *wasn't* snowing, and forecasters were off by hours about when the storm was supposed to reach this far north."

She wasn't trying to convince him, John guessed, but rather herself.

Her voice went quiet. "Maybe I deserve to lose my job. We could have all died. I used poor judgment."

He'd been harsh yesterday, and now felt like the worst kind of hypocrite. His own misjudgment had resulted in horror. Maybe she'd been lucky, but her error had been mild in comparison.

Besides… He'd been surprised himself yesterday afternoon to walk out of the grocery store and see snow falling so soon. His own drive back to the lodge had been treacherous.

They'd reached the hallway above.

"I suspect there are travelers stranded all over. You may not be the only Knowledge Champs team that got in trouble. From what you said, high schools all over Oregon had sent kids."

Her eyes widened. "Oh, no! I didn't even think about that. Two groups came from Portland and one from Lincoln City over on the coast. What if…?" She pressed a hand to her throat.

"Nothing you can do about it." Okay, that didn't help, John saw immediately. He tried again. "Eight kids is enough for you to take responsibility for."

"I can't help worrying. Oh, I wish we could get some news coverage!"

"You can't do anything."

She tried to smile. "I can worry, can't I?"

They'd been standing here in the hall too long. He was becoming uncomfortably aware of her. Of little things: the palest of freckles on the bridge of her nose, the fullness of her lower lip, the single strand of dark hair that curved down over her brow. He resisted the urge to lift his hand and smooth it back.

The effort made his voice curt. "Worrying won't help."

Her pointy chin rose. "No. It won't. Hadn't we better get started? I figure they've already been out there five minutes. By your estimate, Amy will be coming in the door in another five minutes."

"I didn't mean…"

"It's okay. You're trying to help. I know." She smiled, a benediction.

His fingers curled into fists at his sides. She wouldn't be so forgiving if she knew about the death he'd rained on the innocent.

The road to hell was paved with good intentions.

She took the girls' bathroom, he took the boys'. From long habit, he cleaned fast, and then carried a pile of towels and washcloths to her. She was wiping the countertop, which took longer than in the other bathroom because of the amazing array of toiletries and cosmetics scattered there. All of which had presumably come out of their purses and bookbags.

"Oh, thank you," Fiona said, seeing the pile in his arms. "More loads of laundry in the making."

His laugh felt rusty. "You don't look like the half-empty kind."

She smiled impishly. "In this case, the washing machine is going to be a lot more than half full."

Still smiling, although it felt unnatural, John said, "And I seem to remember you promised to load it."

"Yes, I did." Fiona began hanging towels on racks, leaving part of the stack on the counter between the pair of sinks. "What you said earlier, about Iraq… Was it awful? I know a lot of the returning veterans are suffering from posttraumatic stress, just like after Vietnam."

PTSD—Post-Traumatic Stress Disorder—was a fancy way of saying that you'd seen things you shouldn't have, in John's opinion. It was ridiculous to talk about it as a disease, as if the right pills would cure it.

He cocked a brow at her. "Are you asking if I'm one of them? Maybe. Most soldiers do have some symptoms."

She flushed. "I'm so sorry if you thought… I really wasn't asking, even obliquely. You haven't given me any reason… Oh, dear."

Great. He'd been a jackass again.

"That's all right. I…hinted."

"If you need help you can get it from the Veterans Administration, can't you?"

"I don't need it." The gravel in his voice startled even him. He cleared his throat. "What I need is to...decompress. This is my way of doing that. Be around people in limited doses. Get over being jumpy without a barrage of noise around me all the time."

She looked doubtful even though he could tell she was still embarrassed. "Is it working?"

Some days he thought so. On others, when he awakened from a nightmare with his heart pounding and a bellow raw in his throat, he wasn't so sure.

"I feel better than I did when I tried to go back to work at Robotronics." Which was truth, so far as it went.

"It is peaceful up here." Shouts from outside drifted up, and her mouth curved. "Or was, until we darkened your door."

"You've been good guests," he forced himself to say.

"Why, thank you." She sighed. "I suppose I'd better go check on the kids."

He stepped aside and let her pass him, a flowery scent lingering for a moment even after she'd disappeared into the hall. Had she brought perfume...? No, he realized; she'd used one of those fragrant bath beads.

John glanced toward the old-fashioned tub, picturing her letting her bra drop to the floor, then slipping off her panties before stepping in. He'd seen her long legs when she changed yesterday in front of the fire. Imagining the rest of her naked body came easily. Had her hair been loose, to float on the water when she sank down into the tub? Or had she bundled it up?

Loose. Definitely loose. Her hair had still been wet when she came down for breakfast.

A groan tore its way from his throat. Damn it, what did he think he was doing? He had a shaky enough hold on reality.

He forced himself to scan the bathroom with a practiced, innkeeper's eye before following her downstairs.

As predicted, Amy was the one to have come in and was shedding her outerwear in front of the fire. Water pooled on the plank floor around her boots.

"It's freakin' *cold* out there." She shivered and hugged herself.

"It was nice of you to go even though you didn't want to, for the sake of everyone else," Fiona said.

Reaching the foot of the stairs, John paused to hear the girl's answer to the teacher's kindly retooling of motives he was pretty damn sure hadn't been that altruistic.

"Even though I went out to be nice, *Troy,*" she said the name with loathing, "made this big snowball and smashed it against my face. He's a…a *creep.*"

"Well, you did go out to have a snowball fight."

"But he walked right up and did it! He's such a jerk. Him and Hopper, too."

How sad romance was when it died. A grin tugging at his mouth, John crossed the huge great room, opened the heavy front door and went out on the porch.

Snow still floated from the sky, obscuring the landscape. The steps he'd shoveled last night had disappeared again.

There seemed to be a free-for-all going on, snowballs flying, accompanied by shrieks and yells. With the snow still falling, the teenagers were indistinguishable from each other, all blurred in white. They were thigh deep and higher in the white blanket that enveloped the landscape, the shed and the cabins he could usually see from here.

John raised his voice. "Time out!"

The action stopped and heads turned his way.

"When you get cold and decide to come in, everyone go get an armful of wood and bring it. Pile's just around the side of the lodge." He jerked his thumb toward the north corner.

"Girls, too?" a voice squeaked.

"Girls, too."

He went back inside, where Amy was elaborating on what pigs all boys were, while Fiona soothed with common sense. As far as he could see, the girl was a spoiled brat, but what did he know?

Not that much later, the kids did all carry in wood, and all three boys and one of the girls willingly went back for another load.

John nodded his approval as they dumped split lengths in the wrought-iron racks. "That should keep us going for a bit."

"It's a really big fireplace," the girl said. "Have you ever had to cook in it?"

"No. The generator hasn't failed me yet."

"God forbid," Fiona murmured.

He silently seconded her prayer, if that's what it was. He'd be okay on his own with just the fire. But trying to feed ten of them? No ability to do laundry for who knew how long? He remembered all too well what it felt like to go for days without a chance to do more than sponge your underarms and genitals with lukewarm water, to get so you couldn't stand your own stink, to have sand in every fold of skin and gritty between your teeth.

Somehow, he didn't think the spoiled girl would take even three days of sponge baths and half-cooked food stoically.

"I get the first bath," Amy declared, staring a challenge at the others.

Dieter pulled off his wool hat and shook his head like a wet dog. "We just had baths. Why do you want to take another one?"

"Because I'm cold," she snapped, and stomped off.

"Why's she so upset?" Hopper asked in apparently genuine puzzlement.

Nobody leaped to explain. The teacher was too tactful to say, *Because she didn't get her way.* The others were either indifferent or perplexed as well.

"Maybe she's just having a delayed reaction to the fact that yesterday was pretty scary," Fiona said.

"But we're okay," one of the other girls protested.

"Some people are more resilient than others. It's also possible that getting stranded this way reminds Amy of something that happened to her in the past. We all have different fears."

John shook his head. Damn, she was good. He wondered if she believed a word she was saying.

"Now," she said, more briskly, "let's get everything that's wet laid out in front of the fire to dry. Neatly," she added, when one of the boys dumped socks and gloves in a heap. "Then the lunch crew can get started. Ah...who did I assign?"

"You!" they all chorused in glee.

She laughed with them. "Okay, okay! And, uh, Tabitha and Erin, right?"

Erin nodded with composure John suspected was typical, and Tabitha made a moue of displeasure.

"Next question." Fiona smiled at him. "What's on the menu?"

"Soup and sandwiches."

"That we can handle. Right, gang?"

He accompanied them to the kitchen to show them where everything was. Fiona disappeared to the laundry room to move a load to the dryer and start another one while the girls opened cans of cream of mushroom soup and dumped them in pans.

John loitered for a few more minutes, waiting for Fiona to come back. Despite his earlier discomfiture at imagining her naked, he couldn't resist watching Fiona competently slice cheddar cheese and slather margarine on bread to make the grilled cheese sandwiches she'd decided on. He doubted she or the girls were even conscious of his presence. This past year, he'd discovered he had a gift for invisibility.

Damn it, he could have spent most of the morning hiding out in his quarters, reading in front of the woodstove. But Fiona MacPherson intrigued him.

What he couldn't decide was whether it really was her in particular, or whether he'd been quietly healing without realizing it and she just happened to be the first attractive woman to come his way in a while.

Not true, he reminded himself; two weekends ago, a quartet of women in their twenties had spent two nights at the lodge. Apparently they'd been getting together a couple of times a year since they graduated from college. Each took a turn choosing what they did.

A couple of them were married, he'd gathered. One of the two single friends in particular had flirted like mad with him. He hadn't felt even a flicker of interest, and she'd been more beautiful by conventional standards than this slender teacher with the river-gray eyes.

He'd thought rather impassively that the woman who kept making excuses to seek him out was attractive. He'd been bothered then by the fact that he'd felt not even a slight stirring of sexual desire. He hadn't had had a woman since the night before he'd shipped out for Iraq. He'd missed sex the first months there. At some point, he'd quit thinking about it. That part of him had gone numb.

It wasn't that he felt nothing. Grief was his constant companion, anger looking over its shoulder. He had unpredictable bursts of fear. Once in a while, he allowed himself to be grateful that he was alive and that he'd found sanctuary.

Fiona MacPherson's pretty gray eyes and cloud of curly dark hair wouldn't have been enough to draw him from his preferred solitude. Not if something else about her hadn't sliced open the layer of insulation that had kept him distant from the rest of humanity.

So what was different about her? What had he sensed, from the moment their eyes first met?

He kept following her around in search of answers, not out of lust.

John gave a grunt that might have been a rusty laugh. *Well, not entirely out of lust,* he amended.

The sound he'd made brought her head around,

although neither of the girls seemed to hear. When Fiona saw him leaning against the wall, she smiled. As if *glad* he was still here.

There, he thought in shock, might be his answer. She saw him. Really saw him. Not as a Heathcliff she was bent on seducing as part of a weekend's adventure, but as if she were interested in him as a person. As if she might even like him.

In fact, she was the only person outside family and old friends who'd ever bothered to wonder if he suffered from PTSD—and he could tell she had been curious, even if she hadn't meant to ask. He'd only admitted to having served in Iraq to a couple of other veterans who'd stayed at the lodge over the past year. They had recognized each other. If others had speculated after seeing his scar, they'd kept the speculation to themselves.

What he didn't know was whether Fiona MacPherson looked at everyone the way she did at him. Why that mattered, he didn't know. In a few days, she'd be gone.

But he still wanted to know.

CHAPTER FOUR

FIONA COULDN'T BELIEVE John Fallon had thought she would come right out and ask if he suffered from post traumatic stress disorder. She didn't know him anywhere near well enough to be that personal. The embarrassing part was that she *had* wondered, and he could probably tell.

In the privacy of the laundry room—where she was shifting loads again perhaps an hour later—she groaned aloud. He must think she had no better manners than Amy! She couldn't even blame him.

Should she apologize once more? Or would it make things worse if she brought the subject up again?

Definitely worse, she decided.

Folding towels in the same style he did, lengthwise in thirds, she couldn't help thinking about what he'd said. He needed to decompress, which must mean he *was* having trouble with... She didn't know. People, noise, nightmares? Of course, there was his limp, too. She'd seen how much his leg hurt him on occasion. He'd go utterly still, his jaw muscles locking, and a sheen of sweat would break out on his face. Was he continuing to do physical therapy, or had he recovered as much as he was going to?

"Gee, why don't I just ask him?" she said aloud, rolling her eyes.

His voice came from behind her, mild but impossible to ignore. "Ask him what?"

Fiona froze. Her fingers tightened on the towel in her hands and she said the first thing that came to her. "Oh, um, whether you have more laundry soap."

"Why? Are we running low?" He came closer to her and peered into the tall plastic bucket. Which was half full.

Even more flustered by his nearness and the woodsy scent that clung to him, she babbled, "No, no, I'm just afraid we'll use it up. I thought maybe we should start hanging the towels after baths instead of washing them incessantly."

"We have plenty of soap." He nodded past her, where half a dozen plastic buckets were stacked against the wall.

"Oh." She gave a weak laugh. "I'm practically tripping over them. Well, now I feel dumb."

"Don't."

Her laugh became slightly more genuine, if a touch hysterical. There he went again. Anybody else would have said, *It's okay, you were being considerate.* Or, *Anybody could have missed seeing them.* But if John Fallon could compress twenty words into one, he did.

She grabbed almost at random for something to say. "You must get sick of laundry during your busy season."

He reached for a towel from the basket and folded with quick efficiency compared to her more deliberate efforts. He was reaching for another by the time she was half done with one, even though his hands looked too large to be so deft.

"If you're here for long, we'll put the kids to work on laundry, too."

Her embarrassment was fading, thank goodness. She chuckled. "The beauty of unpaid guests."

"Maybe I should lower my rates in exchange for labor."

"You could make the whole stay do-it-yourself," Fiona suggested. "Kitchen privileges, bathroom privileges, but leave 'em clean."

"You can't imagine how appealing that is." His tone was heartfelt, less guarded than usual.

"Oh, I don't know. After a few days of cleaning up after them—" she nodded toward the kitchen "—I'm sure I'll be in complete sympathy."

"They're done in the kitchen."

A non sequitur? Or not?

She braced herself. "Is it clean?"

"I've seen worse."

"But you've seen better."

He shrugged. "They're kids."

She should have continued supervising. "I'll finish up."

"I already did."

She winced. "I wish you wouldn't do that."

He raised his brows. "Do what?"

She forgot she held a towel in her hands. "Work nonstop. I feel guilty."

"You've worked nonstop today, too," he pointed out.

"But they're my job. My responsibility."

"And the lodge is mine." While folding the last towel, he made it sound inarguable.

As, she supposed, it was. He couldn't want a crowd of teenagers trashing Thunder Mountain Lodge, even though he seemed less than enthusiastic as an innkeeper.

"What are they up to now?" she asked.

"I offered some games. Most of them are in front of the fireplace playing them. I think a few are upstairs."

Not one boy and one girl, she hoped.

"Amy?"

"Last I looked, sulking because someone else already took Boardwalk."

"Oh, dear."

He frowned. "Quit worrying about them."

"But they're…"

"Your responsibility. I know. But they're not toddlers."

"No, they're teenagers, which is almost worse."

Why did he look irritated? Was he tired of her fussing?

He picked up the piled towels before she could. "I'll put these away."

"I can…"

He ignored her, of course. Frustrated, she watched him limp out of the laundry room, leaving her to the sound of running water in the washer and the spinning dryer. Why did the wretched man have to be so hard to read? And why couldn't he be, oh, fifty years old, balding and potbellied? Or the wizened old man Dieter had said used to own the lodge?

Fiona sighed and went to see what the kids were up to.

She found them sprawled in chairs and on the floor around a couple of different gameboards. Dieter, Hopper, Tabitha and Amy played Monopoly, Kelli and

Troy Chinese checkers. Erin was curled like a cat in an upholstered chair reading. Only Willow was missing.

"Anybody seen Willow?"

They hardly glanced up.

"Nope."

"Not in a while."

"Uh-uh."

Fiona hesitated, hating to look as if she was following John, but finally started up the stairs. He was just closing the door to the linen closet when she reached the top.

"Missing a kid," she said. "Seen one?"

He shook his head. "Let me know if you need help."

Fiona glanced in the first bedroom on the girls' side—beds still unmade, she saw—then knocked on the door to Erin and Willow's room. "Willow, you in there?"

"Yes." The voice sounded small.

"I'd better feed the fire." John passed her, his shoulder brushing hers.

Even that minor, incidental physical contact made her heart jump. Darn it, he was the sexiest man she'd ever met, even with a scar and limp. And she must be feeling a little more vulnerable than usual.

The kids. Think about the kids.

She took a deep breath. "Can I come in?"

"If you want," Willow agreed.

Fiona pushed open the door. Willow lay on the bed, curled on her side around a pillow she clutched to her middle. Fiona sat on the edge of the bed.

"You okay, kiddo?"

Face wan, she nodded. "I have cramps."

"Period starting?" Thank heavens for the tampons John had produced yesterday.

"Not yet. But it must be."

"Have you taken anything?"

She shook her head. "Do you have Midol?"

"No, but I bet I can find you some ibuprofen or something."

Her expression became anxious. "You won't tell anybody, though. Right?"

"That your period's starting?" Fiona rose to her feet. "Wouldn't think of it. I'll be right back."

Going downstairs again, she reflected on how little she knew this particular student, the youngest of her Knowledge Champs kids. Fiona had never had her in a class, and Willow had just joined the Knowledge Champs team this fall. Fiona had been surprised, because of her shyness. Most of the students who chose Hi-Q, Knowledge Champs or Debate were extroverts, noisy, funny and smart.

Willow had come faithfully to practices, but she rarely joined in the clowning or in taunting the teacher. So far, she was slow hitting the buzzer to answer, as much, Fiona guessed, out of shyness as because she lacked knowledge. Fiona thought she had been gaining a little confidence lately. Willow had confided once that her braces would be coming off in March, which should help.

Bypassing the rest of the kids, Fiona went straight to the kitchen, where she found John sitting at the table with a cup of coffee.

"Do you have some Tylenol or ibuprofen?"

He gave her a lightning quick assessment. "You okay?"

"It's Willow. She isn't feeling great."

He nodded. "Cupboard to the right of the sink."

There was an impressive array of medications and first-aid products there, she discovered. Which made sense, given how far the lodge was from doctors and hospitals.

"Thanks." She took a couple of white pills and a glass of water back upstairs.

Willow swallowed them gratefully. "I wish I didn't get cramps," she mumbled, handing back the glass of water.

"It stinks, doesn't it?" Fiona sat back down on the bed. "Do you get heavy periods, too?"

The girl nodded unhappily.

"Seems to be hereditary. Your mom probably does, too."

"My mom's dead."

"Oh, no! I'm sorry. I didn't realize." The father had signed the release, Fiona vaguely recalled. She didn't think she'd ever met him.

"It was a couple of years ago. She was in a car accident."

"Were you in the car with her?"

Head shake. "No, but my little brother was. He's okay, though. He just had a broken arm. And his collarbone, too. Mom had on her seat belt and everything. But, um, this car ran a red light. They said Mom didn't have a chance."

"Oh, honey. I'm so sorry." Fiona gently squeezed her shoulder.

Willow shrugged, mainly, it appeared, to hunch into a tighter ball. "I really miss her."

"I can only imagine. And it's tough when you're at an age to need advice."

"Daddy…I mean, my dad tries."

"I bet he doesn't know much about buying bras or what you wear to prom, though, does he?"

A tiny smile flickered on her mouth. "Uh-uh. But nobody's asked me to prom anyway."

"They will," Fiona predicted. "Hardly any sophomores go."

"Do you think I'll make the A team someday?"

Surprised, Fiona said, "Sure I do. Very likely next year, with Erin and Troy gone. You just have to get bolder."

"I know." She fell silent for a moment. "What's everybody doing?"

"Reading. Playing games."

"Oh." She sounded wistful.

"As soon as you feel better, go on down. I'll bet you can get in on the Chinese checkers, anyway."

She nodded, but said nothing.

Fiona hesitated. "It's too bad you don't have a friend you could have talked into joining Knowledge Champs with you. With Erin and Troy graduating next year, we could use some more freshmen and sophomores."

"I don't, um, really have any friends. We moved in August. From Denver. Dad took a new job in Portland. I guess he thought we wouldn't be as sad in a different place. You know."

"I imagine that sometimes a change of scene does help. It's hard leaving friends, though."

Her eyes filled with tears. "Nobody is that friendly here! I wish I could go to the public school, but Dad says I'll get into a better college if I stay at Willamette."

The prep school where Fiona taught did regularly send graduates to colleges like Stanford, Columbia and Yale. Still…

"Does he know how unhappy you are?"

She shook her head. "I don't want to make him sad again. He thinks I love it here."

Fiona wasn't sure what to say. Willow, her brother and dad were probably all pretending to be happier after the move, none of them willing to acknowledge anything was wrong with their new life. And, given her grief, Willow might not do any better making friends at the public high school.

With new determination, Fiona decided that she was going to do her darndest to see to it that Willow did make friends at Willamette Prep. A boyfriend would follow. Minus the braces, she'd be a pretty girl if she came out from behind the hair she hid behind and smiled more often.

"Cramps letting up?" she asked.

"Yeah," the fifteen-year-old said tentatively. Then, "Yeah. I feel better."

"Good. You want to come downstairs?"

"Um…I guess." She released her death grip on the pillow and rolled off the bed onto her feet. "I don't think Amy likes Hopper anymore."

Fiona laughed. "I noticed. She's not so crazy about Troy, either."

Willow wrinkled her nose. "He was kind of mean to her. You know. Outside."

"She should have dumped snow down *his* neck."

Willow giggled, then pulled her lips over her braces.

Downstairs, Kelli and Troy had just finished a game and he was saying, "I'm going to go find something to eat."

Kelli spotted Willow, and to Fiona's relief said, "You want to play a game?"

"Sure."

Fiona went to the small-paned window near the front door and looked out. How could it still be snowing? Another twenty-four hours of this, and the front porch would be buried! They might have to tunnel out.

Turning away, she thought of choosing a book from the tall cases along the wall beneath the staircase, but realized she ought to find out first what John planned for dinner and then decide on preparation and cleanup crews. *She* was beginning to feel like an innkeeper. Did they ever get to relax? Imagine if all the rooms upstairs were full, as well as the cabins Dieter had told her were down by the river. John must often cook for a crowd three or four times the size of their group, and this was enough work.

Troy came back from the kitchen crunching on an apple and sank down to sit beside Kelli and watch the game of Chinese checkers.

Fiona went to the kitchen.

John still sat at the kitchen table, but now had a book open. At the sound of her footstep, he looked up. "Hungry?"

"Lunch wasn't that long ago. Only teenage boys are hungry an hour after they get up from the table."

He smiled briefly. Probably longing for her to go away so he could have some peace. Although he could have hidden in his own room if he'd wanted to be left entirely alone.

"No," Fiona continued, "it just occurred to me that dinner also isn't that far away and I should figure out how much help you need and who to assign to you."

His mouth quirked, although whether with a smile or a grimace she wasn't sure. "I keep expecting one of them to chop a finger off when I give them knives."

"They need to learn," she said firmly. "I'll help, too."

He appeared to ruminate. "Why don't you and I make dinner, and let them clean up?"

Inexplicably her pulse speeded up. "We can do that. If you're sure you don't want a whole crew?"

"I'm sure."

"Okay. Well, then." Her feet seemed to be rooted to the floor. "I'll have to think about whose turn it is to have KP duty."

"You sound like a sergeant." His tone was gentle and almost, well, *affectionate*. As if he were teasing her.

"Did you have to peel potatoes when you were in the Guard?"

"Oh, yeah." He shrugged. "Came in handy, though. Taught me how to cook for big groups."

Fiona nodded. "Well, I'll let you get back to your book."

He didn't reach for it. "Why don't you get yourself a cup of coffee and sit down? Unless you're playing Monopoly, too."

"Chinese checkers I could have been talked into. But not Monopoly. It tends to go on forever. When I was, oh, ten or eleven, a couple of friends and I used to start games that went on for weeks. We'd play after school. We got truly vicious."

He was definitely smiling now, although it was more a matter of that hard mouth softening than actually curling up at the corners. "Now that I can't imagine."

"Really." She got a mug down from the cupboard. "We had ever shifting alliances trying to put each other out of the hotel business. Half the time, one of us would go home mad."

"Yet you didn't grow up to be a real estate tycoon."

Pouring herself coffee, Fiona laughed. "I invariably lost in the end. One of my friends was more ruthless."

"And she's now a real estate tycoon."

"Something like that." She splashed milk in the coffee, then returned the carton to the refrigerator. "Carol is a mid-level executive with some division of Procter & Gamble."

Behind her, John's grunt might have been a laugh. "And did you let your friends visit your Monopoly properties free when they were too broke to pay the rent?"

"I told you," Fiona said with dignity, as she set down her mug on the table and pulled up a chair, "I was way tougher than that. I'm no pushover."

"Aren't you." It wasn't a question, although his brown eyes studied her thoughtfully.

"I have a reputation as a tough teacher, I'll have you know. I've heard kids telling freshmen that Ms. MacPherson is nice, but you really have to work in her classes."

"The ultimate compliment."

"I thought so."

"Why teaching?"

Something in the way he still scrutinized her made Fiona feel like a lab rat exhibiting puzzling behavior. She sensed that he really wanted to know.

"Because I loved school," she said simply. "I had a bunch of teachers along the way who really inspired me. I remember one day when I was in high school, I looked around the classroom and thought, Why would anyone want to be anywhere else?"

"You loved the smell of chalk?"

"You're making fun of me. But actually, I did. I do. My elementary school was ancient. Dry erase boards just aren't the same." She brooded. "Really, it's the atmosphere in a classroom I like. The quiet when everyone is fiercely concentrating…"

"Trying desperately to remember stuff they *meant* to study the night before," he murmured.

Fiona ignored him. "The complete engagement in the topic when a debate gets passionate. The look on a student's face when he or she gets something—really gets it—for the first time. Come on," she challenged him. "You must have liked school, too, or you wouldn't have stayed in it so long."

Again, the smile touched mainly his eyes. "You wouldn't believe me if I told you I stuck it out so I could make lots and lots of money?"

"No, I wouldn't."

"Okay. I did like school. Most of the time. But I'm not a teacher."

"You found something else that excited you." She pretended not to see the flash of some intense emotion that he quickly hid. "Me, I just like to get other people excited about an intellectual idea."

"You didn't say what you teach."

"U.S. History and Government."

"Ahh." He took a sip of coffee.

She eyed him with suspicion. "What's that supposed to mean?"

"I said 'ah.' I acknowledged your answer."

"No, you didn't. You said, *Ahh.*" She imbued the sound with a thousand shades of meaning.

"Okay." He set his coffee cup down. "I was thinking that I could see you getting fired up about justice and the wisdom of our founding fathers and the balance of powers."

"You sound so cynical," she said, surprised. "Is that because of Iraq?"

He looked back at her without expression. "Iraq? What's that have to do with anything?"

"Don't *do* that," Fiona exclaimed in exasperation.

His dark brows rose in what was becoming a typical response. "Do what?"

"Go blank. Do you do that when you don't want to think about something?"

She'd actually caught him off guard. He looked startled and perhaps perturbed. "I don't know."

"I wasn't trying to get you to talk about Iraq. I mean, not your experiences. I meant more in a political sense. All the debate about Bush's motives and whether the administration was honest..."

"I thought all Americans got cynical after Watergate."

She flapped a hand. "Watergate wasn't any worse

than the scandals during Ulysses Grant's administration. We Americans are ultimately hopeful."

"Are we."

"You wouldn't have joined the National Guard if you hadn't thought you could make a difference."

"Maybe I just wanted the extra pay."

"Did you?"

In the face of her challenge, he shook his head. "Our decisions are rarely that simple, are they?"

"No, they aren't."

Coming into the kitchen right then, Dieter asked, "What decisions? Do we have to start, like, rationing food or something?"

Fiona laughed. "We've been here less than twenty-four hours. I presume we haven't yet eaten Mr. Fallon out of house and home."

"'Cuz I'm hungry," the lanky sixteen-year-old confessed. "What's for dinner?"

Fiona glanced at the clock on the kitchen wall. "The dinner we won't be having for at least a couple of hours?"

He grinned unrepentently at her. "Yeah. That one."

"Spaghetti," John said.

"Really? Cool! Um—" he looked around "—can I have an apple or something?"

John gestured toward the counter. "Help yourself."

The boy grabbed one from the bowl that sat there. "So what are you talking about?"

"I was telling him why I became a teacher."

He took a bit crunch of apple. Around it, he said, "Yeah? How come you did?"

"Because she liked the smell of chalk," John supplied.

"Really?" Dieter looked from one of them to the other. "You're kidding. Aren't you?"

"I became a teacher because I like to inspire young minds."

He hooted. "Right!"

Fiona only laughed. "So, who's winning out there?"

"Me." He flexed a skinny arm and near nonexistent bicep. "I have ten hotels."

"And Amy?"

"She quit and stomped upstairs."

"Oh, dear." Fiona started to rise.

John's hand on her arm stopped her. "She'll get over it."

She hesitated, then sank back down. "I know she will. I just think it's important that we all get along, stuck together the way we are."

Dieter finished a bite. "Amy's always mad at somebody."

Fiona had noticed that the girl didn't take being teased very well. Later, she'd try talking to her. Maybe she'd open up the way Willow had.

"You may spread the word," she said, "that you're all off the hook for preparing dinner." She held up a hand. "On the other hand, I think we've worked our way around to you, Troy and Hopper for cleanup."

He groaned melodramatically.

"Come on, how long did it take you to wash the dishes after breakfast? Twenty minutes?"

"Yeah, but spaghetti's lots worse than scrambled eggs." Taking his apple, he retreated.

Fiona decided it was high time to do the same. She

took a last swallow of coffee and stood to take her cup to the sink. "I," she announced, "am going to find a book to read. In my room. I might even take a nap."

John Fallon's mouth relaxed into another of those near-smiles. "Good for you."

"But don't start cooking without me, okay? I feel guilty enough at the work we've put you to."

"If necessary, I'll wake you up before I start dinner," he agreed.

"Okay." She started across the kitchen. "Don't let the kids bug you for anything."

"I'll send them to bug you instead."

She gave him a last look, said, "Do that," and pushed through the swinging door. She felt as if she'd just made a near-escape even as she wished she'd stayed to talk. Maybe to ask him what *his* dreams as a child had been.

No, he was undoubtedly relieved to have a couple of hours to himself.

Although...he *had* invited her to sit down with him in the first place.

CHAPTER FIVE

JOHN COULDN'T REMEMBER enjoying a day more since before he'd gone overseas. He was hungry to learn more about Fiona, and regretted it every time she walked away to deal with the kids.

He couldn't figure out why he didn't feel disdain and even contempt for someone who struck him as remarkably naive. These days, most teenagers like her charges had long since shed their innocence. Yet somehow she'd held on to a basically sunny faith that other people had good intentions.

What would someone like her make of Iraq now, he found himself wondering, with its confusion of loyalties and ancient hatreds and modern, militant Islamic fanatics? How would she deal with the sight of a recently beheaded hostage, a man who'd come over with no interest in war or politics, intending only to work in the oilfields and make the extra money that would get his family out of debt?

John found, to his surprise, that he didn't want to know how she'd react. He thanked God she'd never seen anything so horrific, and hoped she never would. There was a place for her kind of optimism in the world, even if he couldn't share it. Her happy little glow was occasionally contagious, and how could that be a bad thing?

He hoped he would have to wake her from her nap. Of course, if she didn't wander downstairs herself, he should send one of the girls, but John persuaded himself that she wouldn't want one of her students to see her so vulnerable. What if she snored? Drooled? Talked in her sleep? Within a day of getting back to Hawes Ferry, every kid in her high school would know. She'd be at the front of the class lecturing, and hear a soft snore from the back of the room followed by an eruption of giggles. He'd be doing her a favor, waking her up himself.

He watched the clock, which moved with infuriating slowness. The moment it reached four-thirty, he rose to his feet. Half the kids still lounged downstairs, while four of them had disappeared. Their teacher would undoubtedly have worried, but John didn't care what they were doing off by themselves.

In the hall above, giggles came through the closed door to one of the girls' rooms, followed by the deeper rumble of a boy's voice. Dieter was still downstairs; Hopper or Troy, then.

Fiona's door was shut as well. John knocked lightly. When there was no response, he opened it, then cleared his throat.

The dark head on the pillow didn't move.

Leaving the door slightly ajar, he crossed the room.

Still dressed, she'd stretched out on top of the down comforter, then pulled half of it over her. She apparently didn't snore and wasn't drooling, but neither did she stir even when he cleared his throat again, more loudly.

"Fiona."

She slept on, lips parted, her expression serene. Clearly she wasn't fighting bad dreams.

He reached out, wanting to push back the curls that had fallen over her face. His fingers tingled from the need to feel their springy texture and the plump satin of her cheeks. But he didn't want her to catch him in the act, so reluctantly he shook her shoulder instead.

"Fiona."

She mumbled something and buried her face in the pillow.

Perhaps he should just go start dinner himself. He wasn't used to help and didn't really need it. Spaghetti was one of his standbys. He had made it weekly for the past year.

Maybe she'd only fallen asleep a short while ago. A trade paperback book lay open beside her, facedown. It looked as if she'd gotten a fair way into it, so she must have read for quite a while. Curious, he tilted his head so he could see what she'd chosen to read.

Generation Kill: Devil Dogs, Iceman, Captain America, and the New Face of American War.

John stiffened at the sight of the faceless soldier dressed in desert camouflage depicted on the cover. He hadn't known the book was on the shelf. He hadn't read it, didn't want to.

Why had she spent her afternoon immersed in the Iraq war? Was she trying to answer questions she hadn't felt she could ask him? Or did her curiosity have nothing to do with him?

A kind of panic flooded him. What had she read in

the book? Did it talk about the price soldiers like him had paid for killing? About the callousness that so easily encased them? Had she read about the way terror made your skin crawl and your bowels loosen, how you had to quit thinking about home, about people you loved, or you got even more scared that you were going to die?

He started to back up. He suddenly didn't want her eyes to open, for her to gaze searchingly at him and see too much.

The foot he couldn't help dragging caught on something and in trying to right himself he put too much weight on that leg. His hip spasmed and he grabbed for the edge of the dresser. The mirror rattled against the wall.

"John?" she said softly, sleepily. "Oh! Are you all right?"

The agony retreated. He unclenched his jaw. "I'm fine."

"You're not."

He turned. "I'm fine!"

Half sitting up, she shrank back from his anger. "I'm sorry."

This was why he stayed away from people. One of the reasons he stayed away.

"There's no reason for you to be sorry." He tested some weight on the leg, which held. "I was a jackass." He hesitated. "I get spasms."

Hair tousled, she eyed him warily. "I can tell it hurts."

"It…happens less often than it used to. Regular exercise helps."

She was relaxing. "Like chopping wood and hauling it in?"

"Not what the physical therapist had in mind, but…yeah."

He allowed himself to relax, too. Despite the way she'd flinched when he snapped at her, she wasn't looking at him as if she saw a monster.

"Did you come to wake me?"

He dipped his head. "I did knock."

Fiona made a face. "I should have warned you. I sleep like the dead."

Not like the dead. He knew what dead people looked like.

She saw his face, and her expression shifted subtly as she remembered what she'd been reading. He could tell; her gaze slid from him to the book beside her. "I'm sorry," she said again.

"Quit that," he said harshly.

Still sitting up in bed, the comforter across her lap, she stared at him with those startlingly clear eyes. "Quit what…?"

"Apologizing." John swallowed, softened his voice. "You didn't say or do anything to apologize for."

"I wasn't apologizing." She swung her legs over so that they dangled off the bed. "I was expressing sympathy."

"Because I limp? Because I'm scarred?"

Her eyes flashed. "Because I could tell you were remembering something bad. Why would you assume the worst of me?"

How did he say, *Because I'm so damned mired in self-pity, I assume that's what people feel when they look at me? He couldn't. Didn't want to.*

"My turn to apologize." He sounded stiff.

She gave him a soft smile. "Don't worry about it." Making a sound of pleasure, she yawned and stretched luxuriantly. The knit fabric of her turtleneck pulled taut over her small breasts. "I may have to start napping every day."

God. Her voice alone, lazy and satisfied, was enough to arouse him.

"I shouldn't have woken you."

"I made you promise." Her eyes widened. "Unless you're waking me because one of the kids needs me…?"

"Nope. Just thought I'd start dinner."

She pressed a hand to her chest. "Thank goodness. I scared myself for a second there."

"They're big kids."

"And my responsibility." Her forehead puckered. "Maybe I should try calling my principal again."

"Did you remember to turn your phone off?"

"Oh, crap!" She scrambled off the bed. "I don't know! And I don't have a charger…"

"The kids have phones. I have one."

She swung to face him. "You said you didn't."

"I said I didn't have a landline. I have a cell phone. It just doesn't work up here most of the time."

Groping in the purse that sat on the chest of drawers, she came up with her phone. "Thank goodness, I did turn it off." She dropped it back in the purse. "I'll try later, once we get dinner on."

He nodded, retreating. "I'll see you downstairs."

She yawned again and nodded. "Just let me get my shoes on."

It took her a bit longer than that to appear in the kitchen; but he'd known she would check on her kids on the way down.

He was setting out onions, garlic and green pepper on the counter when he heard the swinging door and glanced over his shoulder. She'd brushed her hair and pulled it into a ponytail that made her look as young as the teenagers.

"Find them all?" he asked.

"Mmm-hmm," she murmured absently. "Shall I chop?"

"Sure. I'll get the hamburger frying."

He dumped several pounds in his largest skillet.

"Four onions?" she asked, sounding surprised.

"There are ten of us. Wouldn't hurt to have enough left for lunch tomorrow."

"No. That's true. Okay." The knife whacked down on the cutting board.

By the time she dumped the first diced onion in with the meat, her eyes were misty. With the second, tears clung to her lashes and her eyes were red. "I'm going to be wailing any minute," she warned.

"Want to switch jobs?"

"No point in us both crying. We'd scare the kids if they come in."

He gave a laugh that felt creaky. "It's good for teenagers to get jolted out of their self-absorption occasionally."

Whack. Whack. Whack. "Are you speaking from experience?"

He saw more of himself in Dieter than in the others. He, too, had been a nerd despite the fact that he'd played high school sports and therefore achieved a degree of respectability.

"Maybe. Did *you* ever think about anyone else when you were fifteen?"

Her laugh was watery. "Maybe more than most kids do. My family had...problems."

The tiny hitch in her voice gave him an insight. "That's why you loved school so much."

"I suppose so. It was my refuge."

He wanted to know what kind of problems made her want to hide out at school, but knew it wasn't any of his business.

"Not that it was that terrible," she said hastily. "It was just that my parents were fighting. They got a divorce my first year of college."

"Did you wish they'd done it years earlier?"

She dumped more onions in with the browning meat and shook her head. "No. Although that would be logical, wouldn't it? But who's logical about things like that? I knew my father had been having affairs. Even when I hid in my room, I could hear their voices. And then I saw him one day. Midafternoon, coming out of a motel room with this woman who worked with him. He kissed her, then they got in their separate cars and drove away. It was like seeing a stranger. You know?" She wasn't chopping anymore, and John turned to see her gazing into space as if she didn't remember where she was. The knife in her hand was suspended above the onion. It didn't seem unnatural that tears streamed down her cheeks. She continued after a moment, "I didn't know whether I should tell my mother. I was afraid she'd see it on my face, so I bicycled over to a friend's house and begged to spend the night. In the end, I never did tell Mom. I don't think she realized how much I'd heard and knew." Fiona shook her head. "And why am I telling you all this? All you asked was if I wanted them to get a divorce. And here's the thing. When they finally did separate, I was devastated. It was like the bottom had dropped out of my world. Home wasn't home anymore. It was supposed to stay the same forever. Which I suppose answers your question. I *was* self-absorbed. My parents existed to be my bedrock, not as people with their own needs and problems."

"That's normal." Leaning against the lip of the counter, he watched her finish chopping the last onion. "Have either of them remarried?"

She gave a laugh that revealed more unhappiness than he suspected she knew. "Oh, my father has. Twice. He wasn't faithful with number two, either. And probably isn't with number three, which is a shame. Shelly is a nice woman." She seemed to shake herself. "Mom hasn't. I think she might have a hard time trusting a man."

"What about you?" he heard himself ask. "Do you, too?"

She scraped the onions into the hamburger mix with the knife, then set the cutting board back on the counter. As if she hadn't heard him, she said, "I need to go wash my face before I start the garlic."

John nodded toward the door to his quarters. "You can use my bathroom if you want."

"So I don't have to explain why I've been sobbing

to assorted teenagers? Thanks." She disappeared into his small apartment, consisting of a sitting room, bedroom and bathroom.

He didn't have to worry about having left the bathroom tidy; between the military and his stint as innkeeper, keeping his space clean and clear of clutter had become automatic. Wondering how much she could tell about him from his living quarters did make him a little uneasy.

She came back with her face scrubbed, and her eyes still red and puffy. "I've never chopped so much onion before. I guess I somehow escaped that particular job when we had big family Thanksgiving get-togethers."

"I appreciate you doing it."

She worked in silence, adding the garlic a minute later. John was pouring cans of tomato sauce he'd already opened when Fiona said, "What you asked about me trusting— The answer is I don't know. I guess it hasn't come up."

"I shouldn't have asked."

"Why not? I was telling you my life story."

He shrugged. "All right. Doesn't trust always come up?"

"I haven't actually had any relationships that were very serious." She scraped diced green pepper into the sauce. "My mother worries. She's convinced the divorce scarred me, that I'm shying away from marriage. But I really don't think so. I keep telling her I haven't met the right man. Which is just as well. I didn't want to get married at twenty-three, like my best friend did."

John dumped burgundy wine into the sauce with a free hand, then poured oregano into his palm and added it.

"You didn't even have to measure?" she asked, sounding indignant.

"Practice." He stirred in thyme and basil and sniffed experimentally.

"Shall I cut up the tomatoes?" Fiona asked, waving her knife at the row of large cans.

"We can both work on those."

She used a fork to set several tomatoes from the first can onto her cutting board. Then her head came up. "It occurs to me that it's been awfully quiet out there."

He remembered the incredible smells coming from the kitchen on holidays when he was a kid, and his remarkable ability to resist them. "They don't want to be put to work."

She laughed and resumed dicing. "You're right. They're not crazy about this whole KP thing."

"Are their families rich enough that they have housekeepers?" He didn't care, but wanted to keep her talking.

"Oh, probably. Certainly someone to clean. I doubt any one of them has ever scrubbed a toilet bowl."

"Why did you choose the private school then?"

"I started in a public school. That's where I did my student teaching. But it can be frustrating. The classes are too big. Lots of the kids need help they don't get. The advanced placement classes go to teachers with seniority. I saw the ad, and was attracted to the idea of a smaller school and a closer relationship with the students. This is only my second year, but I've been really happy at Willamette Prep."

He nodded.

"We're done," she said in surprise, looking around. "It smells fabulous already. Are we planning a vegetable?"

"Maybe not tonight. I can heat some garlic bread." He kept loaves in one of the freezers.

"O-oh. That sounds good."

"I'll make a cobbler for dessert. I have blackberries, huckleberries…"

"Really?" She looked at him as if he'd offered her a sleigh ride behind white ponies with silver bells on their harnesses. "I love huckleberries!"

This laugh came more easily. "You're easy to please."

"That's not what my mom says. She thinks I'm picky."

He lifted his brows. "About food, or men?"

"Both." She set the cutting boards in the sink along with the paring knives, and began wiping the counter. "Your turn. I've bared my soul, and I don't know anything about you."

"You know I was in the National Guard and went to Iraq." *And was wounded.*

"Yes, but besides that." A wave of the sponge dismissed the transforming events of his life. "Are *your* parents still married? What do they think about you buying the lodge?"

"Yes. They're still married. I can't imagine them fighting." He thought about that. "My mother, maybe. But Dad is the strong, silent type. He nods to whatever she says. She was always telling us kids, 'your father says…' Or, 'your father thinks…' We didn't believe her. We knew he must think something, but we were pretty sure he never told anyone what that was."

Her laugh was a lovely cascade of notes. "But he must have courted her, once upon a time."

"No, I think she courted him. She asked him to marry her, and he nodded."

Fiona giggled. "What does he do? For a living, I mean."

"Plumbing. Has his own business."

"Did he want you to go into it?"

"Fallon and Son? Don't know."

Solemnly she concluded, "He never said."

This time, they laughed together. John was astonished by the sound. No, not just the sound, but the *feeling*. It took him a minute to identify it. Happiness, or something close. He felt carefree.

She'd opened the dishwasher and begun loading it. "So what *do* they think of your taking up innkeeping?"

He tried to stay relaxed. "They're puzzled."

You're not yourself, his mother had said. *Johnny, what happened to you?*

He hadn't been able to tell her. *I killed too many people. Some I didn't mean to kill.*

Mom wouldn't have understood. She wouldn't have had any words to put in Dad's mouth.

"Your brother or sister?" Fiona asked, as casually as if the conversation hadn't become emotionally loaded. "Or do you have both?"

"Two sisters. They're puzzled, too."

That wasn't entirely true. Mary, much like his mother in personality, was. Liz, quieter and more thoughtful like John, had come to him and said, "I've been reading things. I know lots of soldiers have been coming back traumatized. Whatever happened must have been awful, to change you like this."

Words had stuck in his throat, even with his favorite sister.

She'd given him a swift hug. "We love you, John. I'm so glad you're safely home."

He had feared being called up again, knowing he couldn't endure it, but in the end his emotional state was moot; he'd never be physically able to serve again. He was glad, but felt guilty, too, because he had friends who would be going back. That was his idea of hell: another tour in Iraq.

Before Fiona could ask more questions, the swinging door opened and Hopper came in.

"Hey, that smells really good. When's dinner?"

"Gosh, it might be quicker if we had help," his teacher said with clear mischief. "The garlic bread needs slicing, doesn't it, John?"

"No fair! You already said we have to clean the kitchen!"

She laughed at him. "Just trying to scare you. John, when will dinner be ready?"

"An hour."

The boy came over to the stove, dipped a finger in the sauce and tasted, dancing out of the kitchen just ahead of the towel Fiona snapped at him.

"Glass of wine?" John asked.

She looked wistful, but said, "I shouldn't. I'm still on the job. Sort of. I don't want the kids going back and telling anyone I drank when I was in charge."

He nodded, unsurprised when she said, “Speaking of which, let me go count noses. Again.”

Telling himself he didn’t mind some time alone, he went to the freezer and took out bags of the red, high-bush huckleberries he’d picked and frozen that summer. By the time he got back, she’d returned and was getting a pitcher of cranberry juice from the refrigerator.

“All present and accounted for,” she reported. “Nobody seems to need me.”

I do.

John was staggered by the fervency of his reaction. Instinctively he rejected it.

No. If he needed anything at all, it was solitude. He was attracted to her, enjoying the novelty of having lighthearted conversation with a pretty woman. *Need* was gut level. It was the next breath, the next meal, the chance to sink into the oblivion of sleep.

If he already hated the idea of watching her drive away with her vanful of kids, well, that was a good sign. It meant someday he might want to return to his former life. To live normally again—whatever that meant.

He surfaced to realize that Fiona was watching him.

Her voice was soft, her tone tentative. “I could go back to my book if you’d rather.”

If he were smart, he’d say, *Why don’t you do that while I finish up here?* Not being unfriendly, but making clear that he didn’t need her, either.

“Stay.” He sounded rusty again, as if he didn’t know how to ask for what he wanted. He tried again. “Talk to me. Tell me about…” What? Her life? What she expected the 'right' man to be like? No. He'd scare her. He was scaring himself. "A movie. I haven't seen one in a long time. What's the last one you went to?"

She relaxed, as he'd hoped she would. While he measured sugar and flour and put together the cobbler, she told him about a thriller with a huge budget, big stars and an unlikely plot.

At one point he glanced at the clock and thought in surprise, *They haven't even been here twenty-four hours.*

How, in such a short time, had he gotten to the point where he had thoughts like, *I need her?* He hadn't kissed her, hadn't touched her beyond a hand on her shoulder, didn't know that she felt anything at all for him. He suspected she'd have been just as friendly to the codger who'd owned the lodge before him.

Although, she had spent the afternoon reading about the Iraq war.

Maybe because of him, maybe not.

She'd moved on to talking about other things, an exhibit at the Portland Art Museum, music she liked. John guessed he must have nodded or interjected a word here and there, because he didn't want her to quit.

He didn't *need* her; that had been a ridiculous thought. But he wouldn't mind if snow kept falling for another day or two.

And maybe if the state road crew left Thunder Mountain Lodge isolated for a while after that, he'd eventually get his fill and want his solitude back.

Just not yet.

CHAPTER SIX

AFTER DINNER, Willow disappeared again. At first, Fiona didn't pay any attention. She'd probably just gone to the bathroom. But when she didn't come back, Fiona set down her book on the upholstered chair she'd been occupying a cozy distance from the crackling fire, and went upstairs.

The doors to both girls' bedrooms were open, Willow in neither. Only the bathroom door was shut. Fiona knocked lightly.

"Willow? Are you okay?"

"Ms. Mac?" The voice was high and shaky. "Are you by yourself?"

"Everyone else is downstairs."

"My period started!" she wailed.

Surely, surely, not her first one, Fiona prayed.

"I left tampons in the basket on the counter."

"I can't use them." She was definitely crying. "They…they hurt. I never use them!"

Oh, Lord. Fiona stood facing the door panel. "All right," she said. "I'll ask the other girls. Maybe one of them has a pad in her purse."

Otherwise, they might just have to go back to the rags

their great-grandmothers would have used. She decided not to mention that option yet.

"Why don't you just fold a bunch of toilet paper inside your underwear for now?"

There was a pause, then a horrified, *"Toilet paper?"*

Nope. Fiona definitely wasn't saying a word about rags, or the interesting historical fact that women on the Oregon Trail had had to reuse them without washing when no water was available, and had dried them by hanging them on the back of the wagon. Diapers, too. Must have been a pretty sight for the driver of the next wagon in line.

"I'll be back," she said.

She paused for a moment on the stairs, looking at the tableau below her. Everyone was lounging, one group playing poker, a few reading or listening to music. They looked amazingly content, considering they were stranded here and not on vacation. Unaware of her above, John tossed a log onto the fire, raising a storm of sparks. For just a moment, she couldn't help letting her gaze linger on his broad shoulders and—okay, admit it—the way his jeans clung to muscular thighs and butt. His shoulders were nice, too, broad and strong.

Willow, she reminded herself.

Continuing down, Fiona caught Erin's eye. Erin had been reading, sitting on an area rug, legs outstretched, and leaning against the massive leather sofa. Troy lay on the sofa, eyes closed, headphones on, his fingers drumming on the leather.

Erin stood and casually made her way over to the teacher. "Is something wrong?"

"Willow's period started," Fiona said in a low voice. "She's not comfortable using tampons. Any chance you have a pad?"

Erin shook her head. "I use tampons. Besides, I just had mine. I didn't bring anything."

"Okay, I'll ask the other girls."

Tabitha threw down her cards and stood. "I'm going to get something to drink," she announced.

Fiona stopped her on the way to the kitchen and repeated her question.

Tabitha, too, shook her head. "Uh-uh."

Kelli had her back to Fiona, so Fiona signaled to Amy next.

Amy didn't want to be separated from the boys. When Fiona gestured for the second time, she said, "What?"

"Can I talk to you for a minute?"

She was aware of John Fallon turning from the fire and watching them. No surprise—she was *always* aware of him when he was in the room.

Amy rolled her eyes and stood. When Fiona quietly repeated the question yet again, Amy curled her lip. "Why can't she use tampons like everyone else?"

"Is something wrong?" Hopper asked.

Amy looked at something—or someone—behind Fiona, then said deliberately, pitching her voice so everyone could hear, "Willow's having her period. And she doesn't like the tampons the rest of us use. Like it's any of your business."

They all heard a gasp.

Fiona turned to see Willow halfway down the stairs, her face blanched. For a long, suspended moment, she and Amy stared at each other. Then Willow's face crumpled and she turned and fled.

Keeping her voice level with an effort, Fiona said, "That was mean. I thought better of you, Amy."

"What?" she snapped, tossed her head. "Like boys don't know we menstruate?"

Everyone was listening, even Troy, who took off his headphones.

"Willow is younger than you, and shy. You did that deliberately." Fiona shook her head and went to John.

"Nasty little thing, isn't she?" he murmured.

Fiona was mad enough to say, "I'm beginning to think so. Is there any chance you have any more supplies? Uh, besides tampons?"

"I don't know. I'll look." He headed for the kitchen.

Out of the corner of her eye, Fiona was grateful to see Erin quietly heading up the stairs.

With a sniff, Amy plopped down again at the small table where she'd been playing poker with the others.

"That was cold," Troy said loudly.

She spun in her chair and narrowed her eyes to slits. "What do *you* know?"

"I know you like being the center of attention." He sounded thoughtful, as if just realizing. "You get pissed whenever anyone else is."

"I do not!"

"It was mean," Dieter said. "Jeez, Amy."

She spun back to face him. "Because I'm not mealy-mouthed? Why's it a big deal?"

He shrugged. "It's not, except it is to Willow. I saw

you looking at her when you said that. Like, you wouldn't have if she hadn't been there to overhear."

Furious spots of color had appeared on her cheeks. "You're the one who's being mean!"

He just shrugged.

Amy looked at Hopper. He bowed his head.

"Not cool," Kelli said.

Amy burst into tears, scrambled up so fast her chair fell over with a crash and raced for the stairs. Everyone let her go.

Of course, it was Fiona's job to go after her. Eventually. Once she'd taken care of Willow's problem.

So much for the peaceful tableau. With a sigh, Fiona followed John to the kitchen, passing an unsuspecting Tabitha who had a can of pop in her hand, said, "Any luck?" and at Fiona's shake of the head went back to join the others.

John came out of the storeroom with a couple of pink-wrapped items. "These?" he asked, holding them up.

"Oh, bless you!" Fiona said fervently. "My next option was to suggest rags, and I know that wouldn't go over well."

"Rags?"

"Never mind." She took the two wrapped pads. "Is this all you could find?"

"No, there's a bunch of them. Different colors and, uh, sizes." His shoulders moved. "Ones left behind. I save anything like that, if I think it might come in handy."

"John Fallon, you are the best innkeeper in the entire world." Before she could think twice about it, she stood on tiptoe and kissed him on the cheek, then twirled away before she could see how he reacted. Before *she* could react, to the scratchy texture of his cheek, the smell of the wood he'd been handling, his nearness. "I'll take these to her," she said, backing away.

"I'll collect as many as I can find." If there was a slightly odd note in his voice, Fiona didn't pause to analyze it.

Instead she hurried upstairs and knocked on the bathroom door. "Willow?"

Her teary voice said, "Yes?"

"I found some pads."

"Really?" The door opened a crack, and Erin held a hand out.

Fiona gave her the pads. Then, with a sigh, she went to the bedroom next door and knocked. "Amy?"

"Go away!"

"We need to talk."

"I don't want to talk!"

Tough, she wanted to say.

"You can't hide up here for the next three days."

"I want to go home!"

"We all want to go home." Except, maybe, Fiona. She decided to shelve the slightly startling realization to think about later. "Can I come in?"

After a long pause, Amy said, "Oh, fine," a bitter note in her voice. *I can't stop you,* she might as well have said, *but I don't have to be nice.*

Or maybe, Fiona thought, trying to be charitable, *I really do want to talk to you, but I'm sulking so I can't admit it.*

Amy lay flat on her back on one of the beds, staring up at the ceiling. Fiona could tell she had hastily wiped away tears.

"You okay?" she asked gently, sitting on the other bed.

"They all act like they hate me."

"No, they were just expressing disapproval."

"She's such a *mouse,*" Amy spat.

Fiona counted to five. "Not everyone has your confidence, Amy."

"You should have seen her outside. She was all over Hopper."

Ah. Was revenge sweet?

"Are you sure she was flirting, and not just playing?"

"Playing?" Amy rolled a sidelong, incredulous look at Fiona. "Oh, right."

"Willow is young in a lot of ways..."

"Not *that* young."

Willow's confidences weren't hers to tell, and anyway, Fiona wasn't so sure Amy would care that the other girl's mother had died and that might be why she was clinging to childhood.

"No matter what you think Willow did to you, you owe her an apology."

Tears abruptly filled the sixteen-year-old's eyes, and she flipped so her back was to Fiona. "No way!"

"To some extent the decision is yours." Fiona paused. "But I suspect you'll get the cold shoulder from the others until you say you're sorry."

Voice smothered by the pillow, Amy cried, "But I'm not!"

Fiona stood. "If you make your apology gracious enough, everyone will assume they were mistaken about your motives. Think about it."

Quietly she left the room, shutting the door behind her. Had it been smart, she wondered, to give a girl like Amy advice on how to manipulate people? How to get along with other people, yes. But she'd done more than that. She'd as good as said, *Here's how to act out the scene so you'll look good.*

She made a face. It was done, and she couldn't take it back. She couldn't say, *If you're not sorry, we'll all be able to see right through you.*

Willow's and Erin's voices now came from their bedroom.

Fiona rapped lightly on their half-open door. "Can I come in?"

"Sure," Erin said.

Willow's eyes were still puffy. She sat cross-legged on the bed, a pillow clutched to her stomach. "Um… were those the only two pads?"

"No, John has quite a collection, apparently. I'll get them later." She smiled. "I'm going on down. Why don't you two come with me?"

Willow hunched over and squeezed the pillow harder. "I can't! Everyone knows… And I acted so stupid."

"I think you'll find everyone sympathizes with you. And, thanks to sex ed if not their own mothers, boys do know about menstruation."

Erin nodded, her black hair shimmering. "Come on. It's better to get it over with."

"Is Amy down there?"

"No," Fiona said. "Right now, she's…in her room." She'd almost said, *Sulking*. Thank goodness she'd swallowed the admission in time.

Willow finally agreed, and accompanied Erin and Fiona back downstairs. Troy had his eyes closed and was listening to his music again. Only the poker players turned their heads.

Kelli smiled brightly and said, "Hey."

Hopper asked, "You want to play?"

Color high, Willow shook her head shyly. "No, thanks."

Dieter stood, abandoning his cards. "How about Chinese checkers?"

She bit her lip, gave Fiona a desperate look, then took a deep breath and nodded. "Okay."

Erin went back to her book, and peace once again reigned.

John materialized at Fiona's side. "Did you convince the brat to apologize?" he asked, voice pitched for her ears only.

She sighed. "In a manner of speaking."

"What's that mean?"

"You'll see." She tried to shake off her oddly dark mood. "Maybe I'm wrong. She could be genuinely contrite."

He grunted. Fiona had no trouble interpreting the sound.

"Has the snow let up yet?" she asked.

He shook his head. "It's going to be a while before you get out of here."

Of course she felt dismay, because the kids were

going to get bored and have even more trouble getting along. But if she'd been here alone… Well, she'd be *glad* to be stranded for longer.

And she knew perfectly well why.

"Shoot, I forgot to try to call Dave again. My principal," she explained. "I suppose I'd better do it."

She retrieved her cell phone, but this time failed to get the call through. She followed John back to his room, where he took his phone from a bedside table. She succeeded no better with his.

"They know you're here and safe," he said. "Don't worry."

"I'll bet the parents are worrying."

"Because you would if one of them was your kid."

"Well, of course I would! Dave got one call, I kept cutting out, and now not a word."

"You can't do anything."

"No. I know." After a minute, she smiled, if crookedly. "Oh, well. Until Amy's little outburst, everybody looked pretty happy."

"You wearing down yet?" Had his voice softened?

"I'm fine. Oh, let me retrieve the rest of those pads."

"Right." He went into the storeroom and returned with another of the baskets he used for toiletries and soap in the bathroom, this one heaped with small, plastic-wrapped sanitary pads. "This okay? Or should I put them in a brown paper bag?"

She made a face at him. "Girls' bathroom. Boys' bathroom. Remember?"

He grinned, then said, "Sorry I didn't offer any in the first place. I could have saved some trouble."

"Amy was mad because she thought Willow was flirting with Hopper outside. I suspect she'd have figured out some way to get back at her. This was just the first opportunity that arose."

"Ah."

"Makes you glad not to be sixteen again, doesn't it?"

As if involuntarily, his hand rose to touch the scar on his face. "Oh, I don't know."

Feeling insensitive, she said, "I'm sorry," then stopped. "Okay, I'm doing it again.

His fingers curled into a fist and his hand dropped to his side. Face completely blank of expression, John shook his head. "Don't worry. That time, I might as well have asked for pity."

She let out a huff. "I wasn't expressing pity. It was sympathy!"

"Which is completely different?"

"Yes!" she exclaimed. "Don't you know the difference?"

"Apparently not."

"Do you think...that the scar makes you unattractive?" She couldn't believe she'd said that, and almost opened her mouth to once again say, *I'm sorry.* Just in time, she stopped herself.

He gave her a peculiar look that she couldn't read. "It might've looked better if I'd just tattooed one side of my face, or put ten hoops through my eyebrow instead. A scar... I don't know."

She eyed him suspiciously. "You're teasing me, aren't you?"

"No." His voice was flat, hard. "I see people look away quickly. It makes them uncomfortable. They wonder what happened, but they don't really want to know."

Her voice dropped to a near-whisper. "I want to know."

He nodded. "That makes you...unusual."

They seemed unable to look away from each other. His eyes searched hers with an intensity that shook her.

Sounding a little breathless, she managed, "The scar just gives you that brooding, Heathcliff look."

"Don't say that." He sounded disgusted, the electricity abruptly broken.

"It was, um, meant to be a compliment."

"I detested *Wuthering Heights.*"

Actually she wasn't crazy about Bronte's classic, either, although there was something about being forced to analyze theme and characters endlessly for an English class that could ruin the best of books.

"Heathcliff does epitomize the romantic hero, you know," she pointed out.

"The guy was rude and self-pitying. Am I that bad?"

He sounded so appalled that she had to laugh.

"I was just trying to say that a scar doesn't make you any less attractive to women. In fact—" she tilted her head "—it makes you look just a little dangerous."

"Attractive, huh?"

Darn it, her pulse began to bounce again.

"You know you are."

"It's been a long time..." He stopped, obviously wishing the words unsaid.

Was he admitting that he hadn't made love to a

woman since he was wounded? Maybe, since before he went to Iraq?

Fiona asked the only thing she could think to. "Did you have a girlfriend before you left?"

"I was seeing someone, but we were drifting apart even before I shipped out."

"Oh. I, um, haven't actually dated more than casually in a long time, either." Oh God. Why did she tell him that? Maybe he wasn't interested. If she saw boredom cross his face…

He didn't look bored. His voice was low, a little rough. "Why?"

"Well, I've been busy. Working full-time and going to grad school at the same time is a challenge."

He waited.

"Okay, I guess I just haven't met anyone who interested me enough to bother. Which is *not* what I tell guys calling to ask me for a second date!"

He smiled. Really smiled. "Break their hearts, do you?"

"Oh, that's me. A femme fatale."

"I think—" again his voice had roughened "—you could be."

They were flirting, she realized, not just dancing around the possibility, as they'd been practically since she stumbled over the lodge doorstep yesterday. Her heart was pounding, her cheeks felt warm, and despite all common sense she wanted to be snowbound here until she found out if this attraction to him meant anything.

Suddenly a giggle escaped her, as irresistible as a hiccup.

His eyes narrowed. "What?"

"I suddenly realized I'm having this intense conversation with a man who's holding a basket of sanitary napkins."

He looked down. "Uh, yeah. Here. *You* take them." He all but shoved the basket into her hands.

Another bubble of laughter in her throat, she said, "Feel manlier now?"

He was getting better at the whole smiling thing. This one was positively rakish. "Hey, you kissed me because of those pads."

"I *can* be bribed," she said with as much dignity as she could summon.

"And with so little."

She laughed. "I'll take these upstairs."

"You do that."

Fiona backed up a step or two. "And see whether Amy has reappeared."

"Good idea."

"The boys are probably getting hungry again."

With resignation, John said, "Undoubtedly. I'll see what I can find."

"Okay." Even so, it was all she could do to make herself turn away. Pushing through the swinging door, she felt a little flutter of alarm along with plenty of flutters of excitement. Was it really all that smart to be even thinking about falling for a man who'd had to move out into the woods so he could "decompress"? Or—horrors—was that the real attraction? Did she think she could somehow "fix" him? Lord, was she that arrogant?

Perturbed, she took the basket upstairs and left it in

the bathroom, then returned to her book downstairs. She couldn't hang out in the kitchen *all* evening.

If she kept finding herself rereading pages, at least no one else could tell.

The poker game seemed to be winding down. Maybe betting on wood and bark chips was losing its zip. Dieter and Willow were talking now, rather than playing Chinese checkers, and, as Fiona surveyed the room, Troy took off his earphones and sat up.

With an apparent gift for timing, Amy chose just then to come down the stairs.

Fiona felt as much as saw John come from the kitchen and stop in the shadow of one of the rough-hewn pillars.

Everyone looked at Amy, who paused on the bottom step, tears seeming to sparkle on her lashes.

"Willow?" she whispered. Then, as she rushed forward, "Oh, Willow! I'm so sorry!"

Looking wary, Willow rose to her feet. Amy hugged her.

"I have *such* a big mouth. I was mostly annoyed at Hopper—" she cast him a half-stern, half-flirtatious look before turning back to Willow "—and I just wanted to tell him to mind his own business. But I didn't *think.* I never meant to embarrass you. And I'm really sorry I did."

Her voice was tremulous, her expression tragic.

What could Willow do but say, "It's okay. It was dumb of me to be embarrassed. I just…I never talked about stuff like that before in front of…" She bit her lip. "But it's no biggie, okay?"

Amy gave a breathtaking smile. "I've been feeling so awful! Thank you."

Everyone smiled with approval. The performance was beautiful. Fiona was a little bit shocked at her own cynicism.

She turned her head and saw the way John was watching the scene, his expression a mixture of incredulity, admiration and disgust.

Maybe, she tried to tell herself, Amy had learned something from this other than how to feign remorse, assuming she hadn't already known how to do that. Could it be that she'd become just a little more aware that nastiness didn't win friends?

Fiona's inner teenager murmured, *Yeah, right.*

Amy was weepy, glowing with relief and reveling in being the center of attention. Willow, once again colorless, had slipped to the periphery as if trying to vanish. Dieter, bless his heart, had gone with her and was ignoring Amy.

Fiona was exhausted. She had never before appreciated so much that classes were only fifty minutes long. She also discovered that, while she didn't want to go home, she wanted *them* to go home.

Meanwhile she was having a debate with herself about whether to take Amy aside and tell her a little went a long way and she really, really didn't have to lay it on so thick.

She was saved by the necessity by John, who took a few steps forward, cleared his throat and said, "Anyone hungry?"

The boys forgot Amy *and* Willow.

"Yeah!" they said, almost in unison, and stampeded for the kitchen.

"Hot chocolate," John added.

Even Erin put down her book.

"Cool!" Amy said brightly. She looked around for Willow. "Shall we go get some?"

Willow blushed, as if flattered at the attention. "Sure."

Fiona sighed and followed.

CHAPTER SEVEN

JOHN AWAKENED in the morning before anyone else. He'd let the small woodstove in his apartment burn down and, swearing, he yanked on clothes with clumsy haste. He'd get the fire in the great room burning again to supplement the old furnace, then make some bread. They'd gone through more than he had anticipated yesterday.

It wasn't until he'd passed through the kitchen and was in the great room of the lodge that he looked outside. The sky was just lightening, and it seemed to him that he saw some pink.

He unlocked the heavy front door and stepped out onto the porch. No white blur of falling flakes. The morning was bitingly cold, the stillness absolute. He walked to the side of the porch, where he could see to the east. Above the treetops, Thunder Mountain reared as a dark bulk, but around it the sky glowed orange and pink and yellow.

It would be a while before the sun was far enough up for him to be able to assess how much snow lay on the ground, but he knew digging out was going to be a job. Maybe he could put the boys to work today. Or would that constitute child abuse to these private-school kids?

He mixed up bread dough, kneaded it, gave it time to rise and had the loaves in the oven before he heard any stirrings at all upstairs. Willow and Erin were the first to come down.

"It quit snowing," Erin said in her serene way, making it an observation rather than an exclamation.

"Yep."

"How long do you think before the road gets plowed?" Willow asked timidly.

"Probably a couple of days, anyway."

"Oh." Her voice was small. "That smells really good."

"Nothing like bread baking. Want to start with some cereal or eggs, or would you rather wait until the bread comes out of the oven?"

"Wait," they agreed.

"Anybody else up yet?" What he really wanted to know was whether their teacher was up. He'd been thinking about her when he fell asleep, and he hadn't even opened his eyes before he pictured her face this morning.

With faint shock, he realized he was in trouble. He'd be foolish to imagine that any sensible woman would want to traverse his bad moods and flashbacks long enough to build any kind of relationship with him.

"I don't think so," Willow said, in answer to his question.

He got some blackberry jam out of the freezer and set it on the table to thaw.

The two girls continued to hover. After a minute, John felt obligated to make conversation.

"You looking forward to getting home?"

"It's been fun here," Erin said, not really answering his question.

"And we might miss some school," Willow added.

"Don't you have to make up snow days in the spring?"

"Only if the whole school… Oh!" The younger girl's mouth formed an O. "Do you think it snowed enough in Hawes Ferry that school will be canceled Monday?"

"From what your principal said, it's a real possibility." He put hot water on for tea. "You think your parents are worrying?"

"My dad will be," Willow said softly, her head tilted forward enough that her hair veiled her expression.

Erin shrugged. "As long as they know we're safe, mine'll be okay."

John checked the oven. A couple more minutes.

"Do you get snowed in a lot here?"

"A couple of times a winter, I'm told. Not usually so early. I'm guessing this is a record."

"We were so lucky." Willow shivered.

"Good thing you had Dieter with you." He kept an eye on her, aware from what Fiona had told him that the skinny boy with the goofy smile had been Willow's knight-errant yesterday.

She obligingly blushed.

More drama in the making.

John hadn't expected to feel as comfortable as he did with these kids. He supposed it was because they had become individuals to him, taking on personality. The only two he still mixed up were Kelli-with-an-i and

Tabitha, both blond and perky, neither yet the center of a drama that would bring their personalities into focus.

Give 'em time, he figured, resigned.

Fiona appeared next, wearing the jeans and turtleneck she'd arrived in, borrowed wool socks that he thought were his and a bright smile. "Did you see what a beautiful morning it is?"

"Ms. Mac! It quit snowing!"

"I know, I saw." She hugged both girls.

Her cheek was creased from a wrinkle in her pillow. John thought it was cute. She, too, exclaimed over the bread coming out of the oven and waited expectantly.

John sliced the first loaf hot and watched with amusement as they slathered on butter and jam and ate with murmurs of delight. Fiona actually went so far as to close her eyes and moan, a sight and sound that forced him to turn away to hide his jolt of longing.

The others gradually came downstairs, begging to go outside after breakfast.

When John suggested the boys take turns wielding a snow shovel, they all shrugged and nodded.

"Yeah, sure. I mean, I never have, but…"

"Yeah, whatever," Troy agreed.

"I have snowshoes," John said. Then, seeing that they were less than thrilled, he held up a hand. "To get a couple of us up to your van. The snowplow always turns in and clears the road to the lodge. But they won't be able to get past your van. With the snow so deep, it'd be a heck of a trek back up there."

Everyone nodded, remembering that the lodge road descended steeply from the highway.

"I keep my own snowshoes on the back porch, but the ones I own for guests are in the shed. We won't be able to get to them if we don't dig out in front of the doors."

That made sense to them, he could see.

"A path around the lodge to where the wood is stacked would be a big help, too. Oh, and the steps, so no one falls."

"We could take turns, too," Erin suggested.

Small as the girls all were, he couldn't imagine they'd get far lifting heavy shovelsful of snow, but why not?

"What a good idea." Fiona beamed at her. "I think all of us should help."

What could he do but say, "Fine."

As they all bundled up after breakfast, John was reminded that some of them wouldn't be able to stay outside long, not in athletic shoes instead of decent winter boots. He'd come up with pairs for all three boys, two from his own closet. Hopper had to double up on socks to keep his feet from sliding around, and Dieter was clearly scrunching to get his feet in his borrowed pair. Only Troy's seemed to be about right.

There were "oohs" and "aahs" all around when they stepped outside to a now-bright morning, the unblemished blanket of snow sparkling. It had become heavy enough at some point to slide off the peaked shed roof and likely the lodge's as well. He'd have to check the cabins later.

Every tree limb bowed under a cloak of snow. At a thump, Willow jumped.

"What was that?"

"Snow falling off a tree branch," he said. "You'll keep hearing that. Gets worse once it warms up and the snow starts to melt."

"Oh." Hugging herself, she still looked spooked.

"Wow! Can we just, like, dive?" Troy asked, staring at the white expanse.

"I doubt you'd get hurt," John said.

Over the top of his words, Fiona started to say, "But I don't think it's a good..."

Too late. With a whoop, Troy let himself fall backward from the porch.

The girls let out squeaks and gasps and peered over the railing. He rose as if from lake water, looking like the Abominable Snowman, shaking snow from his hair and face as he grinned and called, "Dare you!"

Pretty soon they were all thrashing around in the snow as if they'd never seen any before. Even those who skied were probably used to groomed slopes, not five feet of newly fallen snow. Their shrieks and bellows and squeals shattered the mountain stillness.

Only Fiona remained with him on the porch, watching her charges.

"Dare you," John murmured.

"Ugh. It would go down my neck."

"Come on. Aren't you a little bit tempted?"

"Maybe a little." Her nose was already red, her cheeks glowing. "I will if you will."

He was going to be sorry. Real, real sorry. His hip gave a warning twinge, but he ignored it. He couldn't resist the laughter in Fiona's clear gray eyes or the mittened hand held out to him.

He took her hand and nodded toward the north corner of the lodge. "We'd better find ourselves some fresh snow."

"Yeah, nose first on frozen ground wouldn't feel so good, would it?"

Twenty feet from the front steps, he said, "You first."

"Together?" she challenged.

They stood on the edge with their backs to the snowy landscape.

"One," he said.

"Two."

"Three," he finished, and they fell, still holding hands.

It was like sinking into a giant container of feathers that slowed but didn't stop them. He lost his grip on her hand, and couldn't see her or anything else. Some primitive instinct kicked in and he immediately started fighting the snow that closed over his face. Within seconds, he'd reared to his feet and surfaced.

Laughing, she did the same, although only her head appeared over the top. "That was fun!"

The kids were hollering, "She did it! Yay, Ms. Mac!"

"I give her a ten," Dieter called.

"I don't know," one of the blond girls argued. "Didn't you see the break in her form?"

Ms. Mac stuck out her tongue at her students. "Brats!"

She looked comical covered with snow, her ponytail and eyebrows white. Snow slid from his nose, reminding John that he looked the same. He reached up, pulled off his ski hat, shook it out and put it back on, icy flakes slithering down his neck.

"This is so amazing!" As if she were standing in

water up to her neck, Fiona peered around. "I can see how skiers fall and smother."

"Yeah, not a good way to go."

She shuddered.

He picked up a handful of snow and tossed it into the air. "Lighter than usual for around here, though," he commented. "It's damn cold." Western Oregon wasn't known for powder snow; whatever fell was usually wet and therefore heavy. Operators at Timberline and Mount Hood Meadows must be rejoicing today.

"Yes, it is." Fiona flailed her arms in front of her. "Um…how do I walk?"

"You just shove forward. Or follow me." He stepped into the well her body had created, then bulldozed his way forward toward the kids and the still-hidden porch steps.

By feel he located the steps and climbed to the porch, where he collected the two snow shovels.

"Who wants first turn?" he called.

"Bummer," somebody complained.

"You're going to get cold and want to go in."

"I'll go first," Erin offered. "My feet are already getting cold."

She was one of the girls without boots, he remembered.

"Me, too," said Tabitha. Or was it Kelli?

They groped their way up the steps, too, and he showed them how to wield the broad, flat-bladed shovels.

They cleared a few steps while the others romped. He kept an eye on the two wielding the shovels, and when they started struggling, he had them hand off to two of the other girls. Meantime, he called the boys over.

"Deep as this is, we just need to trample paths. Let's get a good one to the woodpile around the corner first."

They started, half working, half roughhousing. Fiona stood beside John near the foot of the porch steps. She was the only one close to him when two things happened almost at once.

The roughhousing reached a peak, with one of the boys falling to one side and another of them swinging around and taking a step as if he was going to run back toward John and Fiona. At the same time, there was a loud crack.

Not the whine of an incoming artillery shell. Damn, somehow a sniper had gotten a range on them. They were on base and he didn't even have his weapon. John saw blood spurting as the running man took another step and then in seeming slow motion toppled. "Get down!" John bellowed at the one standing soldier, then turned, grabbed Fiona and threw her into the soft snow, going after her to shield her with his body.

She struggled under him. He held her down, listening for the next crack of the sniper's rifle. Where was he? In the stand of trees?

A thud sounded like far-off bombing.

"What are you doing?" she spat.

"Ms. Mac got tackled!" someone called gleefully.

He'd never seen snow in Iraq. Why were they in a snowdrift, waiting for the deadly fire of a Russian AK-47 to find them? Body rigid, he tried to think.

One second, they were under fire from insurgents. The next, he lay atop a furious, frightened woman in the snow outside the lodge.

Crap. Oh, crap. He'd heard a tree limb snap. That's all.

But he'd seen blood. A jet of it, spraying the snow with red. God. Maybe not. More dazed than he usually was when he snapped out of a flashback, he stared at the face of the woman he held pinned down.

She saw something in his eyes and went still. "Are you all right?" she whispered.

"No. Yes. Damn." Voice guttural, he rolled to one side.

"It's okay," she whispered. "Just stand up. No one noticed anything."

Adrenaline still pumping, physically battle-ready, he got up with her. All three boys were on their feet laughing. They weren't soldiers; they were kids. No blood dyed the snow a shocking crimson. He reached up and scrubbed a gloved hand over his face.

"Ms. Mac, we're going in," Erin said.

Fiona had been staring worriedly up at him. He couldn't make himself meet her eyes, but he felt her gaze. Now she turned her head.

"Cold?"

"My feet are *ice* blocks," one of the girls said.

"Mine, too." Willow, he thought.

"I'm going in," Amy declared.

His brain was moving sluggishly, but he realized that Amy wore boots, *and* hadn't taken a turn with the snow shovel.

She'd have been useless anyway.

"Give me just a few minutes and I'll be in as well," Fiona told them.

"First bath!" one of the voices claimed, as feet thudded on the porch boards.

Had to be Amy. Who else?

Fiona laid a mittened hand on his arm. "I'll organize Tabitha and Kelli to start trampling a path toward the shed. If you're okay."

"I'm fine," he said automatically. "It was just, uh…"

"*Just?* You had a flashback, didn't you?" She shook her head in warning and he heard the squeak of booted feet coming toward them. "We'll talk about it later," she murmured.

John could hardly look at the boys. They'd been the cause of his episode. Okay, he didn't do well with loud noises, especially ones that sounded like gunfire. But he didn't usually lose it completely. Not like that. But the boys, the way they pushed and shoved and laughed… And, God, when the one went down…

He felt sick.

"This wide enough?" Dieter asked.

John pretended to study the path. "Looks fine. When you get to the woodpile, we'll all bring in some wood for the night."

"Yeah, sure." He looked past John. "What happened to the girls? Did they wimp out?"

"Without boots, their feet were getting cold." He sounded normal. Sane, he congratulated himself.

"Still wimps." Dieter tromped away.

John turned to watch Fiona and the two girls, three abreast, pushing forward through shoulder-high snow and then stamping on what collapsed around them. The girls in particular were giggling madly, and they looked like the women he'd seen in a movie trampling grapes for wine.

Fiona's laugh floated to his ears, lower-pitched than

the girls's, a little husky. A woman's laugh. But she stomped with all the enthusiasm of the two girls, her arm linked with one of them.

His stomach churned again. Would she think he was crazy?

How could she not? He'd thought insurgents were shooting at them and he'd knocked her to the ground. He wanted to lie to himself and call it a life-saving instinct that had to be retrained: the bang of a mortar, the crack of a rifle, you hit the deck. Returning soldiers from every war in the last century and in this one had the same instinct, one that he assumed dulled with time and then was forgotten.

But it hadn't been just instinct. For a minute, he'd been half there in Iraq, half here in Oregon. He'd known snow was around them rather than sand. He'd known it was Fiona he was throwing his body over. But the boys had suddenly worn camouflage, and the blood… The blood had been as real as his would be if he cut himself open right now. He could still close his eyes and see the moment, a snapshot to join the album full of others he carried in his head.

Hopper's face, mouth open in a soundless cry of alarm as he tried to run toward them. The jerk as the round entered his body, the spurt of blood, the fall.

How the hell could he have made it so real? John asked himself. It wasn't just a memory, it was…a hybrid. As if he'd done a computer search, he came up with the right image, frozen in his brain.

He's in a Humvee, looking up a street in some shithole of a town. Three M-16 toting soldiers ahead, not being careful because why should they? This town is ours. They're joking, shoving. One turns to share the joke when he sees something. He lifts his weapon and his mouth opens. Shouting a warning? Crack. His blood spurts, a fountain that says an artery has been hit.

His shock at dying like that, the fact that he *knew* he was dying, kept his face vivid in John's memory. What sickened him most then and now was how young the boy was. Eighteen? Nineteen?

Rat-a-tat-tat. They'd answered fire with fire, and an Iraqi tumbled in grotesque slow-motion from a rooftop where he had been crouched. As dead as the young National Guardsman who now sprawled in the street, blood staining the packed earth.

There it was, simple. Images superimposing. He had an explanation that still added up to crazy. Can't tell then from now. Counseling. Medications.

John seemed to hear a reassuring voice. He'd be fine if he took his pills and bared his soul upon request to a psychologist and in group sessions. The anger choked him now as it had then. He didn't want to remember. He needed to do some old-fashioned grieving, needed to adapt to an everyday reality that now seemed as bizarre as the one he'd just left. Returning Civil War veterans hadn't had serotonin uptake inhibitors. They'd just gone back to their farms, spent time outside staring at the spangled night sky, letting earth that wasn't blood-stained sift through their hands. John wasn't a farmer, but the lodge had been working for him. What was wrong with that?

Fiona and the two remaining girls went in at last,

their path having reached the shed although he could see they'd have to do some shoveling to get the doors open.

John carried in armfuls of wood with the boys, filling the bin on one side of the fireplace and forming stacks on the hearth as well. Unable to bear the laughter and high, excited voices as they all struggled out of winter gear in front of the fire, he went back out alone to stow the snow shovels, then stood for a minute gazing at the woods leading down to the creek.

What would happen to the deer, with the snow so high on the ground? Would they be able to find anything to eat? If they were smart, they'd stay deep under the trees where the snow hadn't been able to pile up. But there they'd be reduced to eating bark from the trunks of firs and cedar. Maybe it was a good thing that this storm had hit so early in the winter, while the wild animals still carried the weight they'd gained through the warm summer and mild autumn.

He turned and went in, glad not to see Fiona. Alone in his own small apartment, he took a long, hot bath, sinking under to release some of the tension gathered in his neck and shoulders. He dressed, towel-dried his hair and went to the kitchen to consider lunch and dinner menus.

Some kind of stir-fry for dinner, he decided. He'd take chicken out to thaw. He had bags of vegetables in the freezer, and enough rice to keep them from starving damn near all winter long. It would be quick and easy, not requiring any help.

For lunch…

He stiffened when he heard the door swing open behind him. Without turning, he knew Fiona had come in. Erin and Willow were the only other two who sometimes entered a room quietly. But they were less likely to track him down. Besides, his nose caught the scent of gardenias, which meant she'd taken another bath with one of the pearlescent beads.

"Thinking about lunch or dinner?" she asked.

"Dinner at the moment." He faced her, careful to keep his face expressionless. "I have frozen vegetables to make stir-fry. We'll have sandwiches for lunch."

"You shouldn't have to cook all our meals."

"I prefer to stay busy."

"Oh." She bit her lip. "Can I help?"

She was having trouble meeting his eyes. Was she *scared* of him?

Clear the air. "I hope I didn't give you bruises."

She let out an unconvincing laugh. "I deserve some, after throwing myself off the porch."

"I knocked you down hard. I'm sorry."

To his eyes, she was so beautiful right now he ached with it. Her cheeks were rosy, perhaps from the bath. Her hair was caught up on top of her head, but wisps curled around her face. She'd changed into a flannel shirt—his—the sleeves rolled half a dozen times, several buttons undone to expose her long, pale throat and delicate collarbone. Her eyes were uncertain, shying from his, the color seemingly having darkened.

"You didn't hurt me. I was just…startled."

"I'm glad," he said, and meant it.

She bit her lip, nodded and took a step back, as if to leave the kitchen. Then she stopped, and he braced himself.

"Does it happen often? I mean, flashbacks?"

"No. Not like that. I duck when a garbage truck clangs, but so do most vets at first."

Her eyes, perplexed, met his at last. "Then why…?"

"There was an incident…" He cleared his throat. He didn't like talking about the war at all, but he owed her an explanation. "Three soldiers. Something about the way the boys arranged themselves today, their voices…" He stopped, found himself hunching his shoulders. "When Hopper turned back and then fell just as that branch snapped… It was so familiar. I wasn't in Iraq. I knew there was snow on the ground, and that it was you I was throwing down."

"Protecting," she said softly.

"But for a minute I saw blood. I thought two of the boys had gone down." Feeling incredibly awkward, he studied the grain of wood in the plank floor. "It was brief, but vivid."

"You've had things like this happen before, haven't you? That's why you moved up here."

He lifted his head and glared at her. "You think I walk around hallucinating? You're wrong. This was an isolated incident. War messes with your head. It takes time to clear it."

Puckers between her eyebrows showed that she was still troubled as she studied him, but after a minute she nodded. "My father was in Vietnam. To this day he hates the Fourth of July."

"Yeah, that would be even worse for Vietnam vets. We didn't have to deal with constant shelling."

"What was the worst part?" she asked.

Being asked to talk about it made him feel as if his ribs were being compressed. He shifted, told himself he was getting enough air.

What was a short answer she'd accept? One that didn't say, watching kids you've befriended get blown up?

"The fact that you're not fighting soldiers. There's no theater of operations. There's no behind the lines where you can kick back and not worry about dying. It's like Vietnam in that sense. Every car driving up to a checkpoint can be full of guys toting AK rifles. Or it might have a family in it, little kids in the back. Road blocks are a nightmare. Everyone over there drives at breakneck speed. Is a car barreling toward you because that's the way this guy drives all the time, or because he's a suicide bomber? That house with kids playing in front of it might be the meeting place for a bunch of insurgents. You can't assume it's safe because of the kids." He tried to figure out how to make her understand. "Violence can happen anywhere. Anytime. So you never relax."

She nodded. "So after a while you look at all Iraqis as enemies and none as a friend."

Not him. Foolishly optimistic, he had tried to make friends with the people, to build a bridge between the Americans and the locals. He wasn't going to tell her about how that bridge was detonated, any more than he had told a single other soul since he was shipped home on crutches.

"The six-month deployments are smart. Knowing you're getting to go home..." Hands miraculously steady, he took out a cutting board and knife. "Trouble is, going back the second time would be harder."

Alarm flared on her face. "You won't be deployed again?"

"I've been discharged," he said unemotionally. "I'd be a liability now with this leg."

"Oh." Her voice was just above a whisper. "I'm glad."

His throat felt thick. He couldn't say anything.

"I can tell you don't like talking about it. But…thank you for explaining. The look on your face today…" She shivered, seemingly unaware that she hugged herself.

"I'm sorry I scared you." The apology felt and sounded inadequate to him, but he didn't know what he could add.

Generous woman that she was, Fiona offered him a smile that looked untainted by anything he'd said or done. "Not to worry. Now, come on, admit it. Surely you can use some help feeding the crowd."

She wanted to stay here in the kitchen, with him? Stunned, John said, "You're a glutton for punishment."

Now the smile became merry. "No, if I were a glutton for punishment, I'd be in the great room with eight teenagers. Instead I'm hiding out in the kitchen with you. At least, I'd *like* to hide out in the kitchen with you. If you'll give me an excuse."

He didn't know when he'd felt luckier than he did right now, realizing that Fiona MacPherson was giving him a second chance.

"You might collect wet clothes and start a load of laundry. Then you can help me with lunch."

"Oh, good." She sounded buoyant, as though he had

relieved her mind in some way. "I can at least pretend I'm being useful." She headed for the swinging door, pushed it open and gave him a last bright smile over her shoulder. "I shall return," she promised.

For the first time, he wondered if, once the road was plowed and the van back on it, Fiona would think about coming back. Just her. If he asked.

Oh, yeah, his inner voice scoffed. *Just what she'd want: to be alone in the lodge with the guy who'd thought Arab terrorists were shooting from the woods today.*

But she'd seemed to buy his explanation. And a couple of times these last two days, when he'd looked at her and the air seemed to leave the room, he'd have sworn she couldn't breathe, either.

He looked at the pile of frozen chicken breasts he'd brought out and wondered what he was supposed to do with it.

Refrigerator. Oh, yeah. That was it.

As for Fiona, she wouldn't be escaping Thunder Mountain Lodge tonight, and maybe, if he was lucky, not tomorrow. So he had time to…well, hint. See if she was interested, unlikely though that possibility seemed.

CHAPTER EIGHT

FIONA NOTICED that John sat at the opposite end of the table from the boys at dinner and ate quickly, his head down. Trying to pretend to herself that she wasn't conscious of him every single second, she was left to referee the far-ranging discussion and squabbles.

Dieter admitted to liking—appropriately enough—a musical group called Snow Patrol.

"You like alternative?" Troy sneered. "What, do you listen to Modest Mouse, too?"

Dieter was unperturbed. "Yeah, and they're brilliant."

This called for taking a poll of musical tastes, always a delicate matter as it exposed rifts in their world views. Eminem and Hilary Duff might both top the charts but did not otherwise pull up their chairs to the same table. Only Willow's youth saved her from being savaged by her admission that Hilary Duff and Aly and AJ were her favorite artists.

"Oh, and Ashlee Simpson," she added.

Troy opened his mouth.

Fiona interjected, "To each his own. I like Ben Folds."

"Yay, teach!" Dieter cheered. "He's awesome."

Troy turned his incredulous stare from the more

vulnerable Willow to someone who could stand his own ground.

"What, are you like some twenty-three-year-old computer geek?"

"No, then I'd like techno, and I don't."

Fiona let them bicker, so long as they left Willow out of it.

She stole a surreptitious look down at the table. What kind of music did John like? What kind of movies? Books? Was he fan of any professional sports? Given how much she did know about him, it was startling to realize how much she didn't.

She wished she'd known him before he went to war. Had he smiled easily? Laughed? Or had he always been closemouthed, perhaps even a loner?

Why, she wondered, were some people more traumatized by war than others? Was it what they'd experienced? What they'd seen or—worse yet—what they'd had to do? Or did personality predetermine who would suffer from PTSD? Now that he'd made her curious, she would have to find a book on the subject once she got home.

"Dieter, Amy and Erin, you're the cleanup crew tonight," she said, picking the names almost at random—except that she always tried to team Amy up with kids who'd keep her on task.

She'd enjoyed teaching at Willamette Prep in part because she didn't have to use the well-motivated pupils to propel the rest forward. In a school where students were accepted on academic merit, the kids were pretty uniformly motivated and college-bound. Amy, however, was proving surprisingly deft at evading work. Fiona was beginning to wonder whether she was the same with her schoolwork. And if so, how was it that she consistently turned in essays and papers that lifted her grades above the results of midterm and final exams?

And, oh, how Fiona hated to have such a suspicious mind.

After dinner, she had the kids bring the remaining soggy clothes down, and she folded laundry, moved a load to the dryer and started yet another.

Thank goodness for multiple hot water tanks! she thought, passing back through the kitchen to see Amy and Dieter unloading and drying dishes from the commercial dishwasher while Erin rinsed off plates and placed them in a rack in preparation for starting it again.

They had all proclaimed the dishwasher, which did a load in under two minutes, "major cool." The fact that they had to dry dishes rather than leave racks to air-dry on the counter had dimmed its appeal.

"Anyone know where John is?" she asked casually.

"Who?" Amy asked. "Oh. Him."

"I think he went that way." Erin nodded toward the great room.

Surprised he hadn't shut himself in his apartment, Fiona followed. Not because she necessarily wanted to spend time with him—after what happened today, she wasn't so sure that was a good idea—but because she ought to check on the rest of her students.

Kelli and Tabitha were nowhere to be seen, but Willow sat curled in one of the armchairs watching the boys bouncing a hacky-sack between them, using heads and knees. John was just tossing a piece of wood in on the fire, creating a burst of sparks.

"Hey, Mr. Fallon," Troy said, "do you have a soccer ball?"

He turned and stared at the boys, who were still keeping the hacky-sack in the air. "No." His voice was guttural, the look on his face strained.

None of the kids noticed. Fiona started toward him. He walked past her as if oblivious to her presence, unlocked the front door and went outside, closing it behind him. Determined, she followed.

He stood in the dark between bands of light that fell through the windows. His back was to her as he stared out at the night. Fiona didn't have to be able to see him well to know that he stood rigid, undoubtedly wishing to be alone.

Hesitating—perhaps she should have pretended not to notice that something in the exchange with the boys had upset him—she hugged herself against the bitter cold.

"Are you all right?" Her voice sounded as uncertain as she felt.

"Yes. Go back in."

She bit her lip and took a step back toward the door. About to turn, she stopped. "Why soccer?"

For a moment, she thought he wasn't going to answer at all. He didn't move.

A shiver racked her.

"I can't talk about it."

The words sounded torn from him. Painfully, leaving an open wound.

"Are you sure? I don't mind listening, if you want to talk."

He wheeled toward her. "But you're *not* listening, are you? I said, *I can't talk about it.*"

Stunned by the rage and pain raw in his voice, Fiona turned and blindly reached for the door latch.

"*God.* I'm sorry." He reached her before she could lift the latch, turning her.

Without thinking of the illogic, the foolishness, she clumsily wrapped her arms around him as he did the same to her. They stood in the dark, John absorbing her shivers, doing nothing but holding her and saying, over and over again, "I'm sorry. I'm so sorry."

"It's okay," she mumbled against his chest. "You were right, I *didn't* listen."

"You're the only person who has."

"I knew you wanted to be alone."

He made an odd sound, almost a groan. "No. I think I wanted you to follow me. Then when you did… God," he said again.

"You're not one of my students. I should mind my own business." But she didn't want to. And she sensed that John Fallon *needed* someone to intrude on his isolation.

"You're freezing." He tightened his arms.

"No," she whispered. "You're warm."

"Fiona?"

She tilted her head back. "Yes?"

He kissed her, the mouth so often compressed in pain gentle on hers, asking, not demanding. His lips were cold for the first moment, then warmed. She sighed and parted hers.

This sound was definitely a groan. Between one instant and the next, the kiss changed from tentative to wild, hungry, frantic. One of his hands gripped her buttock and lifted her against him as his mouth ravaged hers. Her thoughts blurred, only one having definition: *this* was why she'd followed him out onto the porch. She'd kept pushing so that he would kiss her.

He was the one to break it off. When he lifted his mouth from hers, Fiona sucked in a breath that she'd forgotten she needed.

John sounded hoarse. "The kids'll come looking for us."

The kids. She'd forgotten them. Oh Lord, she thought, stunned. If John had ripped off her clothes, she would have let him despite the cold, despite the teenagers just inside. What if Willow had opened the door and seen them fall apart in confusion and guilt?

"Yes." She tried to pull herself together. "I'd better go back in."

Did she look as if she'd just been passionately kissed? Or would the teenagers assume her cheeks were red from the cold?

What made her think they'd even look at her?

His hands fell away from her. "We'll both go in."

"Yes. Okay." Somehow her arms had come to be hanging at her sides. She sounded shell-shocked, then scrambled in her mind for another word. The irony was too great. She had no real idea what it was like to be shell-shocked. What she was, was overwhelmed, caught off guard. Jolted.

While he, she couldn't help noticing, now sounded remarkably calm.

Reaching around her, he lifted the latch and opened the massive door. His other hand on her back, he urged her inside.

Without pausing in the hacky-sack game, Hopper asked, "What were you guys doing outside? It's cold out there. Or didn't you notice?"

"We noticed," Fiona heard herself say. "But how else can we get away from all of you?"

Hopper laughed, as if she were a comic.

"Hey, Kelli was looking for you." Troy headed the hacky-sack, forcing Hopper to lunge to catch it with his foot before it hit the floor.

Wasn't soccer popular in Iraq? Had something happened at a game there that John had seen?

She started to turn to him, but he was walking away toward the kitchen, his limp noticeable. Fiona felt inexplicably chilled.

For the kids' benefit, she forced a smile. "I'll go find her."

But she wouldn't follow John to the kitchen.

Fortunately Kelli was upstairs with Tabitha and had forgotten what she wanted.

"No, I remember. I was hoping my jeans are in the dryer."

"Uh..." Fiona was blank. "I don't know. I was just throwing wet stuff in. I'll bet the load is dry by now. Would you two mind folding it? And putting the stuff in the washer into the dryer?"

"You okay, Ms. Mac?" Tabitha asked.

She managed another smile. "I'm fine. But, you know, I think I'll take my book—" not the one about Iraq, she'd find something else "—and go take a nice, hot bath."

"You deserve it." Tabitha looked at her skeptically, which meant her smile hadn't been entirely convincing, but she didn't ask any more questions. "We can fold the laundry. Right, Kelli?"

Less enthusiastic, the other girl shrugged. "Yeah, sure."

Fiona ended up skipping the book. Picking one out would have involved going downstairs, which might have meant encountering John or more unwanted curiosity from her students. She doubted she'd have been able to pay attention to a plot anyway.

Instead she brooded as she soaked, reliving the kiss over and over. Now she knew what had been missing from every other kiss she'd experienced. She knew why she was rarely interested in a second date, why her few longer-running relationships had, in the end, not endured.

But why, oh why, did she have to be so attracted to a man who, she was beginning to be afraid, was more damaged by the war than he was willing to admit?

Of course, distance was a problem, too, but she couldn't imagine him staying at Thunder Mountain forever. He didn't love the business of innkeeping, he wanted the solitude. And presumably once he "decompressed", he'd sell the lodge and move back to civilization. Perhaps even to Portland, where Robotronics was located.

Not that he'd actually said a word to suggest he was interested in anything beyond a few kisses—okay, beyond sex—with her.

She flushed at the idea. Of course she couldn't... What if one of the kids needed her? And she hadn't brought any protection— No, that was silly; considering the huge variety of tampons and sanitary napkins he'd produced, he surely had an equal assortment of condoms.

The truth was, she just didn't know him well enough. She'd met him only days ago! And considering she'd had to extract each sliver of knowledge about him as if with tweezers from his flesh, with him flinching every time she tugged, Fiona thought she could be excused for feeling wary.

But then she reflected on how nice he'd been to all of them, even the boys who seemed to stir his memories, and she realized she knew more about the John Fallon who tried to hide behind his self-constructed barriers than she'd thought.

More, maybe. But enough?

She stirred, and water lapped at the porcelain sides of the tub.

Would rescue come tomorrow? she wondered. Did she want to go home yet?

Fiona got out of the tub well aware that she hadn't answered a single one of her questions.

She let the water out, dried and got dressed, deciding to leave her hair bundled up on her head, untidy though it was.

Tabitha, Kelli and Amy were lounging on their beds when she paused in their door.

"Did you find your jeans?"

Tabitha nodded. "I miss my clothes. I may never wear this shirt and jeans again."

Fiona laughed. "I know what you mean. Me, I'm just going to be glad to have clean underwear at hand every morning."

"Are you going downstairs?" Amy slid off the bed. "I think I will, too."

"Yeah, let's all go," Kelli agreed.

They followed her, to find Erin reading and Willow giggling as the boys tried to teach her how to keep the hacky-sack in the air with one knee.

"Like she's *really* that bad at it," Amy muttered.

Fiona had a suspicion she wasn't, either. Willow was blossoming.

"Haven't you ever played soccer, Willow?" Amy asked, as they reached the foot of the stairs.

Dieter deftly caught the hacky-sack with his knee.

Willow shook her head. "It looks fun."

"It is," Tabitha said. "You should come out for the girls' team. If you're willing to work hard, you could play JV."

"Hey, cool!" Dieter grinned at her. "I could teach you stuff."

Hopper made a rude noise. "Like you know any stuff."

Dieter bounded on him, and they began to wrestle. The girls rolled their eyes.

"Boys," Amy said, in a tone of supreme disenchantment.

"Well, there's boys, and then there's *men*," Tabitha suggested.

Amy sneered. "*I* don't see any."

"Mr. Fallon."

"But he's got..." Her hand flapped at the side of her face.

They all knew she was referring to his scar.

"So what?" Kelli said. "He's hot."

"Yeah, he is," Tabitha agreed.

Willow gaped at them, and even the boys stopped wrestling.

"Who's hot?" Hopper asked in bewilderment.

"Mr. Fallon." Tabitha gave Fiona a sly smile. "Don't you think, Ms. Mac?"

What if he overheard this conversation? He'd be hideously embarrassed!

On the other hand…maybe it would be good for him to find out that even teenage girls had noticed he was sexy despite the scar. Or even because of it.

"He's an attractive man," she agreed sedately.

"But…" Amy stopped, and her eyes narrowed. "You *do* think he's hot!"

"I just said…"

"I mean, you really think he is. Wow. That's why you keep blushing. Are you going to see him again after we leave?"

They all stared expectantly at her.

"I don't know…" Belatedly realizing she'd just made a big mistake, Fiona said, "There's nothing like that going on. Anyway, it's none of your business."

"You're blushing right now. Yes! I was right!" Amy crowed.

"Amy, there really *isn't* anything like that…"

In a low voice, Tabitha interrupted. "He's coming."

Fiona raised her eyebrows at her circle of students. "Enough said. Okay?"

"Okay," they chorused cheerfully. Lying, every one of them. She would never hear the end of this.

"Problem?" John asked behind her.

"No problem," she said too hastily, and turned.

The mere sight of him sent her heart skittering again. He *looked* so darn good with his broad shoulders and lean build, shaggy dark hair, a perfectly sculpted face with hollows beneath the cheekbones, straight, narrow nose and unrevealing mouth that, Fiona couldn't help noting, seemed more relaxed than usual.

"We were just talking," Kelli said.

"Yeah," Dieter chimed in. "Do you think the snow-plow will come tomorrow?"

"It's possible. Depends how widespread the storm was."

"How will we know if it comes?" Kelli asked.

"We'll be able to hear it. Sound carries out here."

"I don't care if they don't make it tomorrow," Dieter said. He glanced at Willow. "I'm having fun."

"Me, too," Tabitha said. "Except I wish I had more clothes here."

Troy had apparently wandered down the stairs in the midst of the discussion, because from the outskirts of the small group he said, "Yeah, it's been cool."

"I don't want to go home yet," Willow said with surprising force, then flushed as gazes swung her way.

To rescue her, Fiona said, "I'm in no hurry, either. How about you, Hopper?"

"I'm good."

One by one, the others agreed, Amy last and least

convincingly. And yet, she *did* agree, which Fiona thought might be a good sign. Did she even look surprised, as if she hadn't realized that maybe she'd been having fun, too?

Fiona smiled at John. "See what an extraordinary host you are? We don't want to leave you."

"Glad to know that." His gaze lingered just long enough on her face to cause her cheeks to heat before moving to the kids. "You've been good guests."

"Yay us!" Kelli declared.

"Anybody want cookies and cocoa?" John asked.

He was almost flattened in the stampede that ensued. Only Erin rose from the armchair with dignity, carefully put a bookmark in place and strolled past the two adults toward the kitchen.

Echoing Fiona's thoughts, John murmured, "Forty-year-old in a seventeen-year-old's body."

"Um," Fiona agreed, looking after the petite girl. She and John followed her, Fiona keeping her voice low. "What I can't figure out is whether she's *really* that together. The sad part is, I'll probably never know. One of the frustrations of teaching. You see what they might become, then most of the time, you never find out if they did. If that makes sense."

"Surely in a private school you'll hear."

"Maybe. Yeah, you're right. In Portland it was different."

The kitchen door swung shut behind Erin, leaving the two of them alone.

John gripped Fiona and turned her to face him, his easy manner gone. "We didn't get a chance to talk."

"No. It's okay." What "it" was, she couldn't have said. Her heart? If so, *she* was once again lying. It wasn't okay.

His hand tightened. "Later?"

The door swung open again, releasing a burst of voices. Hopper started to say, "Where's the..." then stopped. "Oh. Sorry."

"Nothing to be sorry about," Fiona said. "We were just talking about how we'd get the van back on the road."

She was a little bit appalled at how readily she'd taken to telling lies, one after another.

"Muscle," John said, putting a hand on the door and gesturing for her to precede him. "Good thing you have the boys with you."

"We can do anything boys can do," Kelli insisted. "Um...what are we going to do?"

Fiona laughed, the pressure in her chest easing. "Hoist the van back onto the road."

"Oh. We can do that. Right?" She looked around the table. "Girl power? And I guess guy power, too?"

Fiona cast John a grateful glance and sat down as he went into the pantry and brought out a container of cookies he must have whipped up during the day. The kids excitedly talked about getting the van on the lane, how they'd turn it around, how weird it would be to go home.

"It's like, *anything* could have happened in the world while we were up here," Dieter said. "I mean, the school could have burned down, and we wouldn't know."

They were all briefly silent, contemplating the possibility with awe.

"I'll try to call Mr. Schneider again," Fiona said.

"If I get him, I'll be sure to ask whether the school is still standing."

"Maybe it snowed so much, the gym roof collapsed." Kelli sounded hopeful. "No more P.E."

"The gym roof *is* kind of flat," Troy said. "Hey, you never know."

They launched into an entertaining litany of other possibilities: the principal had quit, parents had moved and left no forwarding address, colleges had gotten together and announced that henceforth SAT results would no longer be required for admission decisions and the quarterback of the football team had heard that Kelli was missing, perhaps dead, and realized he was forever, tragically in love with her.

"Of course, he'd have to know who I *am* for that to work," she admitted practically.

"He does know, he's just suppressed the knowledge," Tabitha contributed.

"Who is the quarterback?" Dieter the nerd asked.

Even John was smiling as they razzed Dieter.

When only crumbs remained in the cookie container, the kids wandered back to the living room and their various games and books. Erin had found a book of Sudoku puzzles on the shelf, many unattempted, and she and Troy huddled over it. While eating cookies, he'd grumbled about the battery on his iPod being gone. History. No charger. No music. Evidently he was consoling himself with number puzzles.

Fiona pretended to read. It seemed an eternity before, in twos and threes, the teenagers headed upstairs. Fiona had quit worrying about what configurations of gender disappeared into rooms together. Now that the budding romance between Hopper and Amy had cooled, Dieter and Willow were the only potential pair, and they were far too inexperienced with the opposite sex and too awkward with each other to do more than sneak a first, clumsy kiss.

Erin and Troy were the last two to go up. "Are you coming, Ms. Mac?" Erin asked politely, pausing on the first step.

She looked up as if surprised to realize she'd be left alone. "Oh. No, I think I'll read for a few more minutes. Good night, Erin. Good night, Troy."

Fiona waited for several minutes after they disappeared upstairs. Then she set down her book on the arm of the chair and went to the kitchen, where, as expected, she found John.

He looked up. "Kids still hanging around?"

"No, they've all gone up."

Very deliberately, he set a torn slip of paper in place and closed his book. "Can I get you a cup of coffee?"

"No, I wouldn't be able to sleep." After a moment's hesitation, she chose the seat right across the long plank table from him.

John nodded. They sat in silence for a moment.

Fiona was just gathering herself to say something—God knew what would have come out of her mouth—when he spoke.

"When I asked earlier if you were okay..." His turn to hesitate. "I suppose what I was really asking was whether I was out of line kissing you."

"Do you mean," she asked carefully, "did I want you to kiss me?"

He dipped his head.

Fiona took a deep breath. They were being so civil, two near-strangers compelled to discuss the uncomfortable. She hated it.

Lifting her chin, she said, "Yes. Yes, I wanted you to kiss me. So you don't have to feel guilty or…I don't know, whatever you were feeling."

He stared at her, face very still. When he spoke, his voice was hoarse. "Not guilty. Just…afraid I'd misread you. I've wanted to kiss you from the minute you walked in the door. But I didn't mean to do it that way, when I'd been a jackass and was upset."

"It really is all right." Suddenly it was. "I've wanted you to kiss me since then, too."

"Ah."

"I was afraid I'd leave and you'd still be so stiff and polite and I wouldn't know—" She broke off. "Well, what it was like."

His eyebrows rose in that way he had. "You were curious?"

"No, I was in suspense."

His mouth twitched. "And now?"

"I'm hoping you plan to kiss me again," she admitted frankly.

He gave a short, startled bark of laughter. "Yeah, I'm planning." His chair scraped on the floor as he stood.

Fiona pushed hers back, too, and rose to meet him when he circled the table.

He reached out and slid his fingers into her hair, wrapping his hand around the back of her head. "In suspense," he murmured. "I've been in suspense all evening, thinking you'd have whomped me if I hadn't opened the door and escorted you back inside."

"*Whomped* you?" Fiona laughed up at him, even though her knees felt weak. "You couldn't tell I was enthusiastic?"

Any amusement in his eyes vanished, leaving him looking terribly vulnerable. "I thought...but I was feeling so much... God." He closed his eyes for a second. "Quit talking, Fallon," he ordered himself, and bent his head.

Fiona gladly, thankfully, kissed him back.

CHAPTER NINE

KISSING FIONA gave him an adrenaline kick as powerful as going into combat but without the accompanying fear. Just holding her…that reminded John more of those occasional moments when he stood on the front porch watching the sun rise and rediscovering an inner core of peace.

He lay in bed that night with exhilaration coursing through his body and thinking, *She heals me.* He wanted her until he ached with it, something he hadn't felt in so long he actually enjoyed the near-pain. She'd reminded him how to smile, taught him to laugh again. Even her students had been a gift of sorts; once upon a time, John had liked kids. He'd volunteered as a coach in a youth soccer league in Portland, before his ill-fated attempt to connect with Iraqi youth in Fallujah in the same way. Despite some uncomfortable moments and the one, shockingly vivid flashback, he had enjoyed being around her students. Somehow they'd managed to take him back to a time when hideous dreams didn't await every time he slept, when a Friday night date or an exam had filled his world and the tragedies happening in other parts of the world had been headlines on Yahoo and not a landscape he couldn't seem to escape.

He'd be sorry to see them go. But not as sorry as he'd be that Fiona would be leaving as well, robbing him of the anticipation he'd begun to feel on waking in the morning, the erection he had to quell when he went to bed at night, the color and life in between that had replaced his previous days of nonstop work meant to keep him from thinking.

He wondered whether maybe it wasn't just her. He'd come to Thunder Mountain for quiet, hard physical labor, unspoiled beauty and peace, believing they'd work better than the drugs Army doctors wanted to prescribe. Maybe they *had* worked.

But he didn't believe it. Fiona had awakened something nearly forgotten inside him. He would give almost anything to keep seeing her.

He could take a trip to Portland in a week or two. Stay at his parents' or his sister's, give Fiona a call. Good idea, John thought, ignoring the unease that had him rolling over and punching the pillow into a new shape. Yeah. He could do that. Just a short trip. His parents would be thrilled to have him there for Thanksgiving. He could kill two birds with one stone.

Bad analogy. Not just words. Small frail bones. Blood. Stillness.

Don't think of it that way. He'd make his parents happy, *and* get to see Fiona. Yeah. That'd work.

He finally slept, not dreamlessly but without throat-clogging nightmares, and awakened in the early hours of morning still aroused. Or, aroused again. A wisp of memory suggested he'd had at least one good dream—an erotic one.

He took coffee out onto the porch as he often did,

cupping his mug to keep his hands warm, watching the forest around him gradually come into focus as the sky lightened at first imperceptibly until finally it became a pearl-gray shade that allowed the trees to acquire sharp definition. And finally came color: a hint of pink, as pearls sometimes had, then richer and richer colors until they nearly hurt his eyes with their incandescence. The blue of the sky leached the vivid colors away as quickly as they'd been born, and morning had arrived.

For once, the spectacle failed to lift the heaviness in his chest. More aware of the biting cold than usual, John went back in.

The snowplows would come today. He realized he'd been half-listening for the roar even though he knew the highway department didn't start work this early except in emergencies.

He should get the kids out there right after breakfast, shoveling in front of the shed so he could pull open a door and get out the aluminum snowshoes he kept for guests. He needed to go up and see how they'd left the van and what kind of work was needed to get it back on the road. The boys could come with him.

As first a couple of the kids and then Fiona came downstairs for breakfast, John hid his regret.

She smiled at him, her gaze shy.

"Yeah, I'll be surprised if the plow doesn't make it up here today," he agreed with Troy. He half-listened to the kids' excited chatter and watched Fiona to see whether she rejoiced, too, at the idea of making it home or whether she shared any of his regret. She nodded and smiled at things her students said, her expression pensive, but he couldn't decide how she felt about the idea of finally continuing the interrupted trip.

The boys were intrigued by the snowshoes, a smaller, lighter-weight version of the old standard, and did well once they got the hang of lifting each foot.

The van was standard white, with the name and logo of the school on each door. The snow hadn't fallen as heavily up here, deep under the trees, but that was the only good news. The first problem was that the van faced downhill on a steep curve, the second that it canted to one side where a front wheel had gone off the narrow road. If the road crew couldn't help, they might have to get a tow truck up here.

Maybe it was because he'd felt edgy all morning, with the knowledge that something he didn't want to happen was inevitable, but standing up there in the snow with the boys, studying the van, triggered a scene in his head too vivid to be called a recollection, but too brief to qualify as a flashback. It was like one of those ten-second videos a person could take with a regular digital camera.

He and Diego had their heads under the hood of the truck, which had lagged behind the convoy and broken down. Iraqis gathered, probably just curious, but one never knew. The couple of guys facing down the crowd had their M-16s pointing at the ground, but out of the corner of his eye John saw Larson's hand holding the gun, his fingers twitching as if he were typing a coded message.

John shook his head slightly, and the vision vanished. It had been a meaningless scene; someone at the back of the convoy had noticed they were missing and a

Stryker had roared back to recover them. Some kid had thrown a rock; John remembered it banging off the truck's welded armor. He'd said quietly, "Easy," to Larson, maybe because of those restless fingers. But that was it. They'd figured out what was wrong with the truck and had driven off. Ninety percent of the scenes that flashed into his head were like this one, nothing he'd normally recall. Just pulled out of his memory by something—a smell, a movement, a noise—and suddenly *there,* as if he lived in two dimensions.

That disturbed him more than anything, the idea that he just couldn't seem to leave Iraq and was perpetually re-enlisting without conscious volition.

But he shook this minor flashback off. They weren't coming as often anymore. "Healing" meant he was a work in process, not cured.

For several minutes, he and the boys threw around ideas, Troy seeming to have the most experience with cars. Then they headed back down to the lodge. The boys raced ahead, their shouts trailing in the thin, cold air, while he took his time.

When he reported the news about the van to Fiona, she nodded resignedly.

"I had a feeling backing out wasn't going to be an option."

"The road crew might be able to wrap a chain around the axle and pull it out."

While they waited, she threw herself into a frenzy of laundry and cleaning, driving the kids to help with the first hint of sharpness he'd heard from her.

Unaware he was within earshot, she told three of

the girls, "Mr. Fallon has been really nice about getting stuck with us, and we're not going to pay him back by leaving dirty linens or bathrooms that need scrubbing."

"But what if we end up staying another night?" one of them complained.

"Then we make the beds up again tonight and wash the sheets and towels again tomorrow. Boys!" she called down the hall. "Do you have those beds stripped?"

John heated tomato rice soup and made a pile of sandwiches, keeping an eye on her as she passed back and forth through the kitchen carrying heaps of bedding and borrowed clothing, dirty going one way, warm and folded the other.

While they ate, she said, "I'm sorry, we don't know which of the clothes are yours and which from the lost and found. We're just piling everything on the sofa."

"No problem."

"I hope we've folded the linens the way you like. If you want us to make up the beds..."

He shook his head. "I'll do it when guests are scheduled."

"How do you *know* when people are coming?" Dieter asked. "Without a phone?"

"I have a cell phone. Sometimes I can make a call from here. Otherwise, there's a spot down river that usually works."

"But how do people make reservations?" the boy persisted. "Do they have to leave a message and wait until you call?"

He smiled. "No, the real estate office in Danson—

that's the next town west of here—handles my reservations. They get lodge e-mail and answer my reservation line. I check in with them a couple of times a week."

"Oh." Satisfied, the boy nodded. "That makes sense. But you must have your own e-mail address, too, right?"

"Yes, I check that at the library when I'm down in Danson."

"Wow, not having a computer here must be weird."

Everyone at the table except Fiona nodded in amazement and apparent sympathy for him. They couldn't imagine a life so primitive it didn't include unlimited access to the computer.

After lunch, the kids dispersed, and Fiona went back to the laundry room. John followed her, taking the precaution of closing the door behind him.

In the act of moving wet sheets between washer and dryer, she looked from him to the door.

"The kids will wonder."

"They've all set about their appointed tasks. I told them I'd clean up from lunch."

"You shouldn't let them off the hook."

"I was getting rid of them," he corrected. "Washing a few dishes is a small price to pay to get you alone."

"Oh. In that case…" She flung a few wet towels in, shut the dryer door and pushed Start, then came to him. "And just why was it that you wanted to get me alone…?"

"To argue." He reached up and smoothed her hair behind her ear, loving the sleek feel, so different from his own coarser hair.

"Um. About?" she whispered, lifting her face.

"Whether you should hand over the van keys to Dieter and just stick around?"

He hadn't known he was going to say that, or even that he was thinking it. Oh, hell, he knew it was an impossibility, but a damn appealing one. He pictured the two of them standing side by side, waving as the van turned onto the newly packed highway and sped up. He could even see the faces in the window behind circles of steam.

Fiona laughed. "Maybe Dieter could take over my classes, too. I'm pretty sure he's smarter than I am."

He nuzzled her nose. "I'm pretty sure Dieter is smarter than just about everyone."

Eyes closed, she murmured, "Smart enough to realize you were getting rid of him?"

"Probably." About to kiss her, John paused. "Or maybe not. He's a child."

The way his hands moved up and down her arms, alternately caressing and kneading, was meant to be a distraction. Not enough of one, apparently, because she argued, "I'm not so sure about that. He and Willow are definitely flirting."

"They're like fifth-graders. My friend says her friend says Jennifer says Fiona likes me."

Her breath escaped in a warm puff when she giggled. "Fiona does like you."

"Ah. Now we've achieved high school directness."

She stood on tiptoe and nipped his lower lip. "Quit talking."

A rumble of laughter started in his chest. "Careful. We may make it into college."

"Probably not if the snowplow comes today…"

God. He wished it wouldn't come. He wanted to take her back into his bedroom and peel off her clothes, then lay her back on his bed…

Not happening. She wouldn't allow it with her students in the lodge.

He kissed her with an edge of desperation. Maybe similar thoughts were running through her head, because she answered fervently, one hand gripping his hair while the other arm wrapped around his neck. John gripped her buttocks and lifted, hungry to feel himself cradled between her thighs. She moaned and sighed and stole quick snatches of breath when he lifted his mouth, then met his lips as eagerly when he came back for more.

He forgot they were in the laundry room, forgot about the kids. Getting lost in her was so damn easy. The skin on her neck was satin soft, and as he kissed his way down, her throat vibrated with a hum of delight that brought him back up to the lush pleasure of her mouth. Her hips and butt were nicely rounded despite her slender figure, her waist tiny. If her breasts hadn't been squished against his chest, he'd have filled his hand with one, but that would have meant opening an inch or two between them, and he couldn't bear to do that.

A distant sound didn't penetrate. The dryer rumbled, Fiona gasped, he groaned and angled his head to deepen the kiss.

"Ms. Mac! Ms. Mac!" The cries, exultant, urgent, came closer.

Somebody was in the kitchen. Brain like sludge, he slowly realized that several somebodies were there. Calling her. Which meant…

Oh, crap. He was still processing what those voices meant when she began to struggle.

"The kids! They're coming!"

"Yeah." He let go of her and stepped back, shaking his head in an attempt to clear it. "God."

Her hands had gone frantically to her hair. "Do I look…?"

"Yeah," he said again. "You do."

Her finger-combing was making it worse.

He reached up and took her hand. "Stop. They're not stupid."

"Ms. Mac? Where are you?"

"In here," she called. "Working on laundry."

The door swung open, hitting John in the back.

He swore as his hip gave a scream of protest.

Tabitha's anxious face peered around the door at him. "I'm sorry, I'm sorry!"

"It's okay," he said between gritted teeth. "My fault."

Just as well if she thought he was keeping his back to her because muscle spasms kept him immobile. Mussed hair on their pretty teacher was one thing; seeing his erection was another.

"We hear the snowplow," she said. "I mean, it has to be the snowplow, right?"

"Unless a helicopter is passing over, it's got to be the snowplow," John agreed.

A couple of the other kids crowded in behind her. Over her head, Hopper asked, "Should we send someone out to meet them? So they know we're here? Because if they don't plow your road as far as the van…"

"They always do," John said. His erection was dying a natural death. Nothing like half a dozen teenagers squeezing into the small room with him and Fiona to kill the mood.

"But they might be in a hurry or something."

"They probably know we're here," Fiona pointed out. She had grabbed an already folded towel and started refolding it the minute the door opened. "You know Mr. Schneider probably let the highway department know we were stranded up here."

"You mean, you think they're actually *looking* for us?" Kelli marveled at the idea.

"Maybe we made the news," speculated someone just out of sight. Amy. Had to be Amy. "High School Students Stranded." Enraptured, she capitalized every word. "They probably interviewed our parents and showed pictures of us and everything."

"We're famous." Hopper poked his head between Kelli and Tabitha. "Wow. We'll be girl magnets."

"*Guy* magnets," Kelli amended.

A babble of voices ensued. Fiona's eyes met John's, every-so-briefly. Amusement, disbelief. Despite her mussed hair, pink cheeks and swollen lips—and, oh yeah, the closed laundry room door—her students hadn't given a thought to what she and John had been doing.

They were adults. Invisible. Not worth speculating about.

"Okay, okay," she said, raising her voice in that way

only teachers could do, effortlessly slicing through the babble and bringing silence. "John? Should we all bundle up and go out?"

He shook his head. "Not yet. I'll go up and meet them. Dieter, Troy, Hopper. You three, too, in case we need the manpower to get the van back on the road."

"Yes!" They scattered, taking the protesting girls with them. Why couldn't *they* go, too? They were strong! They could…

"You okay?" John asked Fiona.

She nodded and set the now twice—or was it thrice?—folded towel onto the stack. "You?"

He nodded ruefully. "They were good as a cold shower."

"Icy." She sighed. "We're still leaving you with work. Including dirty dishes."

"I'll have nothing else to do after you're gone," he pointed out, resisting the temptation to touch her again.

"Yeah, you will. I'll bet you can hardly wait to reclaim your blessed solitude."

"Right this minute, solitude isn't what I'm craving." He gave her a look that widened her eyes.

But the door into the kitchen swung open, and a voice called, "Mr. Fallon? It sounds like the plow stopped. Do you think they've gotten to your road?"

"I'm coming," he called, then backed a couple of steps from Fiona. Tearing his gaze from her was downright painful. He limped toward his room.

The boys were waiting impatiently when he emerged in boots and shrugging on his parka. Gloves in the pocket—yep. Polartec hat in the other—check.

Pros with the snowshoes, they made it up the hill faster than John would have liked. By then, the plow had reached the van and come to a stop, the blade a foot or two from the bumper.

John greeted the men who emerged, recognizing faces from last winter. “Glad you could make it.”

“Just sorry it took so long. Been a busy weekend,” the bearded guy said.

“Heard even Portland got buried.”

“Six inches. Can you believe it? Damn near closed down the city. Had the traffic slip-sliding away.”

John shook his head. “I can imagine.”

“Well.” The man surveyed the boys. “You three part of the Willamette Prep group?”

They nodded. “Did we make the TV news?” Hopper asked.

“Might’ve.” He chewed for a minute, then spat a stream of brown tobacco juice. “Yeah, a couple of groups from that Knowledge thing… What was it, somethin’ like a football game? Anyway, a couple of groups didn’t make it back.”

“A couple?” John knew the first thing Fiona would ask. “Is the group from the other school okay?”

“Yeah, they were stuck up Government Camp way.” He nodded roughly north, toward Mt. Hood. “That road got plowed a while ago.”

Relieved, he nodded.

They turned their attention to the problem of getting the van back on the road. Finally, Dieter got elected—because he was skinny and capable—of lowering himself into the soft snow and shinnying under the van to wrap a chain around the axle. They dragged him back out, clutching the end of the chain. Then, with the snowplow pulling and the boys pushing, the van bumped back onto the road.

It took a hell of a lot longer to turn it around. The plow widened the road as much as possible. Then John got behind the wheel and backed up, inched forward, backed again, while everyone else pushed, until the damn thing faced uphill.

Predictably the boys cheered and gave each other high-fives. John felt branded as the cripple who hadn't been able to pull his weight. Telling himself none of the boys had the skill to maneuver the vehicle under such difficult conditions helped about as much as a skinny bandage on a bone-deep gash. The truth was, he couldn't have been much use. His leg and hip wouldn't have stood up to the strain at the same time as his feet were slipping in the snow.

Face it: he *was* a cripple.

The highway guys introduced themselves to the kids, and everyone shook hands. John expected to be seeing the two men regularly this winter. Not likely nature would throw a temper tantrum like this in November and then turn mild and easygoing come December and January. John figured it would pay to be on good terms with the guys who had to dig him out every time the snow came down.

After some discussion, they backed the plow out to the highway and John followed with the van so that they could finish plowing his road down to the lodge. Otherwise, he wouldn't be able to get out with his SUV.

Time could be elastic; he knew that. For example, getting stuck on an observation post during your tour in Iraq. You've donned full combat gear and body armor, made sure you have five hundred rounds of ammunition for the machine gun you're carrying, then have to go stand or sit in full sun—120 degrees. Sweat pouring down your face, soaking your uniform. Time didn't just crawl, it eked. What had to be half an hour would pass, you'd look at your watch and see that the hand had hardly moved at all.

In contrast, the next hour here and now sped by. He couldn't believe how fast it passed. Within minutes, it seemed, Fiona and the kids were dressed in the clothes in which they'd arrived and were ready to set out, purses and bookbags in hand. Their faces glowed with eagerness. Fiona was back in teacher mode, worrying that they'd forgotten something, thanking him effusively as if he were their rescuer and not the man who'd kissed her senseless barely sixty minutes ago.

Next thing he knew, he'd started up his 4Runner and driven them in two separate groups up to the van at the top of the hill. Once they were out and waiting for Fiona to unlock, their voices rang out as they shared plans.

"Man, I'm glad I've got TiVo." Hopper slapped his gloved hands together to keep them warm. "I'm going to watch big-screen, plasma TV for eight straight hours."

Several wanted to get together with friends. Tabitha apparently had a boyfriend who was going to be, like, *so* glad to see her. Movies, the mall, their cars.

Dieter was hoping to go skiing. "It's going to be *awesome*," he assured everyone.

Climbing into the van, Tabitha gave him a look over her shoulder. "You haven't had enough snow?"

As usual, Willow and Erin stayed quiet. Erin because—John didn't know. Because she was above their juvenile excitement? And Willow because she had no friends?

Maybe he was wrong. Maybe she had plenty.

John stood beside Fiona as the kids piled in. His hip was giving savage warning that he'd suffer later for today's activities, but he needed to see them off.

Sure, he mocked himself. *That was it. Didn't have anything to do with his unwillingness to say goodbye to Fiona.*

He couldn't tell from her face whether she was sorry at all to be leaving. She'd enjoyed kissing him, he didn't doubt that. She was intrigued by him. Maybe he had some kind of mystique, the physically *and* emotionally scarred veteran. Could be she even liked him.

But she wasn't stealing anguished looks his way, or asking if he'd call. She seemed focused on her students, promising that their cell phones would work in about an hour or two and they could call home.

"Right?" she asked him.

He nodded. "Once you pass Danson."

"Seat belts on," Fiona ordered, as the kids already in the van squabbled about who sat where.

"That was *my* seat."

"What difference does it make?"

"Because I get carsick if I'm not by the window." Amy, of course.

"Amy," Fiona interjected, "there's an empty seat in

the back by the window. You can have it. No, Dieter, you're not sitting in front. School rules."

"But you let me…"

"When I needed another pair of eyes. Now I don't. In back."

He whined, but good-humoredly, not as if he'd actually expected to be able to sit in front. He was just giving Ms. Mac a hard time.

John stood there dumbly thinking, *But I was just kissing her. We just heard the kids yelling, Ms. Mac! Ms. Mac! We hear the snowplow!*

They couldn't already be leaving.

They were. Doors slammed, and, keys dangling from her mittened hand, she turned to face him.

"Thank you again."

"Don't keep thanking me," he said, rough and suddenly angry. "I did what any decent person would have done."

"But you took really good care of us. I can't say thank you for that?"

Her astonishment and hurt helped him recognize his anger for what it really was—panic.

"Yeah. Yeah, you can," he said gruffly. "You're welcome."

Her gaze became shyer. "If you get down to Portland…"

He nodded, took a moment to find his voice. "I'll call."

"Good." Fiona gave him a shaky smile. "I'm glad. And I'll e-mail when we get home safe and sound."

He nodded. She'd promised earlier.

"Then…" She hesitated. "For now, goodbye."

He nodded. “Take it slow.”

“Despite my idiocy the other day, I *am* a good driver.”

He nodded again. What else could he do? Grab her?

A couple of the kids banged the flats of their hands against the windows. “Ms. Mac! Let’s go!”

Apologetically Fiona said, “They really had a good time…”

“And now they want to go home. It’s okay. Go.”

So she did. She got behind the wheel, started up the engine, waved and drove away. Some of the kids turned and waved, too, and John lifted his hand in response. Then—God—he just stood there as the van gradually accelerated into a curve of highway and passed out of sight.

For a minute, he heard the engine. Then he was left with silence, a hip that hurt like a son of a bitch, and the solitude they’d interrupted.

CHAPTER TEN

IN HER REARVIEW MIRROR, John Fallon looked so alone standing there backed only by snow and the deep green of the forest, Fiona had to swallow to ease the pressure in her chest.

He *wanted* to be alone, she reminded herself. He'd bought Thunder Mountain Lodge because of the solitude it offered. It was silly for her to feel sad for him when he'd probably do a little jig the minute they were out of sight and he had his peace and quiet back again.

Still, as she drove down the freshly plowed mountain pass, she couldn't shake the memory of him watching them go, unmoving until she could no longer see him in the mirror.

If he'd been glad to see them go, wouldn't he have turned away as soon as they'd climbed into the van and she had started up the engine? Her heart cramped. Would he have kissed her with such desperation if he'd wanted to reclaim his solitude?

She tried to remember the man he was when they first arrived, spare with words and sometimes curt with her or the kids to the point of rudeness. Somehow, she couldn't quite conjure him up. Instead she remembered the smiling man who persuaded her to dive into the snowbank, the patient man who answered Dieter's endless questions, the passionate man whose touch was also tender.

And, though she talked to the kids and concentrated on her driving, Fiona felt an ache grow under her breastbone, one she could only identify as a kind of grief. She missed him terribly, although she didn't know how she could when four days ago she hadn't known him and would have sworn she was happy with her life just as it was.

They passed through Danson, slowing to obey the posted speed limit of twenty-five. Fiona craned her neck to take in the small business district. He must buy his groceries at that Safeway store, a contrast to the false-fronted buildings on the main street. Was Thunder Mountain Real Estate, housed in a log house, the one that handled the lodge's reservations? She imagined him filling the tank of his SUV at the gas station, going into the old-fashioned-looking drug store, nodding at passersby as he walked down the wooden sidewalk. Did he have friends in town, or did he avoid growing close with anyone? she wondered.

As she accelerated, leaving the small town with its Old West look behind, Fiona felt a sense of loss, as if the last link with John Fallon was fraying. Then she rolled her eyes at her own foolishness. For Pete's sake, she was acting like a lovesick teenager! Symptoms with which she was all too familiar, given that she spent more time with high school kids than she did with adults. Heck, maybe teenage angst was catching!

"Why are you making faces?" Dieter asked from right behind her.

Hastily she schooled her features. "Am I?"

"I saw you. In the mirror. With your face all scrunched up."

"Just thinking," she said. "You know we'll have school tomorrow, don't you?"

Tabitha leaned forward, one hand on the shoulder-harness of her seat belt. "I don't even remember what day it is."

"Knowledge Champs was on Friday, and we spent three nights at the lodge." She counted again, astonished that their stay had been so brief. "Which makes today Monday," she concluded.

"I can do a four-day week," Tabitha decided. "Especially with next week short because of Thanksgiving."

"What about my TV marathon?" Hopper complained from farther back in the van. "Maybe I can act all traumatized, so my parents let me stay home tomorrow."

"But it'll be cool to see everybody," Tabitha argued. "And we've already missed two days. I wouldn't want to get farther behind in my classes."

"We won't in Ms. Mac's!" several voices caroled.

"Do you suppose they had a substitute teaching your classes?" Kelli asked.

"Friday, sure, but there might not have been any school today. Remember, it snowed heavily down there, too."

"Yeah!" Dieter cheered. "We can go home and build snowmen!"

"You are such a little kid," Amy told him dismissively.

In the rearview mirror, Fiona saw him laugh, but she thought Amy's put-down had stung. She wasn't the only one to think so, because Willow smiled at him and said, "I like to build snowmen, too."

He grinned at her. "Hey, cool. Where do you live?"

Fiona tuned them out again. She felt amazingly ill-prepared to teach classes tomorrow. It was going to take some thought to remember where she'd left off last week. She'd have to grocery shop before she went home, or there'd be no breakfast tomorrow. And, oh goody, laundry tonight, too, since she'd meant to do it Saturday. As if she hadn't done nine hundred loads of laundry this weekend, trying to keep up with the towels and wet clothes for ten people. Of course, her housework had been waiting for the weekend, too, but it could wait again until next Saturday.

Real life was such fun.

The kids got out their cell phones and called parents and friends. Fiona waited until she stopped for gas and for everyone to get a chance to use a rest room and get drinks. Then she phoned Dave Schneider, estimating how long it would take them to arrive back at the school and promising to call when they got closer.

They pulled into the parking lot by the gymnasium at Willamette Prep just before dark. Cars clustered by the building. Fiona was surprised to see how much snow still lay on the ground, although the roads and parking lots were now bare except for occasional thin sheets of ice. Her neck and shoulders ached, and she was grateful to pull into a slot, set the emergency brake and turn off the engine.

The principal, middle-aged and balding, broke away from the group of parents and came around to Fiona's side of the van as the kids flung open the side sliding door and bounded out. He looked so relieved to see her, she realized how much pressure he'd been under as the responsible school official here.

As they talked, Fiona was vaguely aware of excited voices and parents embracing their offspring. The only ones whose parents hadn't come were Troy and Erin, who had both left their own cars in the lot. She'd noticed them—with snow still piled atop roofs, hoods and trunks—as she'd pulled in. Her own in the faculty parking lot would look the same. Scraping the windshield was just what she felt like doing.

Fiona handed over the keys to the principal, who nodded toward the group of students and parents. "Doesn't sound like any of you suffered too much at this lodge."

"No, I think the kids actually had a really good time. We were lucky," she admitted. "If we hadn't been able to reach the lodge…" An involuntary shudder ran through her.

"It was a bad decision on both our parts," he said frankly. "I'm as responsible as you are. I looked at a map, too. It seemed logical."

"What I didn't see on the map is that the pass closes for the winter."

He grimaced. "I did notice. But it's only November. I never dreamed…"

"Apparently it often closes in late November."

He shook his head. "Next time conditions look worrisome, I'll authorize you to put up in a hotel instead of trying to make it home."

She gave a weak laugh. "Thank you."

"Do you need some time off? I can get a sub for tomorrow."

The idea was tempting, but she shook her head. "We can't expect the kids to show up tomorrow morning if I don't."

"You're sure?"

She nodded.

"Ms. MacPherson?" Dieter's mom had come around the back of the van. "We just wanted to say thanks. You must be exhausted."

She was, Fiona realized in surprise. She felt as if someone had just pulled the plug, and all the nervous energy that had kept her going was draining out. Even her legs felt a little shaky.

"The kids were great," she said, "especially Dieter. Thank heavens he remembered Thunder Mountain Lodge and recognized the turnoff even though the sign was buried in snow."

She laughed. "Dieter never forgets anything. It can actually be a little bit annoying sometimes. In this case, though..."

"He was our lifesaver."

Other parents came around to thank her as well. Nobody, thank goodness, seemed to think she'd been irresponsible. She was lucky that the storm had hit Hawes Ferry as well, so the parents could imagine the conditions that had stranded their children.

She was especially interested to meet Willow's dad, who was thin, balding and as unassuming in appearance as his daughter. Behind his glasses, she thought she saw some moisture in his eyes. Of all the parents, he had the most reason to have been truly afraid when Willow didn't make it back from the field trip.

As car doors slammed and voices called goodbye, she looked around to see that Troy and Erin were together scraping snow from the roof and windshield of Erin's car. His was already swept clean and idled beside hers, exhaust hanging in the cold air. Apparently they'd joined forces, or else he'd been gentleman enough to insist on driving her to her car and helping her get safely on her way home. Troy had grown on Fiona this weekend; he might be participating in Knowledge Champs only to pad his résumé for college, but he'd been mature and uncomplaining through their whole stay at the lodge, staying out of the occasional bickering. He and Erin were simply more grown up than the others.

With night falling, the sodium lamps around the parking lot began to blink on as cars pulled out. Dave had remained, and he drove Fiona to her car on the other side of the campus, even helping by sweeping snow off it while she scraped the windshield and the engine warmed up.

Then they said good night, the last two cars to leave the high school.

Fiona reluctantly stopped for groceries and carried them into her small, rented town house. She'd turned the heat down last Friday morning, so it was cold and dark but for the one lamp she'd left on in the living room. Even before putting groceries away, she turned up the thermostat, hearing the furnace come on with a muted roar. A fire would feel good, but she had no fireplace. If the builder had bothered, it probably would have been one of those gas ones that were all show and put out no real heat, nothing like the huge, river rock fireplace capable of heating the entire lodge.

She put away the perishables, then went to her computer. It was silly, of course; John had probably gone down to town this afternoon to load up on groceries, and might not make it back to check e-mail for days or even a week. It wasn't as if he was waiting by his computer for her e-mail. But she'd promised to let him know right away when they arrived safely, and she'd do it.

Once the computer had booted and she'd gone online, she skimmed the handful of e-mails that had arrived while she was gone and deleted the spam, then called up the screen for a new message. She typed in the address he'd given her for his private email, then typed "Dear John" before stopping.

Too formal. He'd kissed her that morning, dragged her so tightly against him that she'd felt every contour of his body and the full length of his erection. Even the memory was enough to arouse her.

Why couldn't she feel this way for someone more… *convenient?* Why a man so damaged emotionally, he might never be willing to leave his refuge in the mountains?

She started over.

John,
We made it safe and sound. Roads were mostly bare past Danson, just icy in spots. A happy group of parents met us. I was lucky. They all thanked me instead of asking how I could have been so dumb as to choose some skinny line on the map and assume it was a safe route. And my principal said he was taking responsibility for the decision, too. So I guess I still have a job. One I'll be back at tomorrow morning at eight-thirty sharp.

Too chatty? Fiona reread and decided what she'd written thus far was okay. Now to wind it up on a friendly note that didn't assume anything.

I'll put in a request for some reimbursement for you, as I promised. We ate an awful lot of food! And no, I'm not saying thank you again, because I know you'd hate that. Just...take care. And please do call me if you get down to the Portland area. We could go to the multiplex and watch three movies in a row if you want.

Of course, she could think of other things they might prefer to do.

Her fingers wanted to type "Love, Fiona," but she made herself end with just her name. Not letting herself agonize over what she'd written, Fiona hit Send.

Staring at the screen, her chest feeling hollow, she wondered if she'd ever hear from John again.

JOHN NEEDED TO SHOP in the worst way, but he held off going until Tuesday morning. Just didn't feel like making the trip, he tried to tell himself, but knew better. He wanted to hear from Fiona, and she wouldn't have a chance to e-mail until Monday evening.

The small public library had one computer for private use. When he arrived, it was occupied by a white-haired woman who was apparently receiving her first lesson in Web surfing from the librarian. She kept saying, "Oh, my!" and then, "Oh, dear, what did I do?"

Hiding his impatience, he browsed the small collection of new titles, choosing a couple to check out. About the time he was ready to explode, the old lady finally pushed back her chair, babbling on about what an experience that had been and how now she could understand the fascination the Web had for her grandkids.

"I feel like I'm so behind the times," she told the librarian as he slid into the chair in front of the computer before she was two feet away.

It had been a while since he'd bothered to check his e-mail, and he found he had quite a few. A couple of buddies back for another tour in Iraq had sent e-mails, both short, obscene and funny. He had no trouble reading between the lines, though, and like an old-time, flickering movie projector, he caught scenes of them in uniform, one carrying a woman in full, blood-soaked robes who was obviously dead, the other running with his pants around his ankles when a bomb landed beside the latrine.

But he wrote back in the same tone, keeping to himself the nightmares and flashbacks, instead telling them about the snowstorm and the pretty women he regularly had as guests at the lodge.

Then he skipped over the e-mails from his mother and his sisters, clicking on the one from Mizzmack. Cute, he thought, letting her kids choose her screen name.

His heart hammered as he read her short e-mail, then hungrily reread it. It sounded just like her. He could almost hear her friendly voice, amusement quivering in it. *See?* she seemed to be saying. *I managed to thank you while making a point of* not *thanking you.*

He was glad she wasn't going to be in trouble for making the wrong decision and getting stranded. She clearly loved her job.

John hit Print so he could take her e-mail home with him and read it again. In the meantime, he wrote back, thanking her for letting him know they'd made it and saying,

Do you think there are three movies at the multiplex worth seeing?

Then,

It occurs to me that I can't very well go anywhere over Thanksgiving. I'm expecting a full house here at the lodge. I'll let you know when it looks like I can get down there.

Cop-out? he wondered, remembering the relief he'd felt when he realized going to his parents for the holiday just wasn't practical. But it was true that his rooms were one hundred percent booked over Thanksgiving weekend.

He needed to get going now; a couple was scheduled to arrive this afternoon, two more groups tomorrow. He didn't intend to put any of them in Fiona's room. He wanted to think of it as *her* room for as long as possible. He typed,

Hope Dieter and Willow's romance lasts. They both need it.

John's fingers hovered over the keys. Damn. He couldn't remember ever struggling over a few simple words the way he was now. But something told him it was important that he strike the right balance, sounding friendly but not desperate. *Please come back* would scare her off. He finally settled on,

If you have time, e-mail me.
Place isn't the same without you.

No. He backed the cursor up, changing the sentence to,

Place isn't the same without all of you.

"Send" and it was gone, before he could have second thoughts.

He read his other e-mails and responded briefly. He never knew what to say anymore to his parents or sisters. But they'd worry if he didn't answer at all.

Supplies loaded, he headed back up the mountain, arriving barely an hour before the obviously wealthy couple in a Lexus SUV, who tipped him when he carried their bags up to their room, then wondered how far it was to the nearest restaurant and whether he had a hot tub. His Web site emphasized the isolation of the lodge, the family-style meals and the rustic rooms and cabins. It didn't hide the fact that bathrooms were basic and shared. Maybe these two had just looked at the pretty pictures and skipped the fine print. Yeah, and maybe, he thought hopefully, they'd decide to leave tomorrow.

It had been weeks since he'd had a really ugly nightmare. He had one that night. John woke to find himself rearing up in bed, his throat raw from his shouted warning that came too late. Even in his nightmares, he couldn't let himself see the worst parts. The last thing he remembered was knowing he'd been hurt bad, lying with his leg not right, and staring with bewilderment at the mud-brick wall that had provided meager shade while he gathered the boys for a pickup game. Now…God. Before his dazed, uncomprehending eyes, it was splashed with bucketfuls of blood. So shockingly bright as it dripped.

His stomach heaved, just as it had that day. Then, after staring dazed at the blood dripping from a soccer ball, he had pushed himself to his knees to puke and seen… He lifted a shaking hand and rubbed his face. No. He wasn't going to remember. Not that. Thank God he always awakened before he saw anything worse than the blood.

He didn't know why his life had been spared. Maybe the sight wasn't the point of the nightmares. Sometimes he thought it was his shouted warning that came simultaneously with the blast, as if his subconscious wanted to remind him over and over again that he'd been ineffectual.

As if he didn't know? he raged at himself. He was just goddamned lucky that his subconscious didn't seem to realize that ineffectual was the least of it. In his bumbling naïveté and with his good intentions, he had *invited* the horror.

Sitting there in the dark, still shaking and battling the nausea, he thought, *I am the angel of death.*

Fiona wouldn't have been so grateful if she'd known. She wouldn't have trusted him. She wouldn't so easily have brushed off the incident when he'd seen the boys fall and blood color the snow.

What if he'd told her? he wondered, but was shaking his head before he could pursue the speculation. His life goal was to repress all memory of those few minutes. Only once had he described what had happened, when, from a stretcher, he'd had to identify the suicide bomber's body—the scattered bits of his body. John never intended to tell another soul. Words had power. Stories once told lived on, refusing to be corked inside a bottle.

He got up and went to his bathroom. After splashing water that was just this side of freezing on his face, he looked at himself in the mirror. The angry scar stood out like a brand. How had Fiona looked at his face and seen anything but the scar?

The fact that she had was a miracle. Miracles were rare and precious. He'd be a fool to turn his back on this one.

Go see her.

When was he supposed to do that? He didn't have a weekend until March without reservations. Suppose he drove down on a Monday. She'd be working. At best she'd save an evening for him. He didn't want just an evening, he wanted *her.*

Memories of Fiona haunted him all week. The way she curled her feet under her in the chair. The flash of bare legs when she'd stripped in front of the fire that first night. Her smile, her laugh, the soft grumpy sound she made when she awakened. Every damn thing he did reminded him of her.

Monday he drove back down to town for no other reason than to check e-mail. She'd responded with a chatty update. Willow and Dieter were holding hands in the hall between classes and Willow glowed. Amy was subdued. Maybe chastened?

Fiona, he thought, could never be anything but hopeful.

She wrote about her plans for Thanksgiving and asked if he'd be making a big dinner with all the trimmings for his guests.

He hit Reply and told her about this weekend's guests, including the couple who'd stayed but eaten at the end of the table, keeping their voices low and ignoring the two other couples, and who had complained before leaving that his rates were out of line given the lack of luxuries.

Were you polite? Fiona asked with interest the following week, before describing her Thanksgiving stay with her mother who, astonishingly, had invited a male friend to dinner.

I'm embarrassed at how terribly awkward I found it, even though they were very careful not to even brush hands while passing the gravy. Honestly. I felt like a sullen twelve-year-old!

John reported:

I was one hell of a lot politer than he deserved. I even reduced his bill.

I wish I could have seen your face, Fiona said, and he could almost hear her laughing.

John started driving to town twice a week to check his e-mail and write her. She always responded immediately. He began to resent the lodge's lack of telephone service that would have allowed him to have an Internet connection.

Of course, he could call her. But talking never came easily to him. He could just imagine the silences so long he'd keep wondering if he'd been cut off. She would undoubtedly sound warm and friendly, but without seeing her face how could he tell if it was forced?

Until she'd come to the lodge, he hadn't known he was lonely, but now with her gone, the isolation from any meaningful human contact ate at him. It was almost worse when the lodge was occupied. People rarely came alone. They came in couples, family groups, parties of friends. He would see the way they touched each other or the depth of communication in a smile, hear laughter and a note of intimacy in their voices, and he might as well have been outside in the cold peering through the window, so apart did he feel.

He didn't tell Fiona that, of course. He'd revealed enough to her. She'd seen him stagger when his leg failed. He'd made a fool enough of himself when he'd tackled her during that flashback.

He was getting desperate enough to wonder whether he could tolerate staying with his parents or sister if he went down to see her, when she gave him the idea.

She wrote,

I love getting your e-mails, but I miss you anyway. I imagine us sitting in front of the fire talking—of course, if there are guests they're closeted in their rooms where they belong.

The smile was in her voice, even writing.

Or perhaps we're hiding in the laundry room. I confess, I think about the laundry room often.

His fingers seemed to type of their own volition.

Your Christmas break is coming up. You must have at least a couple of weeks off. Spend them at the lodge with me.

His heart was thudding after he hit Send. He sat and stared at the screen as if he expected an instant reply. Damn. How was he going to wait days? Even one day?

What if she already had plans? What if she didn't feel she could desert her mother? What if she was just talking, and hadn't meant a word of it?

He was back at the library the next morning just after ten o'clock. His only e-mail was from Mizzmack.

I thought you'd never ask, she said simply.

CHAPTER ELEVEN

THE ROAD FELT familiar, but this trip was very different from the one down the mountain, when road conditions had still been difficult and Fiona had been so aware that she was responsible for the lives of the eight teenagers with her. Behind the wheel of her own car, the pavement bare, it seemed no time before she left the placid Willamette Valley behind and began the climb into the forested foothills of the Cascade Mountains. As each mile passed, her apprehension and anticipation ratcheted higher and tangled together.

She meant something to John, Fiona kept reassuring herself. She wasn't alone in feeling this powerful connection, or at least attraction. He had gone to a lot of effort to maintain the e-mail correspondence with her. The e-mails held a whole lot more meaning when she knew he'd had to drive a hundred miles round trip to send each one. She might not have had the courage to make this trip if he'd been able to casually reply whenever he had nothing better to do. The effort required, the fact that he'd driven down the mountain twice a week when clearly he preferred to avoid town, *that* gave her confidence.

On the other hand…she was going to spend as much as ten days with a man she hardly knew. A man who had gotten angry when she pressed him to find out what was bothering him.

Going with the full intention of sharing his bed, although they'd left that open.

I haven't booked your room over the holidays, he'd written.

She had been careful not to respond to that remark. Knowing she could have a room to herself meant she could chicken out. Or at least take her time. Get to know him again before baring herself—literally—for him.

Fiona stopped for lunch in Danson, not wanting to arrive hungry in case John was busy with guests. The choices were a homey-looking café and a burger joint. She picked the burger joint, even though she was tempted to opt for the café and hope she had a gossipy waitress. It would be interesting to know what locals thought of the new owner of Thunder Mountain Lodge. But now that she was so close, Fiona couldn't imagine browsing a menu, waiting for food, then for a bill. The need to *get* there was rising in her, to find out if John Fallon still had that instant effect on her.

So she went in just to use the rest room and order her burger and fries to go.

The forest closed in just outside of town. No more than three or four inches of snow had lain frozen on the ground in Danson, but with every hundred feet of elevation the road gained, the snowbanks grew higher. There was still nowhere near the amount of snow as there had been in November, but there was plenty for cross-country skiers and snowmobilers. She passed several turnouts with a couple of vehicles parked in each and various tracks in the snow leading away.

She came around a curve in the road and suddenly, there it was. Sooner than she'd expected. Thunder Mountain Lodge, the familiar sign announced. Just beyond it, the highway ended against a low wall of snow. Fiona shivered in memory of her stupidity. She and the kids had been the last people to make it over the pass heading toward eastern Oregon, and would be the last until sometime next spring. How long would it have taken for them to be found if they'd gotten stuck up there somewhere, with the snow that fell for two days burying the van?

Thank God for Dieter, she thought, for at least the hundredth time.

The narrower lane had been plowed, too, but patches of snow clung to the hard-packed gravel. She drove carefully on the steep descent, her heart thudding as she waited for the lodge to come into sight. She had grown to love it, Fiona realized; in comparison, her town house was bland. No massive river rock fireplace, no deep, claw-foot bathtub, no peeled log walls and broad plank floors.

One more curve, and the lodge appeared, looking just as she remembered it the day they left, when she had turned back just once, wanting to remember it accurately.

The steep, shake roof was punctuated by dormers with small-paned windows for the bedrooms, a smaller one behind which she knew lay the bathroom with that amazing bathtub. The porch seemed larger without snow cloaking stairs and footings. From this vantage she could see the roofs of cabins amongst the trees, and the shed that had been half-buried in snow and was much larger than she'd realized, the size of perhaps a triple garage.

John's black 4Runner was nowhere to be seen, but a row of other vehicles reminded her that she and he wouldn't be alone. Far from alone. She counted five cars and SUVs.

A couple of kids had a blue plastic disk they were hauling up a short incline perfect for brief runs. A snowman tilted drunkenly in front of the porch.

She coasted to a stop at the end of the row of parked cars, set her emergency brake and turned off her engine. The moment she was out of the car, Fiona breathed in the crisp, clean air scented by fir. She was early. John probably wasn't watching for her yet. She could haul her suitcase herself, or even leave it in the trunk for later…

The lodge door opened and he stepped out, his gaze going straight to her and never leaving her as he crossed the porch and came down the steps.

Her heart seemed to swell in her chest until it hurt. Like the lodge, he looked just as she remembered. No, better. Unbelievably sexy in jeans, boots, a flannel shirt and down vest, his dark hair shaggier as if he hadn't cut it since her visit. As he crossed the snowy ground to her, his limp was scarcely noticeable. Was he working to hide it?

Fiona couldn't seem to move. She simply stood by

the open trunk of her car and waited, drinking in the sight of him.

He stopped a couple of feet in front of her. “You came.”

Hearing the hoarseness in his voice, she said, “You didn’t think I would?”

“I…wasn’t sure.”

“After the way I jumped at your invitation?”

Finally, finally, his mouth softened. “You did, didn’t you?”

“It’s the fresh air,” she teased, finally able to breathe as an amazing sense of sureness filled her. Of course she’d done the right thing, coming as soon as she could! How could she have done anything else, given the way John made her feel without even touching her?

“We do have fresh air,” he conceded. At last, he took another step and reached up with one cold hand to cup her cheek. “God, I’ve missed you,” he murmured, and bent his head.

It was cold enough out here that her lips felt stiff, but he warmed them with astonishing speed, taking her mouth with a thorough kiss in which she felt the same raw need as in that last, memorable kiss in the laundry room.

A rough sound escaped him as he lifted his head, his dark eyes devouring in her face. “I kept wishing I had a picture of you. I ordered a digital camera from Amazon, so I could take one this time.”

“I had a picture of you,” she confessed. “Kelli took it with her phone. She took a bunch of the lodge and everyone, and e-mailed them to all of us. But it was the one of you…” She stopped, not wanting to admit she’d made it her computer screen wallpaper so she’d see him first thing when she turned on the computer, and last before she turned it off. He obviously hadn't known his picture was being taken. It had been out on the porch in daylight, his face averted. Perhaps because he looked away, it had captured the sense he gave of holding himself apart. Even though the photo wasn't great quality, the essence of him was there. She could look at it and remember the rough feel of his hard jaw, the way firelight cast shadows beneath strong cheekbones, the way he guarded himself from revealing emotion.

But not now. Now, he looked as if he'd never expected to see her again. He seemed almost disbelieving.

You came, she heard him say again, with something very like shock.

"You're certainly not alone." She nodded at the row of parked cars.

"No," he said, as a childish shout rang out from the two who were catapulting down the short incline on their disk. "There are two families with kids."

The resignation in his voice was familiar, and she grinned at him. "No. Don't tell me. Teenagers?"

"One. Sullen, a girl. Maybe twelve or thirteen."

Fiona nodded. "The words 'sullen' and 'thirteen' are synonymous when it comes to girls."

"Yeah?" He raised his brows, then evidently searched his memory. "I guess it was that age when Lizzie—one of my sisters—was such a brat."

"That would be normal. Cheerful, willing and thirteen? Call the therapist."

She was pleased by the smile that transformed his face from remote to rakish.

"You're the expert." He reached into her trunk for her bag. "Just the one?"

"What d'ye mean, just the one? Airlines would reject it. It must weigh sixty pounds."

He grunted as he heaved it out of the trunk. "You know, we do have laundry facilities here."

She poked him with her elbow, and he laughed out loud.

The limp was more evident weighted down as he was, and she saw him wince climbing the steps to the porch, but she knew better than to offer to take the bag from him. Besides...she'd had a heck of a time hoisting it into her trunk. She wasn't lying; the darn thing felt as if she'd filled it with books instead of just her winter boots, ski pants and wool sweaters as well as plenty of changes of clothes. Okay, and a *few* books. Presumably she'd have to entertain herself some of the time while he worked.

Inside, heat radiated from the enormous fireplace. The room, too, looked just as she remembered it, except there were strange people here. Unjust, perhaps, but for a moment she resented them, wanting to see Dieter and Erin and yes, even Amy instead of the middle-aged woman who lifted her head from a book and nodded, the kids who played checkers at the table, the couple strolling in from the kitchen.

"A new guest?" the woman, not much older than Fiona, asked with a pleasant smile.

"In a way," she said, smiling in return. "I'm actually a friend of John's."

"Oh, how nice. You'll be here for Christmas, then?" When she nodded, the woman sighed. "We're leaving on the twenty-fourth. Unfortunately. You know the drill. His family Christmas Eve. Mine Christmas Day. Neither satisfied."

Fiona had friends with the same problem, so she nodded sympathetically.

"Well, I'm sure we'll see you around." They started up the stairs to their room.

The moment of truth had only been delayed. Here it was, inescapable.

Face utterly expressionless, voice equally so, John asked, "Shall I take your bag upstairs?"

But she'd known the answer from the moment she saw him. "Your room is fine." Her boldness evaporated. "That is, if…um, that's what you intended…"

The sudden heat in his eyes all but scorched her. "Hoped. Not intended. If you'd be more comfortable having your own room…"

Still shy, knowing her cheeks must glow, she shook her head.

John made a sound that didn't quite take shape as a word, then started for the back of the lodge pulling her gigantic suitcase behind him. Fiona had to trot a couple of steps to catch up and reach the swinging door to the kitchen before him to hold it open.

Three more people sat at the long table eating, a solitary older man reading and a couple laughing just before they turned their heads to see who'd come into the kitchen.

Even as she exchanged greetings with them, she was startled by the dismay she felt. All she wanted was to be alone with John. Being alone was going to be a challenge. They couldn't just go into his apartment, close the door and…well, *do* anything, not when they knew there were people right here in the kitchen.

He didn't seem to give a damn. The moment the door shut behind Fiona, John yanked her into his arms.

"Your guests…"

"To hell with 'em."

This kiss was hungry, raw. He had her plastered against him, and she tried to squeeze even closer. His tongue drove into her mouth, sliding against hers. She whimpered, he groaned. His hair was thick, coarse silk in her clutching hand, the muscles in his shoulder powerful and bunched.

Somebody knocked on the door and they both froze.

John lifted his head to mumble a profanity. Fiona rested her forehead against his chest and seized the chance to breathe.

"Do you know where he is?" they heard a muffled voice ask.

Fiona pushed him away. "You'd better go."

"They'll survive if they can't find me for an hour," he growled.

"Isn't there some kind of innkeeper's oath? 'My guests' comfort shall come first'?"

He gave her a sardonic look as she retreated. "I didn't sign it. Oh, crap." He yanked open the door. "Yeah?"

Fiona didn't listen to the exchange beyond to gather that somebody was looking for snowshoes. John left, closing the door behind him, and she sank down on the bed, feeling shaky. Wow. She'd forgotten exactly what happened when he touched her. Forget sex as a pleasant recreation, a nice bonding with a man she was trying to convince herself she was falling in love with. This was…incendiary. Primal. She felt as if, in those brief moments, he had somehow stripped her of all the small pretences that made up the person she presented in public.

Did John feel anywhere near as profoundly affected? she wondered. The stereotype held that sex was simpler for men, more physical and less emotional. But then, did a man who *wasn't* emotionally involved kiss a woman as if he didn't give a damn if he ever drew another breath?

Fiona didn't know. Her other relationships had been too…well, tepid. Maybe it was fortunate she and John had been interrupted just then, though; mightn't it be a good thing if they had a chance to talk before they fell into bed? Especially given all her doubts about whether he was willing to share more than the moment with her?

It might have been smart if she'd taken the room at the top of the stairs and made sure their relationship had some substance beyond the physical before she agreed to share his bed.

Too late. And anyway… Fiona had a suspicion that if John came back right now and kissed her, she'd forget *how* to talk, never mind that she'd actually wanted to in the first place.

She pressed a hand to her chest to quell the butterflies. Why the cowardice now? She'd come up here to get to know John. Given the amazing chemistry between them, she refused to regret her decision to make love with him. But beyond that… Well, she'd see. When she'd been here with the kids, she and John couldn't find enough time alone to really talk. Now, circumstances were different. They'd have a chance to get to know each other. Yes, he was close-mouthed, but he was the one who'd invited her. That meant something, right?

In the meantime, she'd go out and chat with guests. Find out what she could do to help with dinner. Maybe there was even a load of laundry ready to go in. Lord knew, she was an expert on operating his washer and dryer.

Fiona got her hairbrush out of her purse, gave herself a brief inspection in his bathroom mirror and tidied herself, then went out to the kitchen.

Only the solitary reader remained, a man in his fifties at her best guess who didn't seem interested in who she was, but said aloud, "I wonder if any of those cookies are left."

She looked in the pantry and found two different types. "Chocolate chip or raisin oatmeal?" she called.

There was a pause. "I didn't know there were any raisin oatmeal. Maybe one of each."

She brought out a small plate with a selection, then heated water for a cup of tea for herself. She thought of finding herself something to read, but was content just to sit and sip. She loved this huge, open kitchen with knotty pine cabinets, plank floors, a sink big enough to take a bath in and old-fashioned, small-paned windows that looked out at the wintry forest. It smelled of good things, all probably baked that morning before guests arose: bread, cookies, perhaps pie. Fiona's only companion was peaceful, contributing no more than the whisper of turned pages and a pleased murmur when he took a bite of cookie.

When John eventually returned, his brows were drawn together and impatience made his stride quick. His color was heightened from the cold, which accompanied him with a gust. When he saw her, he checked. “I’m sorry. I didn’t mean to be gone so long.”

“That’s okay.” She smiled at him. “I made myself at home.”

“So I see.” His face relaxed.

“Good cookies,” the guest remarked.

“Glad you think so.”

“What’s for dinner?” he asked.

John stole one longing look from Fiona to the bedroom door. Then, with resignation, he said, “Spaghetti.”

Fiona hid her smile. She had probably sampled his entire repertoire. Let’s see. Spaghetti today means stir-fry tomorrow. Or was she misjudging him?

The reader nodded with apparent satisfaction and went back to his book, oblivious to John’s frustration.

“I suppose I should get dinner started,” he said finally.

Fiona swallowed the last of her tea. “I’ll help.”

“You don’t have to. If you’d rather read, go for a walk, take a bath…”

She almost wavered at mention of the bath. He had one of those sinfully deep claw-foot tubs in his bathroom, too. But there would be time. Right now, she wanted to be with him.

“Never turn down help,” she told him cheerfully.

A flash of humor had that amazingly softening effect on his face. “Even when they break dishes?”

“Not even then.” She stood. “Shall I chop?”

It felt like old times, except that it was other kids—

not hers—who wandered in to see what was cooking and whether they could snitch an illicit, before-dinner goody. Fiona immediately recognized the thirteen-year-old girl from his description. Hair veiled much of her face, her lower lip pouted, and her eyes rolled at everything the boy with her said. The parents were apparently out cross-country skiing, likely enjoying the break from their delightful offspring.

When dinner was ready, guests filled the long table. John and Fiona ate quickly at the counter, keeping an eye on the diners so they could respond to requests. The youngest boy spilled his milk. Fiona smiled at him, told him not to worry, and mopped it up. The teenage girl dipped her hair in her spaghetti and snapped at her father when he mildly suggested she put it in a ponytail. The gentleman who'd read all afternoon in the kitchen remained solitary, as did the middle-aged woman from the living room. Otherwise, conversations crisscrossed, quieter ones between couples and family members, more general observations and questions a little louder.

"Sky felt like snow this afternoon."

John nodded. "We might get some. Just an inch or two, if the forecast is to be believed."

"Would you pass the garlic bread?"

"What wonderful spaghetti!"

"Can you recommend another trail for tomorrow? We'd love to get up higher."

John was hardly effusive, but he answered questions and remained patient, just as he had with Fiona's students.

He cut pie and she served as he set pieces on small plates.

No, he was sorry, no television, he told the sulky girl.

"Not even in there?" She jerked her head toward his room.

"Gretchen!"

In fact, Fiona knew that he had a television and DVD player, although she doubted he bothered often with movies. She waited with interest to hear what he'd say.

John met the teen's challenging gaze. "Those are my private quarters." With no more comment, he moved away to get coffee for someone.

The girl said loudly, "This sucks! A hotel with no TV."

Her brother braved her scathing glance to say, "I thought it was fun to play games."

"Why don't you come out with us tomorrow?" her dad asked. "It was beautiful along the creek."

"And *cold.*"

He sighed and shook his head. Fiona hoped Gretchen wasn't enrolling in Willamette Prep.

Gradually the guests wandered out after compliments on dinner, and she and John worked in tandem cleaning up. In one way, it was so comfortable; they'd done it before, and she seemed to fall into the rhythm as if she'd spent weeks or even months here before, rather than mere days. But in another way…well, she kept thinking about when they could close up the kitchen and retreat to his apartment. When they'd finally be alone together.

The reader closed his book at last, stood, stretched, nodded in their direction as if vaguely surprised that they were there and exited through the swinging door.

"Are they really all gone?" she whispered.

"Temporarily." His tone was wry. "Until they develop a yen for an evening snack."

Her kids had always wanted something later, she remembered guiltily.

"What if we leave out cookies, tea and coffee makings, cocoa...?"

"So it's obvious they're on their own?" He gave her a slow smile that set her heart to thumping. "I like the way you think."

She got out mugs and spoons and filled the teakettle with water while he laid out tea bags and packets of cocoa, a jar of instant coffee and a plate of cookies under clear plastic wrap.

"I need to lock up." He disappeared. When he came back, he said, "I mentioned that the kitchen would be self-service tonight."

"Oh, good." She let him guide her, hand on the small of her back, to his room as if she didn't know where it was. "Would you mind if I take a bath?"

His gaze was heavy-lidded but not so imbued with urgency as it had been when she first arrived. Maybe he finally believed that she truly was here and would be for awhile. "Take your time."

As lovely as the bath felt once she ran it, Fiona wasn't tempted to linger. She'd just wanted to feel clean.

When she came out of the bathroom, she thought for a moment John had fallen asleep. He sat in an upholstered rocker beside the woodstove, legs stretched out, head resting against the back, eyes closed.

They opened before she could feel even a whisper

of disappointment. They were intense, glowing with a fire he had obviously banked, and she saw that his relaxed pose was an illusion. He'd been waiting.

He rose to his feet, the chair rocking a few times behind him. Gaze never leaving her, he crossed the room.

"Your cheeks are pink."

"I think I ran the water too hot." Her voice sounded like someone else's.

He grazed his knuckles down her warm cheek. His voice was a murmur, gravelly enough to make heat pool low in her belly. "I wanted you the first time I saw you."

"I...I think I wanted you, too."

He brushed his lips over hers. "You think?"

In fact, she couldn't *think*.

"I was cold, and scared, and so grateful." She let her head fall back as he moved his mouth down her neck. "And...and you weren't very friendly."

He lifted his head to look at her. "I was scared, too. By you."

A bubble of laughter came out as a hiccup, startling her. "*And* of my horde of teenagers."

"Yeah, of them, too. But—" now he stroked her throat with his fingers "—not the same way."

"I'm...not very scary," she managed to say, the words scarcely more substantial than her exhaled breath.

For a moment, a shadow crossed his face. "Yeah, you are."

"No." She lifted her hands and laid them on his cheeks, feeling the texture of the day's growth of beard. "I'm here, aren't I?"

"Yeah." Just like that, his voice was raw, and the emotion in his eyes so intense her heart cramped. "You are."

He kissed her, his longing plain, but his hands and lips so gentle Fiona felt precious. Even loved.

Her last coherent thought was, *Please. Please let it be love.*

CHAPTER TWELVE

HE'D ANTICIPATED this a thousand times without really believing it would happen. Fiona would e-mail with a last-minute excuse. Half a dozen good ones came to mind without any effort on John's part. She felt bad leaving her mother alone for Christmas. She was having car trouble. Whatever. *Maybe over spring break,* she might say. *But call if you get down my way.*

Or the other possibility was that she'd show up but go for the room upstairs. He'd been prepared for that. Even okay with it. He just wanted her here, laughing at him, kissing him, pushing him to talk even when he didn't want to. *Caring.*

But he'd gotten luckier than that. So much luckier, he was still in shock. Here she was, in his room, fresh from the bath, her hair curling even more from the steam, cheeks rosy, gaze shy. She hadn't gotten dressed again, nor had she slipped into a little negligee. Instead she wore flannel pajama pants and a simple white camisole. Without—a flicker of a glance told him—having put a bra on beneath it.

He'd been aroused even before he kissed her. Now that he had... He wished like hell he'd had sex sometime within the last two years. It had been so damn long, he didn't know if he had the self-control not to come the minute he got inside her.

Slow things down, he told himself, lifting his head. "God, you're beautiful," he murmured.

"You know I'm not..." She stopped, humor briefly lighting her face. "Never mind. I'm not *really* dumb enough to try to convince you I'm ordinary looking. It's okay for you to think I'm beautiful. Gorgeous. Ravishing."

Wanting her to believe him, John covered her mouth. "You have these fine bones." He traced a fingertip over her cheekbone, along the delicate line of her jaw. "Big eyes that flash a thousand emotions. And questions. I can always see them crowding your head."

Right now she watched him helplessly, as if he held power over her.

"Do you know how shiny your hair is?" His fingers slipped into the strands. "You turn your head and it shimmers."

She let out a tiny sound.

"Your voice. Gentle but with steel beneath when you're in schoolmarm mode."

She opened her mouth as if to protest, and he silenced her by kissing her. Lightly, ending with a tug at her lower lip.

"And your lips," he whispered, "are perfect. Not thin, not pouty, just...sweet. And sexy."

"You know," she said, voice thready, "you don't have to flatter me. I was already yours with the 'should I take your suitcase upstairs?'"

"Yeah, I do." John knew he wasn't very good being romantic, but he felt he owed her the words. The next ones, though, he didn't know how to say. They came out sounding awkward. "Mostly, though, it's not the way you look. It's…you."

Her forehead crinkled. "What do you mean?"

"Your optimism. The way you want to believe in everybody. Your honesty, your kindness…" His throat clogged. "You have a gift for seeing people. Looking past the outside."

"You mean, your scar." She reached up and stroked it, her fingers as gentle as an early spring breeze.

"Yeah," he said gruffly. "My scar."

"Well, it's my turn. This scar, it doesn't disfigure you! It made me worry about how much it must have hurt, and how close that shrapnel or whatever it was came to your eye. But you're as handsome as you were before. You're, um, a hunk." She blushed. "Even the girls noticed, believe me."

Crap, *he* was blushing at the idea of teenage girls observing him that way.

"Don't worry." A smile lightened her voice. "They're just hoping the boys their age come out nearly as well."

"God," he muttered.

Any humor fled. "And…and I'm not here because of how you look, either. I'm here because of *you*."

That was the part he didn't get. He knew what he was: bad-tempered, withdrawn, and, yeah, a little bit crazy. Sane men didn't see blood soaking pristine white snow. They didn't wake up shouting warnings that came a year too late.

But he was sane enough to want to take what she was offering. Acceptance, friendship, healing. And, yeah, sex. He wanted the sex something fierce.

"I was afraid you wouldn't come," John said gruffly.

"I was about to make reservations here."

"I haven't put anyone in your room since the day you left."

"Uh-oh." Tears sprang into her eyes. "Darn it, now I'm getting weepy!"

He caught a tear from her lash on his fingertip. "Have I killed the mood here?"

With sudden fierceness, she said, "Not on your life," and went up on tiptoe to throw her arms around his neck.

John caught her close and kissed her. The words made what they did now easier, as if in talking openly they had shed any need to be self-conscious.

She pushed his flannel shirt off, then made him help take off the T-shirt beneath it. Fiona lifted her arms with breathtaking trust so that he could remove her chemise. She did flush when he looked at her small, high breasts, but she arched her back willingly when he cupped them, then bent to kiss each.

He hadn't had the foresight to ditch his boots and socks, and had to sit down to do that. She knelt and helped him, when she wasn't nipping at his earlobe or stroking his thigh. He was so hard by the time he was done, he didn't think he could have gotten his jeans unzipped *without* help. The feel of her fingers as she undid the button, then eased down the zipper, was like coming into contact with a live wire. Felt in every corpuscle of his body, and damn near painful but the best pain he'd ever imagined. He was gasping by the time she freed his erection.

She made choked little sounds as she stroked him. He had to grip her hand.

"I'm...on the thin edge here."

"Oh." A slow, satisfied smile was incredibly erotic. "Shall I make things worse?" Before he could answer, she stood, put her hands at the waistband of her flannel pajama bottoms and pushed them down until they pooled on the floor and she could step out of them.

He growled something; her name, an expletive, he didn't know. She was exquisite. Pale-skinned, fine-boned, long-legged, with those perfect, small breasts and just enough curve at her hips. Hair as dark as that on her head curled at the apex of her thighs. John groaned, gripped the arms of the chair and momentarily closed his eyes.

Then he surged to his feet, lifted her high and deposited her on the bed, coming down on top of her. As naturally as if they'd made love a thousand times before, her legs parted to welcome him, tangling with his. It was all he could do to grope in the bedside drawer, find a condom and put it on.

Foroplay might not have been what it should be, but she didn't seem to care and he couldn't have waited another second to enter her. The feel of her enclosing him, not just her core but her arms and legs, and her mouth open against his, was the most glorious sensation he'd ever known. When almost immediately her body spasmed, and she whispered his name against his lips, he had the dazed thought that he'd found heaven on earth. Then he let himself drive into her once, twice, a dozen times, and empty himself of all his bitterness in a climax that shattered him—and yet left him whole on the other side.

THE FIRST DAYS were wonderful. Fiona didn't think she'd ever been happier in her life.

She got up early and kneaded dough while he heated the ovens and spooned muffins into tins. Once the bread was in the oven, she slipped on a wool sweater and stepped outside on the front porch with him, each of them cradling a mug of coffee, to watch dawn lighten the sky. The first morning it came gradually, charcoal-gray becoming infinitesimally paler shades until they could see fine snowflakes floating toward the ground, moving so slowly it was as if time itself had slowed, too. The second morning, she understood why John didn't care that no movie theater was within driving distance. Hollywood couldn't touch this show.

The colors alone stole her breath. She had seen glorious sunsets, but these colors had more delicacy. She couldn't have named the vivid hues. The words "pink" or "peach" were woefully inadequate. And all the while, the world was utterly silent, as if it, too, held its breath.

When the show was done and morning arrived, she looked up at John and said, voice hushed, "I never knew what I was missing."

"It's not the same down there." He, too, spoke quietly, as if out of respect. "Until I came up here, I didn't know."

"Surely in Iraq, with open desert…"

He shook his head. This time, his voice was flat. "No. Dawn there…it was splashier."

Yes, that was the word she'd have used for sunsets on the coast, where she and her family used to vacation.

"I'd better check the bread." He turned and went in,

leaving her to follow and wonder: had he gone in because the show was done, or because she had made him think of a time and place he wanted to forget?

Worry niggled at Fiona for the first time since she'd arrived. Was it chance that they hadn't yet talked about his experience in Iraq?

Well, perhaps "chance" wasn't the right word. The truth was, last night they hadn't been able to keep their hands off each other. They hadn't done nearly as much talking as she'd imagined.

A smile curved Fiona's mouth. Nope, she didn't regret how they'd spent the night at all. Besides, they still had plenty of time to talk.

She followed him in, almost satisfied that she'd imagined his change of tone at her mere mention of Iraq.

The lodge didn't quite empty on the morning of the twenty-fourth, but over half the guests left. The two singles were still here, still completely uninterested in each other or anyone else, and one couple stayed. They were the ones that surprised Fiona. They dressed well, and had been rather social since she arrived, as if being so came naturally to them. She could picture them hosting Christmas parties, not choosing to celebrate the holidays in a rustic lodge far from the trappings that meant Christmas to most people.

Curious, but trying to avoid being tactless, Fiona asked casually over lunch, "Have you stayed here before over Christmas? It's going to be different for me."

The woman seemed to force a smile. "Our daughter is a junior in college. She's doing the entire year abroad."

"Oh? Where is she?"

"The University of Cape Town."

"Oh, dear. I can see why she didn't fly home for the holidays."

"We talked about going over there, but it's all I can do to make myself get on an airplane to zip down to L.A. It takes something like twenty-five hours to get to South Africa." She shuddered. "Anyway…some friends and she are traveling over the break. It's summer there, you know."

"You must miss her," Fiona said, her gaze caught by the deep sadness in the woman's eyes.

Her eyes filled with tears as she nodded, and a moment later they made their excuses and left the kitchen. Fiona felt bad that she'd reminded them of how far away their daughter was and how unlikely that, having flown the nest, she'd ever come home for long again.

That made her think of her own mother, who would be celebrating Christmas for the first time without *her* daughter. She knew Fiona wasn't likely to call, given the cell phone coverage here, and they planned to get together as soon as Fiona was home.

John had put up a rather pathetic Christmas tree—a scraggly six-footer dwarfed by the high ceiling and massive peeled log pillars in the living area. When she chided him about it, he shrugged.

"Couldn't have put up much bigger with the tree stand I found. Wouldn't have been enough ornaments for a bigger tree, either."

Or lights. Fiona resolved, studying the tree, to hit the after-Christmas sales when she got home and mail him a new string or two of lights and some boxes of ornaments for future holidays.

Their small group gathered in front of the fire that evening, sipped hot spiced cider and talked about Christmases past. With the multicolored lights on the tree, the deep comfortable chairs and the crackling fire, the modest sense of companionship seemed to suffice for everyone. They dispersed at an hour that would have seemed absurd to her at home, murmuring, "Merry Christmas," as if they meant it—and, in the case of the curmudgeon who liked to plant himself at the kitchen table all day, as if he were *surprised* to mean it.

In bed, Fiona and John made love with the same, astonishing passion they'd felt the first time, sweetly tempered with patience and newfound knowledge of where to touch to please each other.

On Christmas morning, while they were still in bed, John presented her with a small, wrapped gift. Smiling, she had to scramble from bed, hurrying with bare feet on the cold floor, to get his from her suitcase.

They unwrapped simultaneously, John seeming pleased with the selection of DVDs she'd bought, all movies she loved and he hadn't seen. Wrapped with them was a pair of tickets to her local multiplex. He stared down at them.

A little worried, she said, "For when you come to see me."

"Thank you." He nodded. "Open the box."

His gift was a pair of earrings, pretty ones with central diamonds surrounded by tiny rubies, but she was oddly disappointed. No, that was silly—how could he know enough about her life to give her something deeply meaningful?

What she wanted most from him, Fiona realized, couldn't have been wrapped and tied with a bow, anyway. What she wanted was for him to tell her why he was wounded so badly in spirit as well as body.

But, goodness—they were still tap dancing around all kinds of intimate subjects! Trust came with time, with knowledge of each other. In the meantime, Fiona settled happily into the lodge life she remembered, except now she got to sleep in John's bed with him.

She waited on guests while he wrestled with a frozen water pipe, coming back with raw knuckles on one hand. She found she didn't mind cleaning the bathrooms or changing bedding when one family left and another arrived and he was busy carrying out bags or hauling in wood.

She remembered from that first time feeling astonished at the quantity of food her group of kids ate, the laundry they generated. But within a day she realized there were *more* people in the lodge now, which meant more food to prepare, more dishes to wash, more towels to wash and dry and fold. And this was *normal.* Three days of working beside him, and she should have been exhausted. Instead she was content.

Mostly she loved being wherever John was. Watching him do the simplest task gave her pleasure. Being able to meet his eyes, even when the kitchen was crowded, in a silent, intimate exchange filled her with joy. The moments when he touched her in passing, his hand possessive and knowing, were almost as good as their kisses when they were alone.

He encouraged her to talk when they had time alone,

as if he were hungry to learn everything about her. She found herself confessing to things she'd been dismayed to learn about herself.

"Thanksgiving was weird," she admitted, when they took a walk down to the creek. Snow crunched under their feet, and ahead moving water burbled in an otherwise silent landscape. The cabins, no doubt inviting in summer, looked cold and empty with unmarked snow burying steps, no smoke coming from metal stovepipes, and windows glinting blankly. Icicles hung from eaves.

"Do you know," Fiona continued, as they followed a path made by cross-country skies and showshoes, "I think I was *jealous?* I told myself I was glad Mom is dating, but then I secretly resented this man because I had to share her with him. I'm so used to having her to myself." She shook her head at the memory and with one gloved hand brushed snow from a bough that sprang higher once released from the weight. "They were really careful not to touch, and we were all so awkward. I'm embarrassed to remember."

"Even if you'd felt comfortable, they might not have." John wore a fleece hat—something he rarely did. It was so cold today.

"I'm sure. But they were awkward because of *me.* Because I sat there wishing Mom hadn't invited him. I felt awful when she made a point of telling me Christmas Eve would be just us. And—" this was the most humiliating part "—even worse when I said I'd be away for Christmas and I heard her voice lighten when she told me not to worry, she wouldn't have to be alone."

"You wanted her to be alone on Christmas Eve?" His glance was quizzical, his voice gentle.

"No! Of course not!" Fiona laughed to hide her discomfiture. "I just wanted her to miss the time when it was enough for it just to be the two of us."

John stopped. "Do you think she doesn't?"

Fiona had to sniff, not sure if her nose was running from the grief of something lost or just from the cold.

"Nope. I know she loves me, and that those *were* genuinely happy times. But knowing and *knowing*..." She touched a fist to her chest. "Those aren't the same thing."

He looked away. "No." For a moment it seemed he wouldn't say any more, but then he continued, "The voice of common sense sounds a lot like a parent telling us what we should feel or think. Of course we don't listen to it."

She blinked. Yes, it was exactly like that. She'd chew herself out for being silly enough to feel something irrational, and that voice was downright irritating. It made her feel rebellious and childish.

"I never realized," she said, nodding, "but you're right. I suppose we internalize everything our parents and coaches and teachers say, and then spout it back at ourselves."

"And, unfortunately, at our kids."

"Oh, ugh. And here I am, a teacher!"

"A good one."

"But I say those kinds of things!"

He laughed at her, whatever had made him seem to withdraw for a moment having passed. "Yeah, but the thing is, it's usually good advice."

"Oh, I suppose." She scowled at him. "Well, great. Now I'm going to have to watch everything I say."

John shook his head. "No. Just go with your instincts. You have good ones. I heard you talking to the kids." He suddenly stopped and lifted a hand. "Shh."

Fiona, too, heard a crunch of snow and rustle of branches. She waited, breathless, looking in the direction of the sound. There was silence, and she might have given up had John not remained so still.

A deer stepped out onto the creekside trail not twenty feet ahead of them, followed closely by a second. She wasn't sure, but thought they were does. Did male deer have antlers year around? One was noticeably larger than the other. Mother and yearling? They looked directly at John and Fiona, momentarily freezing, their haunches bunching as if in preparation for flight, but in the absence of movement they relaxed and crunched forward to the creek, their delicate hooves piercing the snow.

In still spots the creek was iced over, but where water eddied or raced over rocks, it ran free between snowy banks. They both drank, lifting their heads frequently to listen for danger.

Abruptly, either having drunk their fill or hearing something human ears couldn't catch, they sprang back into the woods. Their leaps were awkward, and she imagined how difficult heavy snow must be for them.

"Ooh," she murmured, when they were gone. "They were beautiful."

"Not looking too bad, either. I'll worry if winter gets too harsh."

She reached for his hand, and was warmed by it

despite the gloves both wore. "You're not a hunter, I take it."

"Me?" Recoiling, he sounded repulsed, reminding her of how fresh bloodshed was for him. "God, no."

The shadow of horror in his eyes was something he usually hid from her.

"I suppose you'd have lost your taste for it even if you had been a hunter," she said tentatively.

"I never was." He let her hand drop and said, "We should start back."

That night, her sixth there—with only four more to go—she felt bold enough to ask him about Iraq. It took a little coaxing, but he did talk about life there for the soldiers: the rec center with ping-pong, foosball tables, computers with unreliable Internet connections and free movies every night. The Hajji shops run by locals where you could buy anything from bootlegged DVDs to Welcome To Iraq postcards. The state-of-the-art gym, the food, the ups and downs of laundry service. Telling stories, John was occasionally funny and seemingly relaxed.

It was only as she settled into sleep that Fiona realized he hadn't actually told her anything important. Not about what he'd felt, or done every day. Certainly not about friends he'd lost. He made a joke about how often the gym closed down because of mortar attacks, but had nothing to say about what it was like to live day-to-day knowing you weren't safe even walking to the dining hall.

And, of course, he said nothing whatever about getting wounded.

The next night, beginning to feel frightened by how near the end of her visit they were, Fiona asked about his family. They were lying in bed after making love. He was on his back, one hand propped behind his head, the other arm around her. With her head on his bare chest, she could not just hear but feel his heart beat.

"What do you want to know?" he asked.

"Oh… Are you close? Did they send you care packages while you were overseas?"

He was quiet for a minute. "Yeah. Yeah, they did. My folks are good people. My father owns his own plumbing business. I told you that, didn't I? He encouraged me to tinker when I was little. I could rebuild an engine by the time I was thirteen, fourteen."

"I take it building robots wasn't quite what he had in mind?"

His chest rumbled with a quiet laugh. "No, but my parents were proud of me." He fell silent again, and when she tilted her head, she saw that he was frowning. What was he thinking about? Their pride when he went to college and then grad school, or when he donned his uniform and went to Iraq to serve his country?

"What do your sisters do?"

"Hmm?" He seemed to pull himself back from wherever he'd been with difficulty, but after a minute he said, "Mary—she's three years older than me—she's married, has two kids and, now that they're in school, works at the library. My younger sister was married once, divorced with no kids, and is a journalist with the *Oregonian.*"

Knowing she should remember, Fiona still had to ask, "What's her name?"

"Liz. Short for Elizabeth. My parents believed in the basics where names were concerned. The old ones were still the good ones."

Fiona laughed. "You sound fondest of Liz."

"We're the closest in age—only eighteen months between us. And maybe the most alike."

He talked comfortably about her in particular, telling stories about growing up in a working-class neighborhood in Portland.

"Since you got back?" she asked.

Again, he was quiet for a minute before asking. "They were shocked. They try to be supportive. But, except for Liz, they don't understand damage they can't see."

Fiona was lying on his "good" side, so she couldn't see the scar on his face from here. He always rolled in such a way that she ended up on this side, and she assumed that was because of the pain in his hip. The surgical scar there was horrific, the mass of far-less tidy scar tissue on his thigh even more so. She thought it was astonishing that he could walk, let alone do the hard physical labor he often did.

"They think you should be able to put it behind you?" she said softly.

"They and everyone else." For a moment his voice was harsh with repressed anger, or even violence. As quickly, he buried it deep, tugging her higher. "Hey. Kiss me."

So she did, and ended up learning nothing more.

No, that wasn't entirely true. What she learned was that he was very, very good at not telling her anything meaningful. Evasion, she was frightened to realize, was his way. He wanted to get to know her. He just didn't want her to really know *him.*

Which wasn't entirely fair of her, Fiona knew—that adult voice talking, reasoning with the absurdly emotional part of her that began to resent being shut out. He did share, just nothing beyond the superficial.

She had to keep repeating to herself that they hadn't known each other long. He'd been through so much. Talking about it wouldn't come easily for him. She'd known that about him before she came for this visit. He'd gotten so angry, that night on the porch, when she'd tried to push him to confide in her.

And ultimately, it was the anger that disturbed her most. The horror she understood. The things he must have seen… How could anyone tuck those memories away and go comfortably back to life as if he was still the same person? But who was he angry *at?* The man who'd fired the weapon that hurt him? One faction or another in Iraq? The U.S. government for sending him? Fate? Himself? Fiona had no idea, because he wouldn't tell her.

She was actually starting to feel uncomfortable, as if she should cross her arms and cover herself. She'd told him some really personal and even embarrassing things about herself, like the fact that she was childish enough to be jealous because her mother was dating. But he wasn't at all interested in talking about his feelings in the same way. So there she was, bare, while he hadn't peeled off a single article of clothing. At least, that's what it felt like.

So maybe what they had going was just about sex to John.

Of course, the sex was awfully good. She'd known it would be. How could it not, when the mere sight of him stirred her in unfamiliar ways? And this trip, it was just exploratory, for both of them. She doubted he was ready for anything more than, well, a *fling* with normalcy, anyway. She even tried to tell herself she was okay with that. The way she hurt inside when he evaded a question or even, one night, said, "Not something I want to talk about," and rolled away, that was only punctured ego, not the bruise it felt like.

What she really, truly, wasn't prepared for was what happened on her last night there.

They made love the moment they were alone. She felt John's urgency, shared it; tomorrow night, she'd be home in her town house in Hawes Ferry, miles from here, not knowing when she would see him again. When they were sated, if only briefly, he rolled to take his weight off her and gathered her close.

He nuzzled her hair. She was smiling, her eyelids growing heavy, when he said suddenly, "Don't leave tomorrow. Fiona, stay with me."

Shocked, she whispered, "What? But school starts Wednesday…"

"I don't mean just for another day or two." He reared up on one elbow so she could see his face, his eyes searching hers. "Quit your job. Stay. Marry me."

She gaped at him. Was he *serious?*

Fiona had an awful, awful feeling that he was.

CHAPTER THIRTEEN

JOHN COULDN'T BELIEVE it. He'd asked the woman he loved to marry him, and the first words out of her mouth weren't, "Yes, oh yes!" No, they were a flat and dismayed, "You're not serious."

Still raised on one elbow so he could see her lying beside him in bed, John stiffened. "Why wouldn't I be?"

Her eyes shied from his. "We haven't known each other that long."

"We've spent more time together than most couples do over six months of just dating."

"Well, maybe." She sounded doubtful. "But you've never said..."

Relieved, he realized he'd forgotten the big words. "That I love you? I think I fell in love by the second day you were here back in November."

Her eyes met his, begging, it seemed to him, and her voice was suddenly tremulous. "Really?"

"Yeah." He bent his head to nuzzle her cheek. "Really. You couldn't tell?"

Fiona sat up so fast, her shoulder whacked his nose. "No! No, I can't... Oh." She noticed that he was clutching his nose and his eyes were watering. "John! I'm so sorry. I didn't mean..." She dragged in a deep breath. "But...no. Love means trust. It means sharing. Making yourself vulnerable to the other person. Have you ever voluntarily told me one single really personal thing about yourself?"

Goddamn. He squeezed the bridge of his nose and prayed the blaze of pain would subside.

"Yes. I said I love you."

"And I'm questioning whether you do." She waited, uncompromising. "What else?"

He sat up straight, too. "I told you how I feel about this." He touched his scar.

"No, you didn't. You expressed the belief that women found it unattractive. I trust you're convinced that I don't?"

He nodded. "It's..." He stopped, physically unable to say the words.

She said them for him. "It's a symbol, isn't it? The outward manifestation of...something. Something you won't tell me about."

"Can't." He unclenched his jaw. "Is that what this comes down to? I have to relive it for your benefit, or you won't believe I love you?"

She looked sad. "No. If it was just the one incident, I could understand better. But you don't talk about anything."

Incident? He hardly heard the rest of what she said. The horrific splinter of a moment in time that had killed six teenage boys and maimed four others and him was an *incident?*

Suddenly furious, he got out of bed. "You don't get it, do you?"

"No, I don't. And I won't if you don't tell me."

John was still stunned. He'd been thinking about this all day, feeling something he hadn't in a long time: hope. And it had blown up in his face.

"So we're down to show-and-tell or bye-bye?"

Fiona still looked sad, but also resolute and composed. She wasn't wavering. She wasn't torn. "John, it's not that simple. I have a commitment to be in that classroom Wednesday. I can't walk out on Willamette Prep with no notice even if I want to. It's unrealistic for you to ask me. And you know I'm working on my master's degree at Portland U. Am I just supposed to forget that, too?"

"You could finish the year out…"

"Do you intend to stay here forever?" Her eyes were clear and entirely too perceptive. "Never work again in robotics?"

"I don't know. Maybe I'll go back…"

"How can you, if you can hardly bear to go into Danson?"

"Time heals. Isn't that what they all say?"

"Is that what the veterans' hospital counselor said?"

He didn't answer.

"I didn't think so." There it was again, something very like grief in her voice. In just above a whisper, she said, "I was falling in love with you, too. If only…"

John didn't let her finish, interjecting harshly, "I could be the man I used to be?"

"No. If only you'd take your courage in your hands and work toward being the man you *can* be."

His heart was as frozen as the ground outside. The only heat John felt was his anger. "And who is that?"

"I don't know." She slipped from bed and went to her suitcase. "I can't even guess, because I don't know you well enough."

He watched as she pulled on a T-shirt and her pajama bottoms, then came back to bed.

"I'm going to sleep," she said with dignity, climbed in with her back to him and pulled the covers up around her.

What could he do but the same? He turned out the light and lay on his back, his body rigid as anguish and fury washed through him in turn, the one rolling in and then fading back out as the other crested.

She didn't love him. She didn't know him. No, worse than that—she saw him as a coward, despised him.

A man who'd known pain, he didn't think he had ever hurt as much as he did now. God. She despised him. If she knew…

He seemed to hear her whisper. *How can I?*

If he told her, then she would know. That he had acted, however good his intentions, so recklessly, so foolishly, that he had all but killed those boys with his own hands. Then how would she feel about him?

He hadn't thought he could sleep, but he did eventually, only to awaken shouting. Shouting the warning that would forever come too late.

"John!" Hair tumbling around her shoulders, Fiona sat up beside him. She laid a hand on his forearm. "Are you all right?"

"Yes." He got out of bed, went into the bathroom and shut the door. And he stayed, until she had either fallen asleep or was pretending she had. And then he lay beside her in bed until the time when he could reasonably get up.

He was busy baking by the time she appeared, and guests began trickling in for breakfast soon thereafter. Right after breakfast, Fiona went back to his room to pack.

Once she was done, he pulled her suitcase to the porch steps, then carried it across the now-slushy ground to her car, heaving it into her trunk once she opened it.

She faced him. "John…"

"Drive carefully. It can be slippery when it's melting like this."

"Why won't you listen to me?" she asked, with what sounded like despair.

If she'd just *go*. Not insist on rehashing why he had been so foolish as to believe for a second they could have a future.

Stolidly he said, "I listened."

"Then you didn't hear. I came because I was falling in love with you, too. I gave myself to you because I was."

Yes. That's why he'd believed what he had.

"If…if this was the life you loved, the life you'd chosen, then I would give serious thought to how I could combine mine with yours. But we both know it isn't. You have to be intellectually restless…"

Now, he *didn't* want to hear.

"We both know you're temperamentally unsuited to a service job…"

"Thanks for noticing that I'm surly."

"I feel like I'm talking to one of my students!" she said with exasperation.

Seeing her start to turn away, he panicked. “I’m dealing with my PTSD. In my own way.”

He’d never let himself say, or even think, those words before: *my PTSD.* I *am suffering from posttraumatic stress.* He didn’t stop to consider what it meant that he was saying them now.

Fiona turned back. “Your way is to hide out.”

“It’s healing naturally. With hard physical work, limited noise and stress. The old-fashioned way.”

“Is it working?”

“I’m better.”

“But still suffering flashbacks and nightmares. Still unable to tell anyone about the traumatic events.”

“How do you know I haven’t told other people?”

She refused to play his game, her eyes asking for more than he could give. “Have you?”

John couldn’t lie. He stood there, mute.

“I need to go,” she whispered, and threw herself into the car. Not waiting to warm it up, she backed out as fast as the engine caught. John had to take a couple of quick steps back.

He was left with a last snapshot of her face, wet with tears.

FIONA WAS READY to give up. She’d been happier than she had ever been in her life when she was with John, and sadder and lonelier, too. If he couldn’t even admit that he had a serious problem or that he was shutting her out, she didn’t know what else she could do.

Except get over him.

She went to her mother’s for dinner two days after

getting back, and the first thing she said was, "I ruined Thanksgiving, didn't I? I'm so sorry, Mom! I really, truly, am glad you've found Barry."

Her mother laughed and hugged her. "You didn't ruin Thanksgiving! Barry liked you, and *he's* been apologizing ever since for being so stiff you probably thought he was carved out of wood."

"Really?"

As slim as Fiona, with stylishly cut hair that was being defiantly allowed to go gray, her mother laughed again. "Really."

"Can we give it another try?"

"Of course we can!" Her mother's dark eyes softened. "How was your trip?"

She'd intended to lie, say, "It was great!" But this was her mom, and when Fiona opened her mouth, nothing at all came out. Her mouth worked, and the next thing she knew tears were running down her face.

Her mother took her in her arms and let her cry, just as she had when the first boy who'd ever asked Fiona out had stood her up. This time, because she was an adult—her heart and not just her pride had been wounded—the tears couldn't wash away her misery, and her mother's comforting arms didn't convince her that all would be well.

But she did feel marginally better when she finally drew back. "Oh, no, I can imagine what I look like!" she said, and fled to the bathroom.

Face washed, she sat with her mother on the couch and told her about John, his pride, his silences and the banked anger that scared her, as well as about his kindness, his ready ear, his intelligence and patience.

"I really thought..." She couldn't finish.

"He was the one?" her mother asked softly.

Fiona nodded.

"Maybe he is. Maybe *you* need to be patient."

"I think..." She bit down hard on her lip, tasting blood. "I hurt his pride, Mom. I doubt he can forgive me that."

"Just...leave the door open. Somehow, let him know it is open. That's my advice, for what it's worth. Now—" her tone changed, although her expression stayed kind "—what do you say we sit down to eat?"

On the first day back to school, Erin asked Fiona shyly if she'd seen Mr. Fallon over the break. Several of the students knew that he and she had been e-mailing back and forth.

"Yes, I went up there for a few days," she admitted. "He kept my room for me." So, okay, she hadn't used it. That wasn't the kind of thing you told a teenager. "Wasn't that sweet?"

"That's so cool! I wish I could have gone with you instead of..." She stopped.

"Instead of?"

"Oh, my parents mostly worked. I know they had to, but it was boring." She shrugged. "That's okay. I had to work on college applications anyway."

They talked about those, and about the recommendation Fiona was going to write for her. Then Erin left with her customary poise. Recognizing loneliness when she saw it, Fiona was sad watching her go.

Over the next few weeks, Fiona kept thinking about her mother's advice. Would allowing herself to hope that she and John could somehow reconnect keep her from moving on? If she wanted to leave the door open, what would she use to prop it ajar? A note? An e-mail?

Maybe because of her dad's infidelity and her parents' troubles, of which she'd been all too aware, Fiona prided herself on her ability to accept life as it came. In this case, she had a choice: she could marry a man who would never really talk to her and live in an isolated lodge doing laundry, changing beds and serving guests. Or she could walk away from him, choose the career she loved, the graduate degree that meant something to her, the relationships she had with students, friends and her mother. She'd already made her choice the day she'd driven away from Thunder Mountain Lodge. Now all she had to do was put the sense of loss behind her.

In the middle of January, however, she did send an e-mail.

John...

Even her fingers hesitated.

If you ever want to talk, you know how to reach me.

Resisting tears, she typed, *Love, Fiona,* and hit Send.

Her heart pounded when she checked her e-mail the next day, and the day after that. She felt that same hope every time she went online that week, and even into the next week. But John never replied, and she finally gave up expecting him to.

In mid-March, two things happened on the same day. The first was that she got asked out on a date. Chad

Scammell had arrived at Willamette Prep as a new vice principal the previous fall after having taught math in the public schools. Around her age, he'd been friendly from the start, and she'd reciprocated. She offered insight into the different culture in a high-end private school, while he was available to talk about kids who worried her.

He'd wandered by her classroom during her grading/lunch period that day, as he often did, and sat on a front row desk chatting while she ate the sandwich and sliced apple she'd packed.

She was starting to think that the students would be returning soon when he said, "I keep worrying about things like sexual harassment, so I want you to know that if you say no, I'll listen."

Huh? Fiona blinked in bewilderment.

"I wondered if you'd consider having dinner with me sometime."

Now she understood. No wonder he worried about how she would take the invitation. They weren't just colleagues; he was technically her superior in the school hierarchy.

Have dinner with him?

Fiona hadn't thought of him as a potential date, but now that she considered it, she wasn't sure why. He was handsome—in the way of a high school football player all grown up. A little beefy still, neck thick enough that buying shirts had to be a challenge, but he was also smart, entertaining and nice. She'd never felt any spark, but…

Rebellion stirred. She had to start somewhere, didn't she? What were the odds she'd ever hear from John

Fallon again? So, okay, she thought about him often, worried about him, dreamed about him. It was time she started thinking about someone else.

"Yes," she said. "I'd like that, Chad. I'm free this weekend."

The bell rang, and they were just finishing making plans when students started filtering into the classroom. He covered her hand briefly with his, smiled and left. Fiona sat there for a minute, wishing she could feel a glow of anticipation. It took more than the usual effort to concentrate on teaching the class.

Oddly enough, the second thing that happened was right after that class, when Tabitha and Kelli stopped at her desk on their way out.

They glanced at each other, somehow silently electing Tabitha spokesperson. "We were thinking about Mr. Fallon and the lodge. Some of us were talking about how maybe we'd e-mail once in a while. If you have an address for him."

Her eyes narrowed. Now, why would they be asking about John at this exact moment, when she'd just accepted a date with another man? But she couldn't believe one had anything to do with the other—not in their teen-centered world view—so after a moment she concluded the timing really was just coincidental.

"Who is 'some of you'?" she asked.

"Well...not Amy."

No, of course not Amy.

But Dieter and even Erin. "We were, like, talking the other day."

Fiona wondered what had triggered the conversation.

"Do you ever talk to him?" Kelli sounded elaborately casual.

"You know he doesn't really have phone service."

"No, I mean e-mail or IM or something."

"Not in a long while. I do have his e-mail address at home, though. I'm sure he'd be flattered to hear from you. I'll bring it tomorrow." She nodded at them, and they accepted the dismissal, glancing back as they bumped into each other crowding through the doorway.

What in heck was that about?

But she didn't waste a lot of time speculating. The following day she brought his e-mail address as promised and gave it to Tabitha on a self-stick note. Then she turned her thoughts to the dinner date that might be fun, if only she could get past the idea of Chad wanting to kiss her.

THERE WERE A COUPLE of unfamiliar e-mails, but John ignored them until he'd replied to his sister's.

Business has been slow these past few weeks—this is the in-between season. Not enough snow, not enough sun. Same as last year. But it'll pick up soon.

He paused, then surprised himself by typing,

Why don't you come up for a visit?

John almost backspaced to obliterate the invitation he hadn't known he was going to offer, but, although his finger hovered above the key, in the end he moved his hand to the mouse and clicked Send. Liz was unlikely to come anyway. She sounded plenty busy, and content with their e-mail correspondence if invariably concerned about him in a sisterly way.

He was surviving. There wasn't much else he could say. In some ways, he'd regressed since Fiona left. The nightmares had returned full-force, and he'd had two major, full-color, 3-D flashbacks, although in neither case, thank God, had he actually tackled a guest. Once he had yelled a warning and started running toward two men coming down the porch steps. He'd seen—God, as real as they were—a robed figure skirting the porch to intercept them. He'd seen the odd way the robe draped, the mass of something unnatural around the chest. But in his flashback, there was no explosion, and he reached the foot of the steps to find only the two bewildered guests. Sweating, shaking, he'd looked up and found inspiration.

"I must be seeing things." *You think?* he mocked himself. "I could have sworn that icicle was breaking free."

They both looked up as well, at the dagger of ice that could indeed have done some damage if it had fallen, and one of them said, "You might want to knock that baby off."

He had, because they were right; with the melt, it could fall at the wrong time. Solving the problem of what *he* might do at the wrong time was another matter.

E-mails from buddies. He'd been sending more these past few months—one form of progress—and therefore getting more in return. One guy from his platoon was in a Veteran's hospital recovering from the loss of his left lower leg, shattered by mortar. His e-mails were somewhere between philosophical and pissed. John wondered if Miller would be honest if John were to ask,

Do you have nightmares, too? Ever had a flashback? Can you talk to your family? Girlfriend? I mean, really tell them how you feel about losing your leg, about the stuff you saw over there? Just wondering if all of us are having the same problems.

But of course he didn't, just sent the usual chitchat back.

He'd figured the two e-mails from unknown senders would be some kind of spam. Sure, he'd want to help some poor Nigerian widow get out of the country so she could share her millions with him. Instead he got a surprise.

Mr. Fallon,

I don't know if you remember me. I'm one of the students who got stranded there before Thanksgiving, during that big storm. Ms. Mac, you know, Ms. MacPherson, gave me your e-mail address. I just wanted to say thanks again. All of us had a really fun time there. I'm trying to talk my parents into coming up to stay maybe this summer.

We're doing really good. Erin and Troy and all the other seniors are so worried about what colleges they get into they're like no fun to talk to. I guess I'll be like that next year, too.

Ms. Mac is good, too. You probably hear from her anyway. Did she tell you she's started dating Mr. Scammell, one of our vice principals? He's like the enforcer. You know? He suspends kids and expels them and stuff like that. Maybe he's okay I mean I've never been in trouble so I don't know.

Anyhoo—thanks. Maybe I'll see you this summer.
Tabitha

Untangling a few of the sentences with no commas to help took him a minute, but finally he sat back. He tried to think, despite feeling as if he'd been slammed by a recoil.

Back in November, along with a generous reimbursement check from the school district, he'd gotten a series of dutifully written thank-you notes from the students, each mailed separately. Fiona hadn't gathered them up to send them together, but it was pretty obvious she'd expected each and every one of them to write him. Even Amy had thanked him prettily.

Tabitha had been a nice girl, but he didn't remember making any kind of personal connection with her. Still—maybe she was just being friendly. Wanting him to recognize her if she showed up with her parents.

Or maybe not. Maybe she was trying to tell him something. Burying that something in enough chatter so as not to be obvious.

The something could only be her news about Ms. Mac, her teacher.

She was dating? It was only March! How long ago had she and this Scammell started? The week after she got back, having written John off?

Anger, his familiar companion, stirred. Maybe she'd set Tabitha up to e-mail him, to taunt him. *You blew it, buddy.*

After a minute, he replied, telling Tabitha that of course he remembered her, it was nice to hear from her, and he hoped he'd see her and her family.

Then he moved on to the second e-mail from an unfamiliar address, and was a whole lot less surprised to see that it was from Dieter.

The boy's was even longer, telling him about a later Knowledge Champ competition down in Eugene and how both Willamette Prep teams had rocked, and how he had a girlfriend now.

Willow. Remember her? She might try out for Hi-Q with me next year.

Hi-Q, John knew, was an even more demanding form of academic competition.

Dieter was more straightforward when it came to the news about his beloved Ms. Mac.

I thought you two liked each other, he typed indignantly.

And she went up to see you at Christmas and all. So what happened? I asked her and she won't say.
Your friend Dieter

John stared at the screen, unaware for the moment of the librarian reading to a bunch of preschoolers while their mothers browsed shelves, or of the fact that his allotted half hour on the computer was nearly up.

Yeah, Fallon. What did *happen?*

Multiple choice answer. A, she found him unworthy because he wouldn't tell her in grisly detail about his service in Iraq and how he came to be injured. Or, B, she thought part of love was reaching out to each other, but he'd kept his hands at his sides.

A or B. How to reach out. Now, on a rush of fear and sickening hurt, he was hearing the words: *Too late.*

They pinged around in his head like the shiny metal ball in an old-fashioned pinball machine.

Too late. Ding! Too late. Ding!

He couldn't reply. He closed his Yahoo account, pushed back the chair and walked out of the library, forgetting the pile of books he'd intended to check out but had left beside the computer.

Too late.

Or was it? Key in the lock of his 4Runner, he stopped. Maybe *that's* why the kids had e-mailed him. To say, *We think she liked you better, but...you gotta* do *something.*

He gazed at the hand that held the key and realized it was shaking.

Do something. But...*what?*

CHAPTER FOURTEEN

THE EVENING OUT was okay. Just that, no more. If it hadn't been a date, if she and Chad had been having dinner together as friends, she'd have enjoyed herself more. But as it was, she kept waiting for even a flicker of attraction to manifest itself, and worrying about whether she'd hurt Chad if she told him she didn't want to go out with him again. She knew she was sabotaging herself; if not for John, she'd have been pleasantly surprised when Chad asked her out. She'd have been thinking how much they had in common, what nice eyes he had. She'd have been gearing herself up to *feel* attraction.

But compared to how she had felt from the first moment she'd seen John Fallon… Well, she wasn't sure she should have agreed to this evening at all.

When she'd unlocked her apartment door and Chad bent his head, Fiona let his mouth touch hers lightly, then stepped back.

"Thank you for a nice evening."

"Can we do it again?"

She'd had every intention of using him to get over John, but Fiona found that she couldn't bring herself to continue.

"Only if it's as friends." She put out a hand. "I'm sorry, Chad. There was someone, and…I guess I'm not as ready to start over as I hoped I was."

He nodded, looking regretful enough to flatter her, but also resigned. "I've been getting those signals all evening. It's okay, Fiona. I wanted to give it a shot, but…hey, we were already friends. Let's keep it that way."

"Really? I'd miss having you show up at lunchtime."

"I'll be there Monday." He smiled. "Don't worry. Lock up. See you at school."

She shot the dead bolt once the door was closed, then realized that, after he'd been so nice, she felt even worse about encouraging him. Except…heck, it wasn't like they'd had an awful evening. And at least she'd been honest at the end.

Of course, this didn't bode well for the "moving on" plan. A nice, good-looking guy asked her out, and she couldn't work up a shred of interest.

Knowing it was hopeless but unable to prevent herself, Fiona went to her computer and booted it. She wanted so passionately for there to be an e-mail from John, even a *Hey, I think about you sometimes.*

No such luck, of course. Her dad had e-mailed to let her know he and Shelly, his current wife, were back from Hawaii. He grumbled about how rainy it had been and said they thought next year they'd take a cruise instead.

She sent a brief reply and suggested they have dinner some night at a favorite Portland restaurant, then thought, *I could e-mail John again. Just to say how are you.*

But then she pictured his face as she'd last seen it,

stiff with anger and wounded pride, and knew he'd ignore this e-mail, just as he had her last one. The door was already open.

But he wouldn't be coming through it. That's what hurt so badly.

She hadn't cried over him in a long time, and she didn't tonight, but she did go to bed feeling sad and extraordinarily bleak.

JOHN HAD BEEN taken aback when his sister leaped at his invitation, confirmed that he had empty rooms the very next weekend and showed up midafternoon that Friday.

Their older sister looked more like their mother. Both John and Liz took after their father, with dark hair and brown eyes. Liz possessed an innate sense of style, although he knew well that it was careless; she rarely expended much time or thought on what she wore, and yet she never went out the door looking less than chic.

Unlike Fiona, she'd brought only a small bag. John knew his sister well enough to guess that she was unlikely to step outside until she left to go home. Like a pampered house cat, Liz hated being cold or wet, and her idea of enjoying nature was admiring autumn colors from the comfort of her snazzy Nissan 350Z. She *always* had a cute, sporty car, usually leased so she could move on to a new one every couple of years.

He grinned at the sight of her picking her way gingerly across the wet grass in high-heeled, completely inappropriate boots. Waiting at the top of the steps, shoulder propped against the post, he said, "You know I live out in the woods."

She lifted her head and her face lit. "The very reason I've never visited. I'm terrified to find out what your bathroom facilities are like. Please tell me I don't have to take a cold shower outside while yanking some string."

"Nope." He grinned again. "There's no shower at the lodge."

"What?" His sister stopped dead.

"The bathtubs are nice."

Grumbling under her breath, she climbed the steps and stood on tiptoe to kiss his cheek. "I've arrived."

"So I see." Arm around her shoulders, he raised his brows. "And to what do I owe the honor of this visit?"

Liz never bothered to be less than blunt. "I'm worried about you. What else?"

"You missed me?"

"Well, of course I missed you! The fact that you never visit is *why* I'm worried. Surely you occasionally hanker for a really fine dinner, or a movie, or a trip to Powell's?"

He winced. He did love Powell's, Portland's famous bookstore in which used and new books mingled in a maze of rooms on multiple floors that covered a city block.

"So what's up?" she challenged.

"Can we talk later?" he asked.

"As long as we do it." She marched past him, then waited pointedly until he opened the heavy front door for her.

John showed her to Fiona's room. He still hadn't put guests in here, mainly because the lodge hadn't been completely full at any time since Christmas. Just yesterday he'd made up the bed. Liz nodded her approval, checked out the bathroom and said, “Okay, now *that’s* a tub,” then asked what she could do to help with dinner.

High-heeled boots and all, she chopped and sautéed and with aplomb served the two couples who were currently guests. She helped clean the kitchen after dinner, too. When they were done, she said, “Coffee.”

He poured two cups.

“Sit,” she ordered.

Crap. He sat.

“This is a nice place. It’s pretty.” Her tone said, *For those who like such things.* “Last February, when you bought the lodge, it seemed like a plan. Maybe even a good investment. But now you’ve been here over a year. It’s been almost a year since you visited Mom and Dad.”

“I love them, but I can’t talk to them.”

“A lot of people can’t talk to their parents. They still show up for obligatory holiday visits. You know. Thanksgiving? Christmas?”

“Those are my busiest times of the year.”

Momentarily diverted, she said, “Did you celebrate at *all?*”

“I cooked a turkey at Thanksgiving. And all the trimmings. At Christmas…” What to say about Christmas? *I exchanged gifts in bed with the woman I love?*

“What? You cooked a ham?” His sister wasn’t impressed.

“I put up a tree. We had a party.” If sedately sipping mulled cider and gazing at a poor excuse for a Christmas tree qualified.

Her tone gentled. “Do you ever see friends?”

Nerves were jumping under his skin, making him

twitchy, and it was all he could do just to sit here under Liz's penetrating stare.

"Some are over there on another tour. One's in a VA hospital. A couple of the guys live on the East Coast. Humes lives in Houston."

"What about friends from before the war?"

Of course, he couldn't talk to them, either. Felt completely remote from them as if they were distant acquaintances. Most hadn't understood why he had joined the National Guard in the first place, and had been aghast at the idea of him giving up so much to ship out.

"Lizzie..." He hadn't called her that in a long time. "I can't go back."

Just as quietly, her tone terrifyingly gentle, she said, "Yes, you can. All the way? No. You won't be the same. Nobody expects you to be. But to the point where you can connect with people who love you? Sure you can. You've just...chosen not to."

He couldn't sit for another second. The chair scraped on the tile floor as he shoved back from the table. "I don't...choose..." His voice was strangled.

His sister tilted her head back so that her implacable, yet also kind—even pitying—gaze never left his, even when he backed away. "It's like living with a disease. Or being an addict. The *what* you can't change. The how you deal with it...that you can. You're the diabetic who won't go to the doctor, won't check his blood sugar level, even though he feels lousy. John, you need help. Counseling. Somebody who will understand."

"She wanted me to talk to her." He felt as if he was

listening to somebody else. Somebody in such agony, he couldn't keep his goddamn mouth shut.

His sister's antennae quivered. "She?"

John gripped the back of the chair. Looking down, he saw distantly that his knuckles were white. "I met someone."

He thought he heard Liz murmur, "Hallelujah," but wasn't sure.

"Fiona's a teacher. She and eight of her students were snowbound here during that big storm in November."

She nodded, as if slotting pieces into a puzzle. "So what happened?"

"We e-mailed afterward. She came up to stay over Christmas break."

"Ah."

"She wanted me to tell her what happened." Realizing one hand had somehow come to be touching his scar, John yanked it away and gripped the chair again.

"And?" Liz prodded.

"I can't keep reliving it for everyone who's curious."

"Curious? You want her to love you, but you can't tell her about something so fundamental to who you are now?"

Desperate, he asked, "Why do the details matter?"

"Because they matter to you. If they didn't, you'd be able to talk about it."

"That's simplistic," he argued.

All she did was challenge him with a look, something she'd perfected by the time she was five years old. "Yeah?"

When he didn't—couldn't—answer, she said, "So, you blew it with this—Fiona? Is it a hopeless cause?"

"She's started seeing someone else. One of the students e-mailed me."

"Uh-huh. What's the last thing she said to you?"

"Said, or e-mailed?"

Talking a placid sip of her coffee, his sister said, "So she e-mailed later. Okay. What did she say then?"

"That I knew where to find her if I wanted to talk."

"So, not hopeless."

His spirits rose momentarily, then crashed and burned. "That was three months ago."

"Idiot," his beloved little sister said without heat.

"The price was too high."

Her eyes narrowed. "Actually talking to her. *That's* too high a price?"

John shifted uneasily. "I talked."

"But not about the big pink elephant crashing around in the living room. She was supposed to ignore that."

"She knew…I had issues." The searing pain in his gut was back.

"Issues?"

"Nightmares."

"Before she came up here at Christmas? She knew you had nightmares? Which means she *slept* with you when she had students here?"

He scowled at her. "Of course she didn't."

"So, not nightmares. What?"

"Flashbacks!" he shouted, then closed his eyes. *Get a grip.* "I had a flashback," he mumbled. "Fiona knew."

"And yet, she came to spend time with you at Christmas." Liz sounded thoughtful.

Yeah. There it was, the miracle.

This stare from his sister was almost fierce. "Do you love her?"

He surprised himself with a hoarse laugh. "Why else am I telling you about her?"

"Because you can't resist my persuasive powers?" She gave him an evil grin. "Okay, okay. You love her. You've blown it with her. What's the next step?"

"No next step."

"Because you're chicken?"

She was taunting him, wanting a rise. She struck out. Bleakly he said, "Yes."

"Oh, John." Abruptly she stood and came to him, wrapping her arms around him in a fierce hug. "Oh, John."

He turned to her and held on tight, embarrassed by the fact that his face was wet. "What do I do, Lizzie?"

She told him.

He didn't like it, but the future lay before him, stark and hopeless if he refused—as any future without Fiona would be. And Liz was right in making him admit he was afraid. If he were any kind of man at all, Tabitha's e-mail would have made him determined to fight for the woman he loved.

"Maybe," he mumbled. "Let me think about it."

His sister tilted back her head to scowl at him.

"Okay. Yeah." He squeezed his eyes shut on a wave of vertigo. When that didn't help, he opened them again. "If you mean it…"

"I mean it."

"Then you win," he finally conceded.

She smiled, her face soft. "No, brother mine, you do."

INCREDIBLY his sister had offered to take over the lodge for up to two weeks. She'd taken her vacation with that intention. Yes, she assured him, she had actually brought athletic shoes, jeans and sweatshirts. No, she wouldn't split wood, but she was fully capable of hauling it in, doing laundry and cooking for a dozen, three times a day.

"My dream job? Nope. But that's what I came here to do."

"Wait a minute. You're lying. You don't have room in that bag for enough clothes…"

"My suitcase is in the trunk of the car. If you said no, I wasn't going to bother hauling it in."

Now, having been assured he wasn't needed, John was on his way down the mountain, his own bags in the back of his SUV. He had the key to Liz's condo so that he could stay there, but she'd admitted to telling their parents about how she planned to force him into action. He knew damn well his mother would be hoping he'd choose to stay with them instead, sleeping in his childhood bedroom.

And he had an appointment for Monday morning at 10:00 a.m.—scheduled by his sister—to see a counselor who specialized in posttraumatic stress.

"He's a Vietnam War vet," Liz told him. "He has a prosthetic leg."

In other words, John was left with no valid excuse. His guests were being taken care of. He could stay in solitude at his sister's place if he wanted. And, yeah, maybe the counselor *would* understand everything. But what about the guilt? Could anybody understand that?

John's unease grew as the trees thinned and then opened into the rolling, fertile Willamette River valley, logged and farmed in the nineteenth century by early settlers. Agriculture had long since lost its way to the growing population, pushing suburb by suburb out of Portland.

He saw a sign that said Hawes Ferry, and his fingers flexed on the wheel. But he kept going. What would he say to Fiona now? *I'm trying?* Not good enough.

The big old house where he'd grown up was in the Rose City neighborhood in Portland. He went there first, not wanting to hurt his parents unnecessarily. He parked at the curb in front, and he'd no sooner gotten out than he saw his mother flying down the porch steps.

"John! You came!" Her face was awash with tears by the time she reached him. "I wasn't sure you would."

He returned her hug, feeling a little awkward, and more than a little remorseful. So much for convincing himself that his folks were busy people only mildly concerned by his new eccentricity. It would appear he'd been breaking his mother's heart.

Patting her back, he said, "Liz is a steamroller."

Dashing at her tears, she stepped back. "That's news to you?"

"No. I just didn't expect her to turn her energy onto me. Don't they keep her busy enough at the *Oregonian?*"

"Did you see her series about chop shops? There's talk of a Pulitzer prize."

"Really?" John took his bag out of the back and slammed the door. "I did see it. She's good."

She was drying her tears, thank God. The worst was past.

They walked up the driveway. "Are you worried

about her being able to keep the lodge running?" his mother asked.

"No," John was able to say truthfully. "Pity the guests. She'll dig their life stories out of them, and they'll find themselves on the front page when she gets back."

Connie Fallon laughed. "Probably. Oh, I'm so glad to see you! You look wonderful, John."

His fingers wanted to go to his scar. How had it gotten to be a habit, touching it every time he thought about it? And why hadn't he noticed he was doing it? This time, he resisted by curling his hand at his side. "Thanks."

"In hopes you'd come today, I put a pot roast on. And of course I baked an apple pie. I wanted dinner to be your favorites."

Hell. It wouldn't have killed him to get down here a couple of times this past year. No matter what, he would do better, John vowed.

Forcing a smile, he said, "Thanks, Mom. That sounds great. Uh…where's Dad?"

"Work." She made a face. "Always work. The Hendersons had a burst pipe and their bathroom flooded. He should be done soon. I'll call to let him know you're here."

"No, don't do that. It's good to have time with just you."

She teared up again. "Daddy'll be home by five."

How long since she'd called his father that for his benefit? How long since she'd *thought* of him as John's daddy? Damn, he thought again; he'd hurt her far worse than he'd had any idea.

They had coffee in the kitchen, looking out at the backyard with her carefully pruned roses and the brick patio he had helped his dad lay when he'd been maybe twelve or thirteen. Bricks had weathered and chipped, and moss and some creeper his mother had turned loose now nibbled at the mortar and softened the edges.

He told her about innkeeping and the more unusual guests he'd had, and bragged about his cooking.

Sparkling, delighted, his mother exclaimed, "I'll let you demonstrate while you're home." Her face dimmed. "Oh. I didn't think. You might not be planning to stay with us."

He was lost. He could no more tell his mother he didn't want to stay than he could have gone out and shot a doe for recreation.

"Liz gave me the key to her place so I could water plants." Did she have any? "But I was planning to stay here, if it's okay with you."

His mother gave him a smile so radiant, it made his chest ache. "I can't think of anything I'd like more than to have you here. For however long you want to stay."

His eyes burned. "I don't deserve you, Mom."

She half-stood so she could kiss his cheek. "Of course you do! Never, never doubt it. You were a good boy, and you're a good man, John Fallon."

The women in his family seemed to know how to make him cry. But—funny thing—each time, the tears seemed to cleanse him of bitterness and remind him of a humanity he'd feared he no longer possessed.

"THE DAY YOU GOT HURT."

Until this moment, John couldn't have said what color the counselor's eyes were. They weren't startling in any way. But damn could they pin him to his chair like a butterfly on a board.

Blue, he realized. They were a washed-out blue. To go with an ordinary face, brown hair, a body average in build and height and a rumpled sport shirt tucked into wrinkled khakis.

The guy didn't believe in leading gently up to the hard part. Say, a week from now. Maybe use this first session to get to know John, to exchange war stories. No, he'd asked a few brisk questions. What unit? How much action had he seen? How many friends had died?

Ten minutes, tops. Now he looked at John and said, "The day you got hurt. What's your most vivid memory? Just a snapshot."

John felt like a phobic in a dentist's chair waiting for the drill to descend. Pretending he was just fine, when his body was rigid. God, he wanted to bolt.

Fiona, he thought desperately. Fiona.

Drawing a shallow breath, he said, "Blood dripping down a soccer ball. Lying there wondering why it hadn't popped."

"When you wake up at night screaming, what are you trying to do?"

He started to shove up from his chair. "How the hell do you know? Did Liz tell you…?" He stopped, feeling foolish. "You had your own nightmares."

"We *all* have nightmares." His expression was kind. "Even veterans who aren't suffering from PTSD have 'em. It's the mind's way of processing traumatic memories."

He sank back into the chair, but didn't let go of the arms. "Mine doesn't process them. It's stuck replaying."

A nod. "Like a vinyl record with a scratch. Why do you think you're here?"

Trying to joke, to lighten the mood, John said, "Because my little sister bullied me into it?"

"If that's the only reason, we shouldn't be wasting our time." Apparently Brian Lehr—that was his name—didn't have a sense of humor.

Fiona.

"Because of the scratch." He had to clear his throat. "Because *I* must be damaged."

Lehr nodded. "So let's back up. What are you yelling when you wake up?"

The Arabic word sounded alien when he said it. "Run," he translated. "I was trying to warn them."

"Them?"

"The kids." He closed his eyes, but opened them quickly, unable to bear the scene playing behind his eyelids. "The boys."

"How many?"

"Eleven. It…varied. Eleven that morning."

The voice was both gentle and relentless. "And one of them had a soccer ball?"

"Most of them did. Afterward…" He swallowed. "I just saw the one."

"They were going to practice? Play a game?"

His chest hurt. "Pickup game. The other team hadn't shown up yet."

"How old were they?"

Were. That was the operative word. Six dead. Four

maimed, lives over for all practical purposes. One, Allah only knew why, had walked away unharmed.

"Fourteen, fifteen."

"You saw them regularly."

Breathe, he told himself.

"Couple times a week."

"You play soccer yourself, back here in the States?"

"Yeah. Youth, high school, college."

"Natural that a soccer game would draw you."

Lehr didn't get it, John thought incredulously. He imagined this soldier exchanging a few words with the boys when he happened by.

"What did you see that made you shout the warning?"

"I don't know if I did shout it. It was in my mind. But...things happened fast."

"There's the scratch," the counselor murmured. "You feel like you failed because you didn't warn them."

As if John hadn't figured out that one himself. But the gouge that made the record unplayable...that was something else.

"What did you see?" Lehr asked again.

"A woman. Or a man dressed in a woman's robes. I turned and she—he—was there."

"You think it was a man."

"Yeah. I could just see the eyes above the burqa." He tried to zoom in on the picture. "Heavy brows. Too strong a ridge."

"Is that how you knew something was wrong?"

He shook his head, then said, "Maybe. Part of it. It was so fast. The robe didn't hang right. There was some bulk around the middle. Not…natural, like a pregnant belly. And the eyes. They were wild. Like a fanatic, but scared, too. Maybe he wasn't that old, either. I don't know. Nobody told me."

"A suicide bomber."

The pressure in his chest was near unbearable. "Yeah. I saw him, I opened my mouth… I think I did. And then…boom."

"How many died?"

"Six. Six boys. Four were badly hurt. They lost legs or arms or…" His stomach heaved. "Faces."

"And the bomber died."

"He was torn to bits."

"You were hurt."

"Enough to get discharged and shipped home."

"You said there were eleven."

"One boy wasn't hurt. He was just far enough away. I don't know."

"A miracle."

Did one out of eleven qualify as a miracle? John didn't think so, although that boy's parents might disagree.

"That was a tough thing to see."

"Don't feel sorry for me. It was my fault."

His guts were on fire, his heart hammering so hard he heard it. But *this* was why he'd come. Not to receive pity, understanding, but to say these words.

"Your fault?"

"I was their coach. Their friend. The face of America."

"And you believe the bomb was a message to you."

"No. To the other Iraqis. Hang out with Americans, you will suffer."

"Had it occurred to you that you might be endangering the boys by befriending them?"

"Yes. No." Once again, he squeezed his eyes shut. "I thought…they were children. *Children.* No one would kill a bunch of boys who just wanted to play better soccer to make their parents proud."

"But you found that hate knows no decency." Lehr's voice was soft.

"I found…that I had made a terrible mistake. One that *they* paid for."

He cried again, and scarcely heard the words Brian Lehr murmured.

"And so the healing begins."

CHAPTER FIFTEEN

SOMEHOW, after the date with Chad, Fiona felt even lonelier. It was as if, until then, she'd been able to fool herself that she could easily move on.

The thing with John? Too bad, but… Big shrug. *Win some, lose some.*

Who had she been kidding? she asked herself in despair. She was damaged goods. Heart broken, or at least cracked. Hearts, she had discovered, unlike bones, didn't mend in six weeks.

It didn't help that the kids kept bringing up his name.

Tabitha. "I got an e-mail from Mr. Fallon. He says…"

Dieter. "Dad made reservations for us to go to Thunder Mountain in July. Is that cool, or what? Willow is talking to *her* dad about them maybe going at the same time."

Willow. "Dad says maybe. My little brother thinks it would be awesome!"

Oh, good. Fiona was excruciatingly jealous of two teenagers, because *they* got to go back to the lodge. *They'd* get to see John.

"That's great," she managed to say. "Tell Mr. Fallon hi."

Willow looked shocked, and even accusatory. "How come you don't still e-mail with him?"

"I think maybe to maintain a friendship you have to see each other once in a while."

She immediately regretted what she'd said when the girl's shoulders slumped.

"Yeah. My friends from my old school? It's like, we used to IM all the time. Not so much anymore."

"It happens." Fiona gave her a quick hug. "Important friendships last, even over time and distance. And fortunately, you make new ones at every phase of life."

A quiet glow—and the removal of her braces, leaving perfectly straight, white teeth and a far more natural smile—made Willow considerably prettier than she'd been in early November. "I have, thanks to Dieter and… and to you."

"Me?" Touched, Fiona hugged her again. "I'm glad if I've helped."

The kids who'd been on that trip had become important to her, far beyond the fact that she coached them in Knowledge Champs. It was a combination, she thought, of having faced actual danger together, and of the intimacy of the days that followed. She knew them, foibles, joys and weaknesses, as she rarely knew her students. What she couldn't decide was whether it was an upside or a downside that they felt they knew her, too.

Kelli and Tabitha together stopped at her desk after class perhaps a month after Fiona's date with Chad.

"You went out with Mr. Scammell, right?" Kelli asked.

Her mouth probably dropped open. "How did you…?"

"I heard him ask you. I was waiting in the hall," Tabitha said.

"I really don't think my personal life…"

"He is so into rules." Kelli wrinkled her nose. "It's like, who'd want to be the vice principal in charge of discipline?"

Fiona had wondered that herself.

"Besides, he's not hot like Mr. Fallon."

No. He wasn't.

"Girls." She schooled her voice to be pleasant but steely. "It's not in any way appropriate for me to discuss my dating life with you."

Looking worried, Tabitha said, "But are you still dating him?"

"What did I just say?"

They both looked crushed. "You are," Kelli mumbled.

"As it happens, I am *not* dating Mr. Scammell. Which would seem to be a really, really good thing, if the entire school gossips every time two teachers have dinner together."

"You're not," Tabitha said in a rush of what appeared to be relief. Both their faces brightened. "Cool!"

Before she could ask them what that had all been about, they dashed out, claiming they were going to be late although she realized the minute they disappeared into the hall that they had lunch this period.

Oh, well, she thought philosophically. Perhaps she should be flattered that they even noticed she *had* a personal life—and even more that they worried about her. So much for the self-centeredness of teens.

Her mom worried about her, too. She'd been calling more often lately, even though she had a busy social life. She and Barry went to a movie, play or concert at least a couple evenings a week, and had joined a Saturday walking group. They often asked her to join them, which she had a couple of times. She and Barry had relaxed around each other, and even joked about the Thanksgiving debacle. Nice as it was to get to know him, Fiona couldn't help feeling as if she was being included out of pity.

She could just hear her mother telling him, "Poor Fiona! The first time she's been serious about someone in…oh, forever, and to have it end so badly."

She had to roll her eyes at her own imagination. Her mother had probably never said anything of the sort! And if she had…well, it was true. Every word.

Mid-April, the seniors received their acceptances and rejections from colleges across the country. Troy would be going to the University of Oregon, and was happy about it.

"Dad wanted me to get into someplace like Stanford. That's why I joined…" He looked embarrassed.

"Knowledge Champs." Fiona nodded. "I guessed. It's okay. Most high school kids are thinking about how to make their applications look good."

"Yeah. Thanks. I guess I didn't join enough things." He grinned. "Stanford said no."

She smiled back. "As long as you're satisfied."

"Yeah, this is what I wanted to do."

Erin, in contrast, *was* accepted by Stanford. *And* Princeton.

"I also got into this college in southern California." She had asked to talk to Fiona during her grading period. She sat at a desk facing Fiona's, her back straight, her demeanor dignified. "Scripps College. It's really small…"

"And a women's college." Fiona nodded. "I know of it."

"I don't know how to tell my parents, but that's where I want to go. *Because* it's small. Students were really friendly when I visited. I felt like I belonged. At Stanford *I* felt small and unimportant."

"Have you told your parents that?" Fiona asked gently.

Her black hair shimmered when she shook her head.

"They took you to visit Scripps."

"Actually we went to see Pomona. You know, they're right next to each other. But it's a bigger deal. So, while we were there we toured Scripps and Claremont and Harvey Mudd. They all kind of share facilities, and students can take classes at any of the colleges."

Fiona nodded again.

Erin looked down at her hands, pressed flat on the desk. "I didn't tell them I'd applied to Scripps instead of Pomona."

"Ah."

Her eyes were filled with desperation when she looked up. "So you see…"

"I don't know your parents well, but they have always seemed to want the best for you."

Erin bit her lip. "That's why…"

"Have they ever given you reason to think that they wouldn't be happy with what *you* think is best for you?"

That seemed to confuse Erin for a moment. "No-o," she finally said, doubtfully. "They just were so excited when I got the acceptance from Stanford."

"Talk to them," Fiona advised. "If they have problems with your decision, I'd be glad to speak to them."

"Okay." Erin took a deep breath and stood, her poise restored. "Thank you. I needed someone to tell me I'm not making a really horrible decision."

Fiona laughed. "You're not. Come back tomorrow and tell me what they said."

The next day the girl stopped by Fiona's desk on the way into class. Her smile was shy but happy. "Mom said she loved Scripps, too. They don't seem disappointed at all!"

"It *is* in the top tier of liberal arts colleges in the nation."

"I just thought...Stanford sounds more prestigious. But I mailed my acceptance to Scripps today. I'm really excited."

It was as if all their lives were coming together, Fiona reflected, paying attention that day as she saw them coming and going. Willow and Dieter had blossomed because of their romance, Hopper was his usual happy-go-lucky self, Kelli and Tabitha both seemed to be working harder this semester with a resulting improvement in grades, Erin and Troy were prepared for the exciting step of leaving for college, and even Amy, another teacher reported, seemed to have a better attitude.

Only mine sucks, Fiona thought, checking her e-mail before she put away the milk she'd bought on the way home. And, of course, being once again disappointed.

She had a good life. A satisfying life. But aside from that, she'd been right to say no to John. She knew she had. The decision *hadn't* been about what she would be giving up. It had been about what kind of relationship they would have, and whether either of them would have been content with whatever that had turned out to be.

Unfortunately knowing she'd been right didn't seem to lessen her depression.

She had an exciting dinner of tomato soup from a can and a grilled cheese sandwich, then tried to work on a paper she was writing for a class in educational psychology.

Fiona was about to give up after struggling first with a paragraph for what had to be half an hour, then searching for another fifteen minutes for a reference she *knew* she'd jotted down. Somewhere. The sound of the doorbell was a relief, even though it was unusual enough on a weeknight to make her a little apprehensive.

She looked through the peephole and stared. Distorted though the face was, it looked for all the world like John Fallon. How could he be here? Had she ever even given him her address?

Her knees felt weak and her heart drummed as she fumbled with the locks and flung the door open. "John?"

He looked like himself, and yet…not. For one thing, it was April, so instead of a heavy sweater or down vest over his jeans, he wore only an oatmeal-colored thermal henley T-shirt, with the couple of buttons unfastened to expose his sinfully sexy throat and chest. And athletic shoes instead of boots. He'd had a haircut, too. Recently, she thought. And he was so clean-shaven, he had to have taken a razor to his five o'clock shadow. Which meant… She couldn't think what it meant.

"How did you find me?"

"Dieter." He shrugged apologetically, his eyes wary. "You're unlisted. He, uh, hacked into the personnel records…"

She flapped both hands. "Don't tell me! If I know, I might have to do something."

"He thought it was a good cause."

"It?"

"Me."

"Oh." Warmth crept over her. He'd enlisted Dieter's help… Her eyes narrowed. "Wait. Did you ask Tabitha or Kelli if I was dating anyone?"

"Uh…"

"You did!" she accused.

He glanced each way, at the neighboring town houses. "Do you suppose I could come in?"

Of course she wanted nothing so much in the world as to have him come in, but she pretended to frown. "You used the kids!"

"If you let me in, I'll explain."

"Oh, fine." She stood to one side, then closed the door behind him. "I'm their teacher. You asked them to pry!"

"They're the ones who e-mailed me when you started dating the school Mussolini."

"Chad is very nice… They e-mailed *you?*"

"First, Tabitha and then Dieter. They apparently felt I should rush to rescue you. Or rush over here if I wanted to have any chance whatsoever with you."

Fiona felt a funny shift in her chest that felt very like the crumbling of hope. "That was almost six weeks ago. You didn't rush here. Or even e-mail."

"No." His eyes were very dark and intent on her face. "I thought, uh, that I wouldn't be welcome. Not if I hadn't dealt with any of my issues. But their e-mails scared me, Fiona." He reached out and clasped her hands. "If that's what they meant to do, they succeeded."

"But..." Tears stung her eyes and she knew any minute her nose would be running. "It's been months!" She couldn't seem to help wailing. "You never...never even answered my e-mail."

"God," he said, and enfolded her in his arms.

She cried quietly for a minute, her tears soaking his thermal shirt. All the while, he held her tightly, his cheek pressed to the top of her head.

"I'm sorry. I'm so sorry, Fiona. If you only knew..."

When she thought she could hold herself together, she straightened and stepped back. She heard in her voice a dignity that reminded her of Erin. "That was the trouble, wasn't it? I couldn't know, because you didn't tell me."

Any guard had slipped, leaving his face haggard, unhappiness—equal to hers—in his eyes. "That's why I couldn't rush over here six weeks ago. Why I never answered. I was...struggling with anger because you were asking me to do something that was painful. I couldn't come to you until I could admit that I had a problem."

"But..." The words caught in her throat, emerged as a whisper. "Have you now?"

"I spent two weeks in Portland in March. I saw a counselor who specializes in PTSD three times a week. Since then, I've been making the trip once a week."

Now she was afraid to hope. "Has...has it helped?"

His mouth twisted. "I still have nightmares. I haven't

had a flashback in maybe a month. That's not long enough to assume they're gone for good. But...I've been able to talk to people. First him, then my sister and Mom and Dad." He hunched his shoulders. "Is your offer still open, Fiona? Because I'm here to talk."

Darned if she wasn't crying again. She didn't even try to hide her tears or wipe her nose. "It's still open. I said whenever, and I meant whenever. Even if it took..." She couldn't finish.

Once again his arms were around her. "Months?"

"Forever," she choked out.

HE WIPED HER TEARS and grabbed a paper towel from her kitchen so she could blow her nose. Then he had to kiss her, of course. These last six weeks, it had been all he could do to stay away from her. He'd lived for the moment he could kiss her again. He'd prayed it would come.

He'd known all along that she might reject him. She'd driven away almost four months ago. In that time, he'd neither e-mailed nor called. It had come to seem foolish even to imagine that he could knock on her door out of the blue and be received with any kind of joy.

But in this kiss she gave herself with all the générosity that had drawn him to her in the first place. She held him tightly, she murmured his name, she pulled back to look up at him with something like wonder.

"I can't believe it."

He grimaced. "That I'm here? Or that I was ever willing to admit what a jackass I've been?"

She laughed, as if she was too giddy to prevent it. "Well...both."

"Thanks," he said wryly, and she laughed again.

He ran his knuckles down her cheek, stunned by the amazing softness and by the trusting way she tilted her face to meet his touch. "You busy?" His voice emerged gruffly, and he nodded toward the laptop open on her table. "I could come back…"

"Don't be silly." Fiona grabbed his hand and drew him into the living area. "Do you want coffee? Soda?"

He shook his head as he sat on the couch. *You. Only you.* "I just had a *latte grande.* My equivalent of a drink for courage."

"Well, then." Fiona sat, too, on the middle cushion so she was close enough to touch. She tucked one foot under her and turned to face him. "You really just packed up and went to Portland for two weeks? Did you close the lodge?"

"No." He shook his head in remembered bemusement. "My younger sister, Liz—I told you about her."

She nodded.

"Liz grew impatient with me. She came for a visit. So I thought. Turns out she'd gone so far as to make me an appointment with the psychologist, and to take two weeks of vacation herself. She gave me the key to her condo, told me if I wasn't comfortable staying at Mom and Dad's I could go there and sent me on my way."

"Just like that."

"I'd gotten those e-mails from Tabitha and Dieter not long before." Because he couldn't help himself, he reached out and took her hand. "I was scared. Which meant I was ready."

"Was it hard?" she asked, her eyes meltingly soft. "Talking to the counselor?"

Even remembering was enough to bring a shadow of the tension that had made his body rigid. "Yeah." He moved his shoulders, trying to release the strain that memory—and the knowledge of what he still had to say to her—had brought to his body. "Yeah, I wanted to run out of there so bad I could taste it."

"But you didn't."

"No." He looked down at their linked hands, where his thumb was tracing circles on her palm. "I thought about you. Over and over again."

Her smile was tremulous. "I've tried so hard *not* to think about you. And failed. Over and over again."

"I thought you'd put me out of your mind," he admitted. "Hope was…a little hard to hold on to."

Her eyes shimmered with tears again. "Yes. It is."

"There are things I need to tell you, Fiona."

"You don't have to right now. Maybe I shouldn't have put that kind of pressure on you…"

He was shaking his head before she'd gotten half way through her speech. "No. You were right. I need to get this out of the way. I think I locked it away for a lot of reasons. One was that I felt so guilty, on some level I didn't think anybody would—or *could*—love me once they knew how arrogant I'd been, how I risked the lives of a bunch of kids."

She stared at him with wide, now wary eyes. She had to wonder what in hell he was going to tell her.

He cleared his throat and began. "Somewhere I read recently that there may be personality types more at risk of developing posttraumatic stress disorder. I think I'm one. I mean, I didn't handle war very well from the beginning. The things you see." He looked down, startled to realize his hand had tightened on hers to a point that had to be painful, and muttered an oath. Letting her go, he said, "God, I'm sorry!"

Fiona shook her head. "No, it's okay. Really." She touched his thigh in reassurance.

He kneaded the back of his neck. "I probably would have come home a normal, screwed-up vet if it weren't for this." He gestured at his scar and all it symbolized. "Maybe I'd have had nightmares. Some pictures in my head I couldn't get rid of."

The compassion on her face was almost his undoing, but he forced himself to continue. "But me, I decided I could do some good while I was there." He gave a harsh laugh. "Prove that Americans were decent."

He told her about the nearby field, if you could call the bare, dusty ground a field. About the makeshift goals that had caught his attention. How there were often boys there, kicking soccer balls around.

Expression arrested, Fiona said, "That's why it upset you so much when Hopper asked if you had a soccer ball."

"Yeah. Having them around awakened enough unwelcome memories. Having them heading a soccer ball…" He almost shuddered, even now.

"Did you start playing with the boys?"

He nodded. "I'd played in college, so… We worked on skills. Eventually I organized them into a team. We started playing some games with other teams. Nothing official, not like a league. Just pickup games." He tried to smile, God knew why, maybe still deluding himself that it was possible to lighten the tragic results of his heedlessness. "Word got around. An American soldier was coaching Iraqi boys."

"Were they Sunni or…"

"A mix. I was never really sure. I have no doubt they were aware—how could they not be, these days?—but the neighborhood was integrated and they'd grown up together. In the end, it didn't make any difference. They were just…convenient material for a lesson."

"Oh, John," she whispered, awakening horror on her face.

He went on and told her the grim story. They'd been talking, doing some warm-up exercises while they waited for the other team to arrive. He'd turned, aware of the approach of a woman in the dark, enveloping robe and burqa. The sense—articulated too late—that something wasn't right. The "Oh God, what have I done?" moment.

The warning, never uttered.

He told it as unemotionally as he could, trying not to be graphic about the sights that had met his eyes when he'd lifted his head afterward and peered through the blood that bathed his face. Even so, she had one hand pressed to her chest and the other to her stomach, as if to quell both horror and nausea.

"Children," she whispered once.

"Object lessons," he repeated. "Do not consort with the enemy."

"I don't know how you survived."

He knew she didn't mean physically. He still wasn't altogether sure he *had* survived emotionally. But maybe…maybe he would make it. Because of her.

"I was able to visit the survivors in the hospital. Except for one. He, uh… It was touch and go. I guess he did make it. I don't know if that's such a good thing. He lost his eyes, and his face is just…" God. He was touching his scar again.

"Oh, John," she whispered again, and this time she took his hand.

"I screwed up bad. I was so full of myself that I didn't listen to warnings."

"You were trying to do something very, very good."

"Was I?" he asked out of anguish and a painful need to be honest. "Or was it all arrogance? Was I doing it for me? So I could go home filled with pride because I'd left a mark, I'd somehow changed the path of history. How bad can Americans be?" he mocked himself. "That soldier, he was great with the boys. The boys are the best, they're champions, because of him!"

Now she had both his hands. She squeezed until he met her eyes, his own undoubtedly revealing more of himself than he'd ever meant to bare.

"Was that it?" she asked. "Or did you need to feel human? To have something outside the suffering and the politics and the hate? To offer that to them, too?"

He stared at her. Yeah, that's what the boys had been to him. A slice of something remembered, something enjoyed. Adults sharing their skills, boys challenging each other for their places in the pecking order, preening for girls, thrilling to demonstrate their supremacy on a field.

Just like that, he bent his head and wept. Fiona scooted closer, wrapped her arms around him, and held him.

"They were…such great kids," was the only coherent thing he said.

"You would have done anything to protect them," she murmured as she held him. "They knew friendship when they saw it. Even their parents must have known it, or they wouldn't have let them come."

"Why?" he begged. "Why, God? Why?"

She was silent for a moment, the hand that had massaged his shoulder pausing. "There aren't always answers," she said at last. "But that doesn't mean you have to bear total responsibility, either. That kind of hatred is…is unknowable, I think. To us, at least."

Her simple, sad words touched a chord in him. Was it possible to accept that he never would understand in any way he could get his mind or heart around? That he could live anyway, even find happiness despite guilt and grief that he might never quite lay to rest?

Was she offering him that happiness? Was that what her kiss had meant? What she'd intended when she said her offer would remain open, "Even if it took forever"?

John wiped his face roughly with his shirtsleeve, then asked, "Can I use your bathroom?"

"Second door on the left."

Washing his face didn't improve materially how he looked; his eyes were still too swollen and bloodshot. But, hell, he couldn't hide in here, not like he'd done on her last night at the lodge when he'd awakened to the hoarse sound of his own yell. Then, he hadn't been able to risk sharing his past with her. At least he'd come that far. Now he needed to find out if she was willing to consider a future with him—a man who'd taken only a few baby steps toward recovery.

She was still sitting where he'd left her on the sofa. Her anxious gaze went immediately to his face. Starting to stand, she asked, "Are you all right?"

"Yeah. I'm, uh, beginning to get used to this. I've cried more these past two months than I have since I was five years old."

She smiled, as he'd intended her to, but her eyes kept searching his.

Get right to it, he thought. Prolonged suffering was something he knew too well. A clean, sharp hurt was better.

He stopped a few feet from her. "I love you, Fiona. But I'm probably not going to be ready to go back to any kind of life we can share," he gestured vaguely to take in her town house, including in it her job, her graduate schooling, everything he'd asked her to give up. "Not for a while, anyway. I get pretty stressed when I'm back in Portland. But you were right." He tried out a smile, probably a poor excuse for one. "I'm not meant to be an innkeeper, either. I'm thinking...maybe another year. I could stop by regularly. You could come up on school breaks. If..." His voice failed him. "If you're willing."

"Oh, John." Her voice cracked, too, and now *her* eyes filled with tears. "Of course I'm willing!"

Somehow he cleared the coffee table to take her in his arms. They kissed… Not simply thankful to be together. But rather with desperation, as if they'd never expected to have the chance again.

They got to the bedroom, too, and made love the same way. But at some point—before he stripped her of her clothes and she stripped him of his—she told him she wouldn't just be coming up to Thunder Mountain on breaks. She would take a year's leave of absence from Willamette Prep. She wanted to be with him. She could finish her master's degree long-distance, and be an innkeeper's wife.

Sometime *after* they made love, she also told him Willow's father had agreed to make a reservation for one of the cabins the same week Dieter's parents had already booked another one. "And I was thinking," she said.

"That we could invite all the kids to come? Their families, too?"

"Something like that, I guess."

"What do you say," he suggested, "that we hold our wedding then? Where we met? The lodge is big enough to house our families, our friends…"

Fiona cried again, but from happiness.

And in between her offer to bury herself in the wilderness with him, and his idea of a summer wedding, they did make love. In those moments, as close to her as it was humanly possible to be with a woman, John knew for sure he, too, could be happy. It was even possible that what he felt now was richer, because it hadn't come easily.

Wouldn't come easily in the future.

"I'm going to backslide," he warned, holding her

sprawled atop him, a few curly strands of her hair wandering to tickle his nose.

"Um," she murmured in agreement, seemingly undisturbed. She rubbed her cheek against his chest, then lifted her head to smile at him. "But, you see, it won't be the same. Because I'll always be there to catch you."

She couldn't have offered a declaration of love that meant more to him. John's heart squeezed and he closed his eyes, wishing the boys could know.

Wondering if they did.

Brad shoved the truck into gear and drove to the bottom of the hill, where the road forked. Turn left, and he'd be home in five minutes. Turn right, and he was headed for Indian Rock.

He had no damn business going to Indian Rock.

He had nothing to say to Meg McKettrick, and if he never set eyes on the woman again, it would be two weeks too soon.

He turned right.

He couldn't have said why.

He just drove straight to the Dixie Dog Drive-In.

Back in the day, he and Meg used to meet at the Dixie Dog, by tacit agreement, when either of them had been away. It had been some kind of universe thing, purely intuitive.

Passing familiar landmarks, Brad told himself he ought to turn around. The old days were gone. Things had ended badly between him and Meg anyhow, and she wasn't going to be at the Dixie Dog.

He kept driving.

He rounded a bend, and there was the Dixie Dog. Its big neon sign, a giant hot dog, was all lit up and going through its corny sequence—first it was covered in red squiggles of light, meant to suggest ketchup, and then yellow, for mustard.

Brad pulled into one of the slots next to a speaker, rolled down the truck window and ordered.

A girl roller-skated out with the order about five minutes later.

When she wheeled up to the driver's window, smiling, her eyes went wide with recognition, and she dropped the tray with a clatter.

Silently Brad swore. Damn if he hadn't forgotten he was a famous country singer.

The girl, a skinny thing wearing too much eye makeup, immediately started to cry. "I'm sorry!" she sobbed, squatting to gather up the mess.

"It's okay," Brad answered quietly, leaning to look down at her, catching a glimpse of her plastic name tag. "It's okay, Mandy. No harm done."

"I'll get you another dog and a shake right away, Mr. O'Ballivan!"

"Mandy?"

She stared up at him pitifully, sniffling. Thanks to the copious tears, most of the goop on her eyes had slid south. "Yes?"

"When you go back inside, could you not mention seeing me?"

"But you're Brad O'Ballivan!"

"Yeah," he answered, suppressing a sigh. "I know."

She rolled a little closer. "You wouldn't happen to have a picture you could autograph for me, would you?"

"Not with me," Brad answered.

"You could sign this napkin, though," Mandy said. "It's only got a little chocolate on the corner."

Brad took the paper napkin and her order pen, and scrawled his name. Handed both items back through the window.

She turned and whizzed back toward the side entrance to the Dixie Dog.

Brad waited, marveling that he hadn't considered incidents like this one before he'd decided to come back home. In retrospect, it seemed shortsighted, to say the least, but the truth was, he'd expected to be— Brad O'Ballivan.

Presently Mandy skated back out again, and this time she managed to hold on to the tray.

"I didn't tell a soul!" she whispered. "But Heather and Darlene *both* asked me why my mascara was all smeared." Efficiently she hooked the tray onto the bottom edge of the window.

Brad extended payment, but Mandy shook her head.

"The boss said it's on the house, since I dumped your first order on the ground."

He smiled. "Okay, then. Thanks."

Mandy retreated, and Brad was just reaching for the food when a bright red Blazer whipped into the space beside his. The driver's door sprang open, crashing into the metal speaker, and somebody got out in a hurry.

Something quickened inside Brad.

And in the next moment Meg McKettrick was standing practically on his running board, her blue eyes blazing.

Brad grinned. "I guess you're not over me after all," he said.

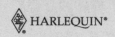

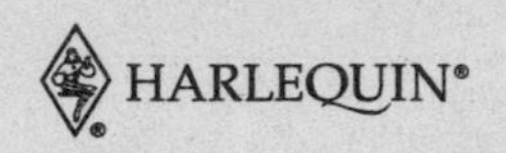

American ★ Romance®

Kate Merrill had grown up convinced that the most attractive men were incapable of ever settling down. Yet the harder she resisted the superstar photographer Tyler Nichols, the more persistent the handsome world traveler became. So by the time Christmas arrived, there was only one wish on her holiday list—that she was wrong!

LOOK FOR

THE CHRISTMAS DATE

BY

Michele Dunaway

Available December wherever you buy books

COMING NEXT MONTH

#1458 GOING FOR BROKE • Linda Style
Texas Hold 'Em
Jake Chandler swore he'd never return to River Bluff, Texas, after being run out of town when he was eighteen, wrongfully accused of arson. But a funeral brings him back. And Rachel Diamonte, the witness to his supposed crime, just might be the woman who keeps him here. Because when it comes to love, the stakes are high....

#1459 LOOKING FOR SOPHIE • Roz Denny Fox
Garnet Patton's life hasn't been the same since her ex-husband abducted their five-year-old daughter and left Alaska. Then Julian Cavanaugh, a detective from Atlanta, comes to town, claiming he might have some new information. Will he be able to find her daughter...and will he be able to lead Garnet back to love?

#1460 BABY MAKES THREE • Molly O'Keefe
The Mitchells of Riverview Inn
Asking for his ex-wife's help is the last thing Gabe Mitchell wants to do. But he needs a chef, and Alice is the best. Working together proves their attraction is still strong. So is the issue that drove them apart. Is this their second chance...or will infertility destroy them again?

#1461 STRANGER IN A SMALL TOWN • Margaret Watson
A Little Secret
Kat is determined to adopt Regan, her best friend's child. Only one thing stands in her way—Seth Anderson. Seth has just learned he is Regan's father, and even though he's no family man, he wants to do right by the little girl. Especially once he realizes Kat is a suspect in the investigation he's conducting.

#1462 ONE MAN TO PROTECT THEM • Suzanne Cox
He says he can protect her and the children, but how can Jayden Miller possibly trust Luke Taylor—when the public defender is clearly working for some very nasty men? With no one else in Cypress Landing to turn to, Jayden is forced to put their lives in his hands....

#1463 DOCTOR IN HER HOUSE • Amy Knupp
When Katie Salinger came back to recuperate from her latest extreme-sport adventure, she didn't expect her dad to have her childhood home up for sale. The memories tied to it are all she has left of her mom. Worse: there's an offer...from the mysterious Dr. Noah Fletcher.

HSRCNM1107